MIDNIGHT SALVATION

A SMALL TOWN WHY CHOOSE ROMANCE

ROSEWOOD
BOOK 3

PENELOPE BLACK

*for everyone who longs for motherhood
and for every woman who's been told she's too loud, too opinionated, too stubborn. for every single one of us who has been made to feel like we take up too much space.
I see you and I hear you.
also fuck those people, they're the worst.*

PLAYLIST

"Solas" by Jamie Duffy
"The Winner Is" by DeVotchKa, Michael Danna
"Eyes on Fire" by Blue Foundation
"Lonely" by Noah Cyrus
"Moral of the Story" by Ashe
"Lost at Sea" by Rob Grant, Lana Del Ray
"Remember That Night?" by Sara Kays
"TV" by Billie Eilish
"Talk Show Host" by Radiohead
"Beautiful Things" by Benson Boone
"State Lines" by Novo Amor
"Can You Hear the Music" by Ludwig Göransson
"Mountains" by Hans Zimmer
"What Was I Made For?" by Billie Eilish

PROLOGUE - SILAS

I take the fastest shower of my life, and considering I used to regularly crash in the clubhouse with twenty other people and very limited hot water, that's saying something. Exhaustion weighs down my limbs, and it takes more effort than I'm comfortable admitting to step into a relatively clean pair of sweatpants.

I hang my towel on the back of the bathroom door and flick off the light, stepping into my bedroom. Hunter's cries assault my ears instantly.

Exhaustion forgotten, adrenaline pumps through my veins so fast I feel dizzy as I run down the hallway toward his nursery. It's not much, but Ma assured me that he won't even remember the fact that he sleeps in a glorified walk-in closet. I gently lift him from his crib, careful to cradle his head as I tuck him against my chest. His little face is scrunched up with distress, and my heart thumps uselessly inside my chest. The sheer force of the panic I feel every time he cries is alarming.

Damn, this kid has a set of lungs on him.

"Shh, it's okay, Hunter. It's alright. Daddy's here." I cradle my newborn son to my chest, trying out that rock-sway thing and adding a little bounce I saw someone do on a YouTube video. His cries feel like needles piercing my heart. Death by a thousand cuts.

It feels like it lasts for hours, but my reality is warped by lack of sleep and the most anxiety I've ever experienced in my whole goddamn life. I'm scared and worried all the time.

Is he sleeping enough? Is he sleeping *too much*? Does he get enough food? How many times did he shit today, and what's his weight at? The doctor told us he needs to gain some more weight back before he sees him at his one-month checkup in a few weeks.

By the time he calms down, I'm sweaty and ready for another shower. But Hunter is snoozing on my chest, wrapped up like a baby burrito, and I can't bring myself to put him down.

"Let's go find your mama, son," I whisper, brushing my lips over the top of his head. He has that brand-new baby smell. I thought it was a fucking weird thing for people to talk about all the time, but I get it now. It's intangible, and it doesn't even smell like something familiar as much as it makes my heart squeeze with some unknown emotion. It's hard to describe, but I just know that I'm going to miss it when it's gone.

I head toward the kitchen, expecting to find Gloria at the table with one of the casseroles Ma keeps making and dropping off. But the kitchen is quiet.

"Gloria?" I keep my voice low, though a quick glance at my little football baby tucked into my arms shows his little mouth pursed open like a baby bird.

When she doesn't answer me, I head down the hallway toward the bedroom. Maybe she fell asleep.

Gloria's in the bedroom, but she's not napping or even resting. She's standing at the foot of the bed with an open duffel bag half full.

"What's going on?" My brows sink into a deep V as i try to make sense of what I'm seeing before me

"Prez." She stills, looking over her shoulder at me.

"C'mon, Gloria. I told you to call me Silas." It's not a reprimand, just a gentle reminder. We made a kid together, for fuck's sake. I don't want her calling me by my position within the Reapers.

"Right," she says, swallowing audibly. "Well, I was going to leave you a note but . . ." She shrugs half-heartedly.

"Hunter was crying, like really crying. Didn't you hear him?" I tilt my head to the side, my brain not quite catching up with what I'm seeing.

She glances at him almost curiously. It's the same kind of look she's given him since we came home from the hospital five days ago. Mildly curious but mostly disinterested. "He seems fine now."

"What's going on?" I ask again, suspicion creeping along my back and loosely wrapping around my throat.

She sighs, setting down the sweatshirt on top of her duffel. "I'm leaving."

"What do you mean *you're leaving*? What about Hunter?" I lift my arm up an inch to emphasize our perfect and adorable sleeping boy.

"Look, Silas. I'm not . . . cut out for this, okay? I did the right thing. I told you when I was pregnant, and I stayed here like you asked. But now he's out and so am I."

"What the fuck are you talking about?" I hiss, tilting my body away from her, as if it shield Hunter from hearing her talk so indifferent about him. "You're his *mother*."

She shakes her head, her eyes sagging with pity or acceptance, I can't tell which. "I'm not his mother. I just gave birth to him."

"I . . . I . . . can't believe this." I feel tongue-tied and speechless at the same time. My brain is demanding I say all these things to her, but shock holds my tongue hostage. With panic swiftly on its heels.

"I'm sorry, okay? But I never wanted kids. And I don't want to play house with you, no offense. So I think it's time I move on now, okay?" She sends me this sort of half-smile like she pities me.

"What am I supposed to tell him?" My heart aches at the fact that someday I'm going to have to tell my son that his mother willingly left him because she simply didn't want to be here. Didn't want him or me or this life.

She tucks her sweatshirt in the duffel bag, zipping it closed. She tosses the strap over her shoulder and looks at me. "I don't really care what you tell him. That's not really my business."

I shift to the side, curling my body around my son as much as I can. He lets out this little squeak, and my heart seizes inside my chest for a second, sure that she's going to grab him out of my arms and run off. I back up until my back hits the wall, tilting Hunter away from her and giving her plenty of space to walk down the hallway and out of our lives.

I shouldn't have worried though, she walks by both of us without so much as a word, let alone an affectionate touch or a last-ditch effort to snatch him away from me.

I make myself watch her from my front porch until long after I can't see her tail lights. I sear these images into my brain so if the day comes that she wants back in our lives, I always remember that she left us so easily.

1

SILAS

"SILAS, they've breached the compound. Get home, son."

Ma's words seem to echo around the car. Each word, each syllable, pinging off of me. Bouncing off of Bane, and rebounding off of Nova. Just ricocheting around like pinballs in that old arcade game Hunter's been asking me to buy ever since him and Evangeline talked about two weeks ago.

Hunter.

I suck in a breath like I'm doing eighty up a mountainside and the air is thinning by the second.

I thought I knew what anxiety was. That I'd spent too many moments in my lifetime with it, too many days submerged in its thick, syrupy exhaustion. But all of that was nothing compared to what's flooding my veins and short-circuiting my brain right now.

My father was never going to win any parenting awards, and it sure as fuck didn't feel like he ever put his kids first. But maybe he did the best he could with the tools he had. He was a fucking outlaw in every sense of the word.

I didn't quite understand it until now—I didn't understand *him*. Until I'm slipping through the quicksand of terror over my boy's safety. And the cool clarity hovers above the anxiety like mist on the lake.

There is nothing I won't do for Hunter.

No piece of my soul I won't corrupt to save his.

Maybe my father and I aren't all that different after all.

How many days did he wake up and think: *Is today the day? Is today the last day I get to see my sons?*

How many days should a man wake up and think that before he does something about it? How long can a heart last under that kind of stress?

This kind of all-consuming emotion is so much more potent than anxiety. It's weaponized terror wrapping its barbed wire talons around my throat, squeezing tighter and tighter and tighter.

The silence crackles, and I swear fragments of Ma's words float around the air like microscopic particles. It's only been a minute since Ma's voice filled the car, telling us to come home, but it might as well have been an eternity.

The sharp prickling sensation of goosebumps erupts across my skin, followed by shivers that cascade down my spine. My knuckles turn white as I clench the steering wheel, weaving through the sparse traffic on the highway. Thank fuck for small miracles.

"Call Ma again," I tell Nova, meeting his gaze in the rearview mirror.

He holds his phone up to his ear, his eyes narrowed with worry. When I meet his gaze again, he's already shaking his head.

"I'll keep trying," Nova says.

The sense of urgency in the air is palpable, thick enough to choke on. My muscles tense reflexively, the adrenaline and flight or fight instinct riding me hard.

Nature's fucked-up game of survival. I thought we were the predators today. But I'd been wrong.

So fucking wrong. And fucking naive to assume they were playing by the rules. And all I can do now is pray that the damage done is survivable.

Bane's phone rings, slicing through the mounting tension like a hot knife on butter.

"Who is it? Ma? Evangeline?" Nova asks, leaning forward between the seats.

I keep my focus on the road ahead, refusing to take my eyes off of it as I pass the slowest fucking driver on the planet. I press the gas pedal down harder, pushing the limits of the car and completely disregarding the speed limit.

"Hello?" Bane answers, pressing the speakerphone button immediately.

"I'm looking for Lincoln St. James." It's a woman's voice, but I don't recognize it.

More importantly, it's not one of the only two women I want to hear from so I don't really fucking care who it is.

"Who is this?" Bane asks.

"Is this Lincoln St. James?" she insists, her voice lowering to near whisper.

I can feel Bane's gaze on me, and I glance at him briefly. His face is carefully neutral, shoulders high and tense.

My cousin and I have always been on the same wavelength. It's part of what makes us such a formidable team. Nova and I are a team in our own right, but he's unpredictable to Bane's reliability.

"Yes, who is this?" he says. There's a quiet, cautionary bite in his voice.

It's better than I would have given her. My nerves are fucking shot, and I don't have the bandwidth for much else right now.

I tighten my grip on the steering wheel and focus on the road in front of me. There's a fine line between urgency and recklessness. And I'll be damned if I crash our truck right now. I don't have time for a car accident or a speeding ticket or being stopped by anyone for any reason.

Unless it's to get Hunter and Ma and Evie out of danger, I couldn't care less right now.

So it takes all of my concentration to keep us on this road safely and get us the fuck back to town.

But the next words float in this tumultuous, charged space the three of us are occupying nearly have me swerving into the shoulder of the road.

"This is Elizabeth Carter and I messed up. I-I need your help."

My neck spasms as I whip my head toward Bane, and the car swerves along with me. Of all the people I could've guessed, a Carter didn't even come close to being on the list.

"Oi," Nova grunts from next to me, his shoulders jamming into the passenger seat.

I jerk the steering wheel left, righting us on the road. A grimace pulls the corners of my mouth down and I blow out a breath. My eyes narrow as they fixate on the phone clutched in his hand. The bright screen illuminates the quiet fury in his gaze. But it isn't directed at me or Nova—it's focused on the screen.

"Start talking," Bane snaps.

I chance one more glance at him, trying and failing to read his vibe, get any sort of clue to what the fuck is going on.

Shame drags its forked tongue up my spine. I recognize the last name, but that's it. That's fucking *it*. And it's so goddamn unacceptable that they know more about her than I do.

I have no idea who Elizabeth Carter is in relation to Evangeline, and I fucking *should* know.

By the way Bane and Nova have reacted, they both know, and it's far from good.

I adjust my grip on the steering wheel and shift in my seat, a lame attempt at dislodging the barbs of jealousy stuck in my back.

I don't have time for this. I don't have time to feel shame or space to feel jealous. I don't have time to be worried about who Evangeline's relatives are.

Right now, my sole focus is getting back to the compound—to *Hunter*. Checking on Ma. And making sure Evie is okay.

There's rustling on the other line, and her voice quiets further. "I can't talk now. It's not—I can't—just meet me in an hour at Maple Leaf Diner. Over in Brookhaven."

"Tell me what this is about," Bane demands. The leather creaks beneath him as he shifts forward.

"One hour. Maple Leaf Diner," she says,

Bane shakes his head and glances at the clock on the dashboard. "I know where it is. I'll need three hours."

More rustling fills the line, and I hear shouting in the background, but it's muffled, and I can't make anything out.

"Fine," she whispers. "Three hours."

"We'll be there," Bane says.

"No," the woman whispers. "Just you—you came for my sister once. Now I need you to do it again."

The call ends, leaving the weight of her ominous call in the air. It tangles with Ma's voicemail, churning over one another until nothing but strained tension remains around us.

I can't fucking take it any longer.

"Who the fuck was that?" I grit out.

Bane shakes his head, tapping the end of his phone against his thigh.

"And before either one of you think about running your mouths about how I should know who that was, I fucking know that already. So spare me the lecture and remember who the fuck you're talking to." The words come out a little more heated than I meant them to, but I don't take it back.

"Huh. Remind me. Who are we talking to?" Arrogance drips from him like water rolling over a cleaver. I've become more than familiar with his sharp edges over the last few months. Ever since *she* got here.

I clench my molars until I feel them ache, and I take the exit off the highway and get onto another one.

Nova tsks from the back seat. "That's what I fucking thought."

"Nah, I don't think so, brother. That's not what I meant, and you fucking know—"

"Elizabeth Carter is Evangeline's sister," Bane says, wading in the middle of our shit like he's been doing his whole life.

"Okay." I nod a few times, glancing between the rearview mirror, my side mirror, and the windshield, making sure there are no threats coming for us. I'm riding a razor's edge of paranoia, half-convinced this is part of their plan too. Another fucking trap.

I clear my throat and keep my gaze straight ahead. "I didn't know she had a sister."

Nova grunts, but he doesn't offer anything else.

"That's it?" I arch a brow and glance pointedly at Bane.

He's still tapping the edge of his phone against his thigh in a quick, steady rhythm. His face drawn, brows furrowed and mouth pressed into a thin line.

"Yeah," Bane says with a sigh. "I think you need to get us to the fucking compound before we lose everything."

I exhale through my nose and curb every instinct I have that's telling me to snap at him. Now is not the time for fighting between us, even if it is the petty bullshit we've been slinging at one another our whole lives.

"If you have something else to say, now's the time. We've got sixty miles before we even reach Rosewood city limits."

My brows sink low over my forehead as I try to understand why the fuck Evangeline's sister is calling my cousin. Does she play a part in this fucking mess, or are we about to be pulled into Carter family drama?

Bane stops tapping his phone against his thigh and leans back in his seat. "Elizabeth Carter is a fuckin' snake."

"Just like her asshole parents," Nova chimes in.

Bane nods. "They're a whole goddamn nest of vipers. And how our girl turned out as sweet as pie, like a fucking adorable little bunny in the middle of a snake pit, is a fucking miracle we should be thanking God for every day."

My chin dips a few times, my thoughts tumbling over one another. But they keep snagging on one unimportant detail: Evie's not a rabbit. She's a butterfly. Soft and pretty and delicate. But if you get too close, if you try to consume her, she'll flay your skin from the inside out with her poison.

The road stretches endlessly ahead, the only sound is the low hum of our truck on the asphalt.

"Well, we know how to kill a snake, don't we, boys?"

I feel it then. A sort of grainy haze flows over me, molds around my muscles, and adheres to my skin like a sticky web.

Washed-out fragments of who I was before.

Before Evangeline, before Hunter. Before the tentative peace we fought so hard for.

I let it settle over my skin like armor. Because I fear I can't do what I need to do to protect my family without it.

I put away Renegade five and a half years ago. Tucked it away in a box and put it in the back of the closet. Like that one pair of dress shoes you wear only to funerals. And it's been collecting dust ever since.

"We cut their fucking heads off."

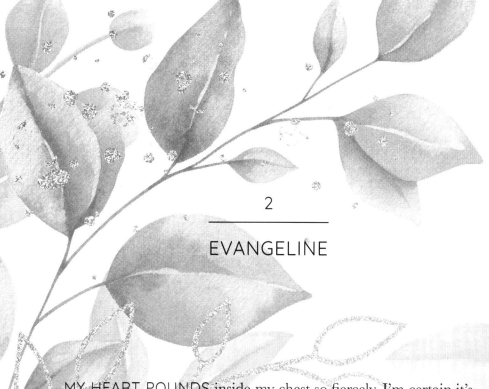

2

EVANGELINE

MY HEART POUNDS inside my chest so fiercely, I'm certain it's going to thump right out of my ribcage. I have half a mind to hope it does just to save me from whatever miserable fate the assholes in leather storming inside my house are plotting. Nothing good can come from it, and in one shot, I'm officially out of bullets.

And options.

Someone kicks open the door, and I pull the trigger.

"You motherfucking bitch," some asshole in leather yells, clutching his bleeding stomach and sagging against the busted doorframe. He grunts, lifting his free arm and pointing his gun at me.

My heart leaps into my throat as I try to calm my breathing. I will not leave this world a scared, frightened animal.

Before the intruder can take aim, another man appears in the doorway behind him. His dark blond hair covers his forehead and shields his eyes from this angle, but not enough for me to miss the glare he shoots at me. As if I'm the problem.

It happens so fast, my brain can't keep up with what I'm

witnessing. One moment I'm staring down the barrel of my demise, and the next, the intruder hits the floor with a resounding thump, a hunting knife in his temple. Blood pools underneath his stomach and his head, spreading across Silas's blue rug like some macabre painting.

My mind has been reeling with shock and adrenaline and fear so potent, I could taste its bitterness in the back of my throat. But I honestly thought I was full, that I couldn't be anything *more*.

But I was wrong. And I think—I think this might've tipped me over the edge. "Who the fuck are you?"

"I'm your white fucking knight, princess," he says, his voice low and calm like he didn't just stab a man's head. Like what the fuck is happening right now?

He steps over the body, bends down to retrieve his knife and slips it into a holster on his belt. He springs to his feet in one smooth movement and prowls into the room, a fucking semiautomatic weapon strapped across his back and right hand gripping a gun.

My sense of self-preservation overrides my shock, and I dig my heels into the floor and maneuver myself backward, inching toward the opposite side of Silas's room. I keep myself low, mindful of the windows to my left.

"We don't have a lot of time. Help me move this," he snaps, rolling the body over and flinging the bedroom door closed. He doesn't spare me a glance as he pulls Silas's dresser across the floor and shoves it flush against the wall.

It won't stop anyone from coming in, but it will slow them down. Even if just for a minute.

I don't help him, holding onto the gun as I continue to half-crab-walk around the perimeter of the room. If I let myself think about it too much, then I'll get lost in the swirling panic of this entire fucked-up situation.

"All you've done is trap us in here. We're sitting ducks." I'm close to the closet now. It's ridiculous as far as hiding places go, but maybe I'll get lucky and find some kind of weapon. Or more bullets.

He pushes off the dresser and flicks his hair back from his face with a hair flip Cora would be envious of. He exhales slowly, as if I'm testing his patience. "Don't insult my intelligence, Carter."

The use of my name seizes my muscles for a precious moment. It's just long enough for the ringing to start fading from my ears. Just enough for me to recognize that the thundering booms echoing in my ears isn't my heartbeat, but several pairs of booted feet pounding on the floor.

"Fuck," I curse, pushing to my feet and spinning toward the closet door.

"See, I knew you were smarter than you're acting." There's entirely too much praise in his voice, and it deepens my growing confusion.

"I don't know what the hell you're talking about, but if you're not going to kill me, then shut up."

He rears back a step, his neck jerking like I slapped him. "*Kill you*? I'm not going to kill you. I'm going to take you home."

"I don't know who the fuck you are, but *this* is my home," I snap, jamming my finger toward the floor.

I twist open the doorknob and yank open Silas's closet door. An empty plastic dry cleaning bag, white plastic hangers, and a few suits. My head whips from left to right, scanning the small space like a portal will suddenly appear and solve everything for me.

My heart races as I push aside the hangers, revealing two stacks of storage totes. The kind you pack your sweaters in during the summer months. I stare, practically panting as I scramble to figure out how the hell I'm going to use storage boxes to help.

"Huh, would you look at that," he drawls, sounding entirely too smug. "Get the fuck out of the way." He shoulders me to the side and shoves the storage boxes to the right.

Revealing a small door just big enough for an adult to walk through if they're hunched over.

"What the fuck?" I whisper, shock stealing my voice.

"Some fuckin' home, huh? Guess you don't know as much about them as you think you do," he muses, dark mirth dancing on his tongue.

I jerk my shoulder away, rage making my tongue sharp. "You don't fucking know me, asshole. And I'm getting really fucking tired of reminding you of that. I'm not diving headfirst into some dark hole with you in the back of a closet."

He bares his teeth at me in a manic sort of grin. "I've been patient. Bided my time. So I'm sure as fuck not going to lose you to some backwoods club feud. Not when you're within my grasp. So get your ass in St. James's escape hatch before those motherfuckers break down the door and we both fucking die." He punctuates his point by curling his hand over my shoulder again and jerking me toward the open door.

It's then I hear the pounding. Great big thumps against Silas's bedroom door.

Oh fuck.

Now I'm *really* out of time and options. With a silent prayer for Nana Jo to look out for me, I dive into the closet. I lean into the open doorway, peering over the side and seeing nothing but darkness. A flashlight clicks on over my head, and as much as I don't understand who this asshole is or why he's here or spewing half the things he is, I decide I'm going to be grateful for the small sliver of hope he's given me. The soft yellow light illuminates a silver ladder in what looks like some kind of metal tunnel.

I reach behind me and yank the flashlight from his hands. He grunts something too low for me to hear as he steps into the closet, pulling the closet door closed behind him. The lock sounds ominous in this confined space, but I don't have the luxury of overthinking right now. I spin around on my knees, tucking my gun into the back of my jean shorts and start my descent, gripping the cold metal rungs of the ladder with trembling hands.

The passage is narrower than I thought it would be, but still big enough to accommodate Nova's broad shoulders. The air is damp in here, stale and sort of musty like an unused basement.

"You're not claustrophobic, so stop fucking wasting time and get moving," he growls from above me, his voice like razor-wire over my already-fried senses. "One little lock isn't going to stop them. And it's only a matter of time before they find your little boyfriend's secret hatch."

I ignore everything he's saying, shove the words and sentiment somewhere outside of my body to deal with later. When I'm on the other side of this.

If I survive.

My hands start sweating, my grip loosening every few rungs. Adrenaline floods my system in a desperate attempt to ward off the inevitable shakes that happen when it dissipates. My heart kicks inside my chest as I near the bottom, and I continue ignoring whatever this asshole is grumbling at me about. Any minute now, my focus is going to shift from getting away from the assholes on motorcycles with guns to getting away from the asshole above me with a gun.

And a fucking hunting knife.

I shiver at the reminder. Of all the things I could've done

today, I hope this right here, climbing into a metal tunnel with a bonafide psychopath, isn't the worst decision I make.

My gaze travels up from his scuffed boots to the faded symbol on the back of his worn leather jacket. His dark jeans and black boots make him blend in with the other men on this compound, but something about this expression sets him apart.

As my feet hit the ground, I spot a gray metal door to the right. It's not your typical door though, because of course, this secret-hatch thing couldn't be this easy. This door is more like a hidden panel, no traditional doorknob or even a keypad. Just a small rectangular hole beneath the curved handle close to the center of the door.

Dread coils in my gut like a pissed-off snake. If this door doesn't open or it's locked from the other side, then I'm worse off than I was in Silas's bedroom. I exhale a breath at the same time he comes up behind me.

He reaches around me and yanks something from the wall above my head. He pushes it into the rectangular hole and grabs the handle. "If I would've known you were such a coward, I might've rethought my plan, Evangeline. But don't worry, princess, I'm going to help you."

3

EVANGELINE

HE SAYS *help you* the same way my mother offers a compliment. It's laced with poison and ill-intent. And it's precisely this moment I realize the shift happens.

Every hair on the back of my neck rises to attention, and I shuffle to the side. If he wants to be the first person walking into the unknown on the other side of this door, that's fine by me. Shouting echoes down from above, and I angle the flashlight toward my feet, making the beam a small circle.

He snatches it from my hand without a word, but I assume he's throwing me a harsh glare. As if his emotions bear any weight on me. The metal door opens with a small whine, like the hinges haven't been used in a while.

He steps through the doorway, and I follow behind him, urgency pounding inside my blood as the shouting gets louder and louder. Or maybe that's the tunnel playing tricks on my hearing. It feels like everything echoes in here.

I try to look around him, but all I can tell is we're in some kind of underground tunnel with metal walls with wooden beams every few feet. It's tall enough for him to walk through without hunching over, but it's not wide enough for two people to walk side-by-side. Unless one of them was a child.

Emotion wraps itself around my heart and squeezes fiercely at the thought of Hunter. I can only hope that Dixie got him far enough away from this in time.

I'm giving myself whiplash with these mental gymnastics. I went from thinking I'm definitely going to meet my end to finding the smallest glimmer of hope to crippling worry in three minutes flat.

The man in front of me picks up his pace, the leather of his jacket squeaking as he breaks into a light jog. Even this close, it's too dark for me to make out the faded design on the back. And for one heart-stopping moment I wonder if he is some kind of special Reaper. If Bane or Nova were able to get word out and he came to help me.

My pace matches his out of instinct, my pulse a constant drum beating inside my ears.

He slows down soon, and I don't stop in time, stumbling into his back. My hands fly to his back reflexively, and I stop my face from smashing into him. My fingertips glide over the material, and I can make out the muted colors of red and orange this close. My mind spins as I realize it looks familiar. Confusion slithers between the adrenaline and determination, sending my thoughts scattering as I try to place the familiarity.

The whine of another metal door draws me out of my spiral. My attention snaps to him as he glances over his shoulder. His brows are a harsh slash across his angular face. "Quiet. We don't know who's inside."

I arch a brow and keep my questions to myself, mindful of how anything I say can be used to glean information out of me. Later, when I'm clear of all of this, Cora and I are going to have a great laugh at how easily I slipped into this role like I'm starring on some drama series on TV. As if anyone is going to interrogate me or try to get information out of me.

And not because I don't know anything of value, but because this is fucking Rosewood and this crazy shit isn't supposed to happen in this town.

I follow silently behind the man as he steps into what looks like the storage side of a basement. And like a lightbulb went off inside my head, I realize with sudden clarity that this is Bane's house—his *basement*. And this is exactly the boon I needed. My confidence and determination inflate a little. Asshole Reaper or not, this is my chance to get the hell out of here, and I'm going to take it.

Silas, Nova, and Bane built an escape tunnel between their two houses. Which is somehow brilliant and scary, and I'm honestly surprised that Nova didn't tell me. An escape hatch seems like something he would have loved to show me.

But more importantly, it means there are things here I can use as weapons.

He closes the metal door shut and leans his hip against it. "Grab me that wrench," he says, pointing to the workbench along the left-hand wall.

I jog over to the bench and make a big deal of pushing onto my tiptoes to reach it. The fingertips of my right hand graze the bottom of the wrench while my left hand curls around the handle of the flathead screwdriver on the top of the workbench. I grunt a little bit, enough to vocalize that I'm trying but struggling.

As predicted, the man sighs like I'm the worst inconvenience and storms across the room. I wait until I can feel his breath on the back of my neck, until he's reaching up for the wrench.

Until he leaves his right side open.

And then I pivot on the ball of my foot and slam the screwdriver into his side as hard as I can.

He roars, dropping his outstretched hand to curl around me.

I try to dislodge his grip, pushing off the workbench and slamming my body into his. I aim for the screwdriver, using my legs to push against the tool. He cries out in pain and lets go of me, his hands flying to his side.

I've seen enough horror films to know what happens to girls who dawdle. So I don't hesitate. I spin on my heels and run like hell across the basement. I keep my gaze on the door, flat-out running toward it like it's some kind of holy grail. It might as well be backlit with gold for the way it holds my salvation.

I ignore the part of my brain that's insisting I look over my shoulder, drowning her out with the sound of my breath panting through my teeth. If he's going to shoot me, it doesn't really matter if I'm watching or not. I can't dodge a bullet.

My palm slides over the cool metal of the doorknob and another burst of adrenaline floods my veins. It's tainted with elation, like I'm going to actually make it out of here. I don't know how I'm going to get past the throng of angry asshole bikers, but I know that Bane has weapons all over this house. And in the time it takes me to turn the knob and pull open the door, that tiny little seedling of hope sprouts.

And that, that was my fatal flaw.

Something tackles me from behind, rolling to take the brunt of the fall as we slam into the concrete basement floor. The door flies toward the wall, hitting the drywall with a resounding thwack before ricocheting back into the side of my head. It's enough to stun me, freezing my muscles as stars twinkle across my vision.

He doesn't hesitate, taking advantage of my inaction and springing into motion. "Remember, I wanted to do this the easy way. But you made me do this."

I groan, pressing my hand against the tender spot on my head and twisting away from him. I try to bring my legs up for leverage to get him off of me, but I'm not fast enough. My movements are sluggish and slow, hindered by pain and disorientation. We grapple for a few moments before he ends up on top of me, sitting on my stomach with my arms pinned at my sides beneath his legs. The wound on his side bleeds freely, but he doesn't seem concerned with it.

His hand grasps my chin, covering my mouth with his big palm, holding my head still. His dark blond hair hangs over his forehead, his lips a cruel slash across his face. Deja vu washes over me like a tidal wave, bucket after bucket of the icy sensation slipping into my nose and over my eyes and covering my mouth. It suffocates me in its intensity.

I stop struggling as the realization floats toward me on a brutal flood of recognition. Closer and closer. It's just outside of my grasp when the syringe comes into view.

He uses his grip on my chin to tilt my neck to the side, and I start struggling again. Desperation leaks from my pores in droves, it's tangy and sticky and coats the back of my throat.

"Stop, stop!" I yell from behind his hand, but it comes out as muffled nonsense.

"I fucking told you to knock it off. I never should've left you here for so long. They told me to let you come to me, but I fucking knew better." He removes the syringe cap with his teeth, spitting it to the side. "If you don't hold still, I might accidentally slip and this will kill you." His tone is so even, so matter of fact. So devoid of emotion that it shocks me into submission.

Because despite everything, I don't want to die. I want to hug Cora again. To listen to Nana Jo's favorite records and dance with Bane. To bake chocolate chip cookies with Hunter. To go to the movies with Nova and kiss Silas in the rain.

I force myself to still. Anger and regret and outrage tumble over one another like the plastic cap rolling over and over across the cold concrete floor. My eyes fill with tears as I exhale through my nose.

"There. That's not so bad, hm?" His voice doesn't change, still the same even delivery as a moment ago. And somehow, that makes it all the more worse.

It's the last thing I hear before I feel the prick of the needle in the side of my neck.

And then I don't hear or see anything at all.

4

SILAS

TIME IS A FICKLE THING. It's fluid and static at the same time. It's too long and never enough. And when your time is up, fate snaps your strings with a flick of its wrist and the world keeps spinning.

I don't remember much of the drive, only that Bane and Nova tried calling them over, and over, and over again. No one ever answered. At some point, I tuned it out for self-preservation. The perverse kind of self-preservation that protected me from their collective escalating anxiety, but only so I could turn on myself.

What-if scenarios play before my eyes for an eternity, each one more devastating than the last. And then when I've worked myself up to expect the absolute worst, my mind flips a switch and the self-loathing drips into me like a leaky faucet.

Every mistake I've made, every time I lost my temper, every moment I failed. I took all those sleepless nights with baby Hunter in my arms for granted.

Each moment in time feels like acid falling into the roiling mess of snakes inside my gut. And I force myself to live in it for the rest of the drive. If something happened to my boy or Ma—or even the woman who has become so much more than the fucking nanny—I'll never forgive myself.

I blink, and I'm in front of the compound. We pull in, and the first thing I notice is the gate hanging off the hinges and the security hut absolutely wrecked.

People fill the courtyard between the clubhouse and the garages, and I slow down, scanning their faces. But I don't spot any children, so I don't bother getting out. I already know they're not here. Red and blue lights bounce off of everything, the pulsing tempo adding to the whole idea that this is some fever-induced nightmare.

"Stop here," Nova barks. "I'll check the clubhouse. You assholes better call me if you find them at the house."

Bane nods. "Likewise. Don't fucking forget, either."

Knowing my brother, he'd probably pin Evangeline up against a wall and get lost in her. He was always too wrapped up in her, blowing shit off and forgetting his responsibilities. Or maybe I'm projecting a little bit. Despite everything and the tangled mess that is sharing a single woman amongst three men, I know he loves my son. And if he found him inside, he would call me without hesitation.

I ease off the gas pedal, tapping the brake long enough for Nova to jump out of the backseat. He slams the door shut without another word, sprinting toward the clubhouse. I catch a glimpse of him in the side mirror, face pinched in determination. Some people break off the crowd and jog toward him, but then I lose sight of him as I curve around the bend in the road.

I accelerate past Ma's house, knowing she'd either go to my house or be at the clubhouse. She wouldn't stay at her place.

Astonishment washes over me as I take in the scene in front

of me. The chaos and destruction are like something out of a movie. Bodies lie scattered on the ground, smoke streams from something smoldering on my front lawn, and bikes are haphazardly strewn above.

A moat of men and bikes draw a line separating us and my house. Fear soaks my skin in a fine sweat as I stop. I'm paralyzed for a moment, disbelief and panic oozing out of my open mouth. I can't believe this is happening again.

There are plenty of ways to incite war, to fight for cities and territory. But this? This is more than a declaration, this is a fucking massacre. Not a message or a warning. There's nothing covetous about this play. There's only devastation.

"Fuck," Bane exhales, pushing open his door and running toward his house.

I throw the car in park and fling open the door in the next breath, not even bothering to remove the keys. My sole goal is finding my family. Even though I know—I just fucking know—they aren't here. Either they fled or they're—

No. I won't let myself think of the alternative. Ma called me. That means she had some warning. And in this game, a minute can mean the difference between life or death.

I step over a few bodies and tipped-over bikes, ignoring all of it. Including the groaning coming from Bane's lawn. I don't give a fuck about him or anything else. Later, when we're all safe and together again, I'm going to have some fucking choice questions about who's dropping bodies on my lawn. Last I heard, Evangeline was a city girl and Ma just had shoulder surgery.

I take the porch stairs two at a time. The sight of the front door, splintered and damaged as if someone kicked it in sends a chill down my spine. My boots crunch on the shards of wood and broken glass that litter the floor.

"Hello?" I call out, my voice echoing through the empty

house. "Hunter? Ma?" I frantically search every room on the first floor, checking in all of Hunter's usual hiding spots.

My heart stutters with worry. "Evie?" I shout, racing up the stairs in a desperate attempt to find any signs of them.

But the second floor looms just as desolate and abandoned as the first. The once pristine hallway is now littered with debris, evidence of a violent struggle.

My footsteps echo loudly against the walls as I make my way toward my bedroom. My steps falter when I find a face-down Savage Soul in my bedroom. Dresser tipped over, the closet door flung open, and all my shit tossed around the room. My heart slams against my ribs, the flimsy thing beating with the strength of a butterfly.

Hope surges as I dive for the back of my closet, where a hidden door awaits. I can't remember if Ma knew about the real reason Bane and I built a tunnel between our houses. It's another exit point, but more importantly, it's built to withstand any attack or collapse.

It's essentially a bomb shelter.

And the perfect place for my family to wait it out.

I wrench the hidden door open, revealing the pitch black hole. I pull my phone from my back pocket, hitting the flashlight app, and peer over the ledge. Adrenaline makes my fingers tremble as I reach for the steel ladder bolted to the wall. I'm at the bottom in what feels like seconds, my heart pounding in my ears like a drum.

The hook next to the metal door is empty, which means someone was definitely down here. I try to open the door, but it doesn't budge. Urgency beats against my skin, and I pound my fist on the door. "Ma! Evangeline! It's me, open the door!"

Silence fills the small space, the air thick with fragile hope. Time seems to slow down as I wait, and my breath turns ragged in my chest.

I slam my fist against the door again. "Hunter, it's me. Open the door, son."

I try the handle again, but it remains locked. The silence presses on me from all sides, and cold sweat trickles down my forehead as I wipe my brow with the back of my hand.

Heaving a breath, I thumb open Bane's contact and climb the ladder back to my bedroom.

He answers on the first ring. "Did you find them?"

"No, but I think they're in the tunnel. Door's locked from my end." I throw my leg over the top and step into my closet.

"Heading there now."

"And there's a Savage Soul bleeding out on my carpet," I tell him as I step over him once more. There's gotta be something I'm missing. "Heard from Nova?"

"Nah, but he would've called by now if they were there."

My heart seizes at his words, and I grunt a response. "I'm going to keep looking here."

"I'll call you if I find them," Bane says.

"Call me if you find anything." I hang up and jog back downstairs and into the kitchen. Evangeline and Hunter spent a lot of their time in the kitchen, and I don't know what I'm looking for, but maybe there's something.

A clue or a piece of evidence—something to tell me where the fuck my family is.

I comb my hands through my hair, pulling at it in frustration. I stand in the middle of my kitchen, spinning in a slow circle and trying to spot anything out of the ordinary.

Thank fuck most of it escaped unscathed.

On my second rotation I see it. A piece of paper underneath a turtle magnet in the middle of the fridge.

It's not the soft swirly letters I'm used to seeing. It's hurried flicks of the pen, her penmanship messier than I've ever seen. Like it was written in a hurry. Like she wanted to tell me something, but I . . . I don't understand what the fuck she means by any of it.

YOU AND I ARE FATED, *written in the stars.*
I was awake, but I was too scared to say it back and I should've.
We could've been epic, baby.
Watch Coco and eat the three dozen cookies I hid in the freezer for you.

5

BANE

I END the call with Silas and grip my phone in my fist and look around at what's left of my house. The first floor is a chaotic scene of destruction, with furniture overturned and walls filled with bullet holes. A puddle of coffee stains the island from a broken carafe. Bits of ceramic plates and mugs litter the kitchen floor.

The room is filled with the eerie sound of broken glass crunching underneath my boots, the faint whistle of the wind through the shattered windows.

Their message is haphazard in its delivery, but fatal in its execution.

The upstairs is relatively unscathed, but strangely I find myself discovering a thread of gratitude underneath it all, because now—now there's no excuse for me to hold on to this house.

No guilt when I raze it to the ground. But those feelings, they're for another day. I inhale deeply, my mind swirling with thoughts as I try to piece together what could have led to this moment.

My senses hone in on the smallest details, searching my memory for what I missed as I race down the stairs to my basement. I don't hesitate by the open door, even though I rarely leave it open. My heartbeat matches the rhythm of my footfalls crashing down the stairs. I rush to the middle of the finished side of the basement, spinning in a circle and looking for . . . I don't know what. It's not like I expected her to be huddled in the corner with Aunt Dixie and Hunter.

I exhale sharply and drag my hand over my face, the scruff on my chin scraping at my palms. I guess, maybe I *was* expecting that. But it's clear they're not here, and worse, I can't even tell if they were.

Disparaging thoughts that sound a lot like my mother's voice flick across my consciousness, embedding themselves in the soft tissues of my brain where I'm most vulnerable.

You should have prepared her, protected her.
You failed her and your aunt and your nephew.
You failed them all because that's what you do.
You're a failure just like your father.

I grunt at the mental onslaught, shouldering open the door to the storage side with more force than necessary. The door handle slams into the drywall with a low thunk, and I stare around the room. My chest heaves with exertion like I just ran a marathon and not across a basement.

The unfinished side of the basement was like a forgotten realm, where shadows crept along the forgotten memories shoved in plastic storage totes.

At a first glance, it looks exactly the same. The wall of shelves on one side, a rarely-used workbench on the other. And the door to the underground tunnel connecting my house to Silas's.

I open the door to my side of the tunnel with ease. It's not even locked. I squint, staring at my hand wrapped around the metal handle and try to remember if I had locked it.

I don't know if I did. It's one of those things I don't think about often, since we've never had to use it before. We tried it out, of course, when we built it. But we haven't needed it.

I step into the tunnel and cup my hands around either side of my mouth. "Evangeline! Aunt Dixie! Hunter!"

But only silence answers as I stand at the entrance of the dark tunnel. Flipping open the flashlight app on my phone, I cautiously make my way inside, my heart pounding. My footsteps echo slightly against the metal walls, the only sound down here. I walk all the way down to the locked door that connects to Silas' house.

It's . . . empty. They're not here.

"Fuck," I bark, fisting my hand against the door and closing my eyes for a second.

I didn't realize it until this moment that I had quietly hoped that I would find them in here, safe and sound. But I fucking know better than to hope.

You would have thought that this life would have burned the last vestiges of hope right out of my bloodstream but no, there it was, flickering like a dying candle in the wind.

That little voice in the back of my head isn't wrong, no matter how much I wish it were. I *didn't* protect her, and I *should've* prepared her more.

But we've grown complacent in recent years. Content to live our lives on the fringe of criminal activity. Our instincts grew dull in the midst of peace.

Regret is a ruthless siren, she'll drag your ass into the depths of your own hell. And then she'll drown you without remorse. And she's doing her fucking best to sink her talons into me right now. I don't have the luxury of time. Besides, I try to make a habit of not giving in to the temptation of regret.

But there are moments, however infrequent and fleeting, when the weight of it all comes crashing down on me. The burden of everything I've done in the name of the Reapers is heavier than I ever imagined.

And eight years ago, I found myself thanking a god I didn't believe in for putting her in my path, for snuffing out the burning embers of regret and reigniting the spark of life within me once more.

It's fucking lame and corny and a thousand other adjectives that paint me as a cliche, but it's the truth.

I . . . I thought she was a gift for all the shit that I had endured, my personal image of hope in a world where savagery was the norm.

But if the universe was merciful enough to grant me her then, what have I done to deserve this?

What have I done to deserve her being taken?

I rake my fingers through my hair, tugging at the roots and willing myself to think.

Think harder, think faster.

Time is an invisible noose cinching around my neck with every passing heartbeat. She's slipping through my fingers. I swallow the scream of frustration that gurgles up my throat, clawing its way free. Anxiety given sound.

I pace inside the tunnel. Five steps, turn, five more steps, turn.

There's gotta be something I missed, some small detail. Evangeline wouldn't just *leave*. I know that as well as I know my middle name. And there's no fucking way Aunt Dixie would just disappear either.

But if they're staring down the barrel of the proverbial gun, they would leave in a heartbeat if it meant protecting Hunter.

So either they left in a hurry and I need to keep looking, or someone took them.

I jog back to my house, stopping inside the storage area. My chest heaves with breaths far too deep to warrant such a small jog. But my anxiety makes the air feel thin and my throat feel tight.

My gaze flies around the small room, and then I see it. There, in the middle of the hanging tools above my workbench, is an empty hook.

Why the fuck would a screwdriver be missing?

I spin in a circle, my eyes scanning every inch of the area around the door. Was the door locked and she tried to jimmy it open with a screwdriver?

I drop down to my hands and knees and shine my phone's flashlight underneath the workbench. The yellow beam of light reveals nothing but dust and cobwebs, so I move to the other side of the room.

And there, illuminated underneath the storage shelves, is the familiar glint of metal. The missing screwdriver, marred with dried blood. My hand trembles as I pick it up, praying it's someone else's blood. Didn't Silas say there was a bleeding Savage in his bedroom? Maybe Aunt Dixie used this on him and they fled through the tunnel?

As soon as the thought crosses my mind, something catches my eye from across the room. I sprint toward it, heart pounding in my chest, until my hand wraps around a small, familiar object. The plastic cap of a syringe digs into my palm, bringing a rush of fear.

Sweat dampens the back of my neck as my mind spins wildly. My stomach pitches at what this offending plastic means.

This wasn't just a message or a warning or even a first strike. Storming the compound wasn't the play and opening fire on our homes wasn't the message.

It was a fucking *distraction*.

6

SILAS

I TRACE my finger along the edge of the piece of paper, my brow furrowing as I try to read between the lines. But these four lines aren't hidden clues to where they went.

A low whistle breaks the silence, and I look over my shoulder and see a figure standing just inside my kitchen. Anthony Redford stands in the doorway, his salt-and-pepper hair cropped close like he just came from the barber shop. His narrowed brown-eyed gaze sweeps around the state of my house like he finds it lacking.

Hands tucked into his pockets, rocking back on his heels like he's going out for a casual evening stroll and not witnessing the attempted murder of my family.

Because that's exactly what the fuck happened here.

"Looks like you got quite the mess on your hands, huh, Silas?" He scratches absentmindedly at his overgrown gray beard, his bloodshot eyes surveying my kitchen instead of looking at me. "See, the problem is we got a lot of bodies in your front yard."

I'm already shaking my head, reminding myself that I need

to tread carefully here. I'm not in a position to be collecting enemies like fucking trading cards. But if this asshole doesn't get a fucking clue soon, I'm going to forget that I'm the clear-headed one running this club. And then we're all fucked.

I turn around, feeling my blood pressure rise with every second that I'm here and they're *not*. "What did you say?"

Redford clears his throat, his gaze skipping around like a rock on the lake. "I can't ignore those bodies, you know? It's not good for the town and all that."

I tongue the inside of my cheek, my body wired. "Not good for the town, huh?"

Redford nods, like I'm agreeing with him. "You understand."

Disbelief carves lines between my brows, dragging a scoff from my mouth. "Nah, Redford. I don't understand what you're saying. Why don't you spell it out for me how you, the sheriff we pay to avoid shit like this, let this happen in our town, at my house. To my fucking son, and my mother, and my goddamn nanny. Where the fuck were you while they were being taken." It's not a question. It's a fucking demand.

Redford drags his hand along the back of his neck, perspiration on his forehead gleaming in the afternoon light streaming through the broken facade of my house. "Well, now, see, Silas. You know I leave you to your club business, but this here"—he motions to the front of the house—"this can't be covered up as club business. So I'm afraid I'm going to need to take someone in for this, son."

I cross the room in three steps, grab the old fuck by the collar of his brown shirt and haul him against the wall. I look down my nose at him, letting him look at the monster swimming at the surface. The part of me that doesn't give a fuck about politics or arbitrary rules. To the beast inside of me who will stop at nothing to get his family back safely.

"I am not your fucking son," I seethe through gritted teeth.

"Those motherfuckers came into my town, onto my property, and drove their asses right up to my house before they unleashed a barrage bullets on my fucking house." I jostle him against the wall. "Where my fucking family was. Do you understand what that does to a man, Sheriff?"

Redford swallows. "Yeah, I understand."

I shake my head, dismissing his empty words. "It's got me feeling like I have to reevaluate who I trust. Can I trust you, Redford?"

He nods. "You know you can, Silas. We've had a mutually-beneficial relationship for years. Why would I jeopardize that right before retirement?"

I release my grip on his shirt with a sharp exhale and take a step back. "Why indeed, Sheriff. What are you planning to do to make this right, hm?"

Redford's eyebrows shoot up, his gaze shifting around once more. "*Me?* This is a club issue, so—Silas. This kind of thing isn't part of our agreement."

"It is now." I grin at him, flashing a feral sort of smile. "These motherfuckers won't stop with us. They'll hit Main Street next, then the residents. If they haven't already. That's how they work. They're fucking parasites, feeding off of destruction and chaos. And they'll tear apart every good thing just because they fucking can."

"Well, now, see you should've told me that right away, Silas. No need for the . . . theatrics," Redford says, glancing over my shoulder.

"We good, brother?" Nova asks from somewhere behind me.

I fold my arms across my chest and stare at the sheriff. "Are we good, Redford?"

The sheriff runs a trembling hand down the front of his shirt and clears his throat. "Yeah, we're good, so—*Silas*."

I nod a few times, but the movement is all sharp and fueled

by anger. "I was having quite the chat here with the sheriff about how he wants to take one of us in for the mess in the front yard. Despite the fact that we're the fucking victims in this situation, so anything that happened after the fact is considered self-defense."

"Is that right?" Nova drawls, his slow cadence a facade. "How nice of our sheriff to come to our aid in our time of need."

"Mm-hmm. Almost as nice as the amount of money we've paid him over the years. You know, Nova, it'd be a shame if that gift turned into a debt. One that needs to be repaid starting today."

Redford shifts his weight from one foot to another, his shoulders curving over a little. "Nah, no need to get hasty, boys. I'll make sure Sheriff Bellfleur gets the details right in the report. And I'll send the team to clean up for ya."

"And where is that shithead Ethan today, hm?" Nova asks, cocking his head to the side. "Seems kind of like the thing the next sheriff should be overseeing, yeah?"

I recognize that faux-casual tone and the almost innocent curiosity in his gaze. My brother has had it out for Ethan Bellfleur since freshman year when he caught him shoving a kid inside a locker like it was some high school sitcom. Nova didn't even know the kid, but if there's one thing my brother hates, it's a fucking bully.

"Oh, ah, Ethan?" Redford asks, scratching his jaw with his index finger. "Yeah, he's handling a dispute by the edge of town."

Nova saunters across the kitchen, stopping a few feet in front of Redford. He arches a brow and flashes a charming smile. "Is that right? Give him my regards, yeah?"

Redford clears his throat, his gaze bouncing from Nova to me and back again. "Right, well. I'll be around if you boys need something."

I wait for the sheriff to leave, before I turn to face my brother. "No sign of them at the clubhouse?"

He shoots me a glare. "Would I stand here and fuck around with the sheriff if there was?"

"Nah, I know. I'm just—fuck." I exhale and shake my head, looking at my boots.

"What's this? Is that Evangeline's handwriting?" he asks, walking to the refrigerator.

The hope in his voice snaps my head toward him. "Yeah, I thought it was clues or directions or something at first, but this" —I stab my index finger on the first line—"I don't fucking know what this gibberish is. Or when she wrote it. For all we know, she did this weeks ago and it has nothing to do with any of this."

He knocks my hand away. "It's not gibberish. And it's from today. I would've noticed it if it had been there before." He takes another step toward it, his expression deepening as he studies the scrawled words.

"How?" The word hangs in the air like a skeptical echo.

"Because that's what I said to her that night at The Wild Boar," he murmurs. "And this, this is from the night Bane said those infamous three little words and she pretended to be asleep. Guess she was scared to say it back then," he murmurs.

My head rears back, and my brows crash into an angry V between my eyes. "And how the fuck do you know that?"

He lifts a shoulder, his gaze focused on the words. "Bane's not the only one who can hack a security system. I liked to check in on her from time to time."

"Am I the only fucking normal one in this family? Why the fuck are you watching Bane and Evangeline *sleep together?*"

He looks up at me, raising a single brow in challenge. "I don't think you're in any position to camp out on your moral high ground."

My blood hums inside my veins, hungry to expel some of

these volatile emotions churning in my gut. Jealousy and worry make excellent bedfellows apparently.

I rock back on my heels and appraise him. "You know what? I'm not going to say *I told you so*. Instead, I'll say *good luck*, brother, because you're going to fucking need it when Bane finds out you've been watching him fuck our girl. And when everything goes to shit, you'll only have yourself to blame."

A knowing smirk curls up the side of my mouth, fueled by a perverse desire to goad him. Just a little bit. The asshole has been off for months now, ever since *she* got here. But since it's been established that they're not giving her up, then he's gonna have to work through whatever the fuck causes him to glare at me when he doesn't think I'm looking. The kind of look he usually reserves for plotting how to rearrange someone's face .

He smirks, but it's laced with spite. "You sure use a lot of words to say 'I'm jealous,' brother."

I rock back a step back, my back snapping to a straight line. "I'm not fucking jealous."

Nova places the note beneath the magnet, ensuring it's secure before he snaps a photo on his phone. Head bent and smile tipping up the corner of his mouth, he whistles softly as he strolls out of the kitchen.

"What the fuck are you whistling about? And where are you going?" I snap, disbelief tightening my shoulders.

"That woman loves us. Even you, you grumpy asshole. And I'm going to go find her."

"Yeah? And how the fuck are you planning on doing that?" I snap.

He flashes his teeth at me, pausing at the threshold. "By any means necessary. Starting with that Savage Soul bleeding out in Bane's front yard."

7

NOVA

THE BROKEN SCREEN door slams against the frame behind me as I stand on what used to be the front porch of our house. Technically, it's still a porch, but it's taken the brunt of the attack today. Bits of wood everywhere, the deck chairs a heap of splintered remains. The fact that they were so fucking close and still had such shitty aim tells me these aren't all seasoned brothers. These might even be fucking prospects in on this.

I shake my head. "These fucking assholes."

I'm sure it's in my head, but I swear I can smell the scent of blood in the air. Hanging around like an unwanted guest and a reminder of what transpired. As if I could ever forget.

I look out over the compound, worry eating a hole inside my gut. It's unfamiliar in its intensity, which is a little ironic for a man who found himself in the emergency room with a gunshot wound not that long ago. But this kind of destruction with Evangeline and Hunter inside the house is . . . unthinkable.

Panic seizes my chest as I scan the horizon, searching for some kind of sign of them.

"Where are you, Evangeline?" It's a murmured plea, carried away on the wind as soon as it leaves me.

Wherever you are, you better be okay, sweetheart. Because I don't know what I'm going to do if you're not.

I've never really been the praying sort. It's not that I don't believe there is a higher power, more like I wasn't really sure if it mattered or not. Evangeline Carter is the only altar I willingly worship, so it seems fitting that I find myself praying to her now.

I cross the sparse lawn, stepping over bullet casings and a couple of prone bodies until I reach the low moaning of one of the pieces of shit who opened fire on my house today.

"P-please," the man begs, sprawled out on his side on my cousin's lawn. His right hand presses tightly against his shoulder, the slow gurgle of blood slipping between his fingers. "I-I need a doctor."

I suck my teeth, resting my boot on his hip and nudging him over, so I can see his kutte properly. My lip curls up when I spot the Hell Hound patch on the left side. Huh, guess I was wrong. I thought only the Savage Souls were fucking dumb enough for this move, but that's what I get for assuming, I guess.

"What's your name?"

He grunts, sweat blooming across his brow as he squints up at me. "Richard Miller."

Asshole is probably baking in this sun, and I can only hope that infection has already started. Which means that I've got to get to work.

"Well, Richard Miller, looks like your shitbag club left you to die." I bare my teeth in a wild grin, the kind that makes people take a step back. It's one of my favorites, a little unhinged and a lot menacing. It feels good to wear it again, like I'm tapping the keg of my boiling rage inside. "But don't worry. I'm going to bring you to my studio."

"Are you some kind of doctor?" He squints up at me, pain tightening his mouth into a scowl.

I rest my boot on his bicep, applying pressure and relishing in the sound of his strained grunt. His face turns a deep shade of crimson as he fights to keep any more noises from escaping him. I let out a sharp whistle Ma would be proud of, and two of the sheriff's most trusted deputies look over their shoulders at me. They're halfway down the road, no doubt heading this way before the sheriff waved them off.

"I need some help with this one," I call out, jerking my thumb toward the guy still beneath my boot.

The deputies jog up the road, their footsteps in an eerie unison for a few seconds there. They stop on the other side of Richard, their expressions drawn and determined. I recognize them in the way you recognize most of Rosewood's residents. And while they're not as trustworthy as a Reaper, I don't want to fucking wait for someone to wander up here or pull someone from the clubhouse.

They didn't raid it or rob us, but the front of the building caught a few bullets. Nothing like what they did here, but enough that it needs to be cleaned up and repaired.

"Nova," the deputy on the right, Wheeler, says. "Sheriff Redford said you had it under control here, so we were heading back to the gates."

"You got a live one, eh?" Thompson muses, looking down his nose at the asshole on the ground between us.

"Seems that way. You two mind helping me for a second? I have a few questions for him, and I think he'll be most comfortable in Southern Steel."

"You sure you don't want us to bring him in? Might be hard to clean all that"—Thompson pauses, tsking from the back of his throat—"blood outta your carpets."

I grin at the deputies, all sharp edges and blunt teeth. "Nah, my studio has an in-floor drain I think will be extremely useful today."

The deputies' faces contort in amusement. Their eyes dance with dark mirth as they both take in Richard's form, his palm still pressing against his shoulder. They exchange a look with one another.

"Sure thing, Nova. I'll grab my truck, it's easier with the open bed," Thompson says.

I observe with a mix of satisfaction and detachment as the deputies roughly shove him into the bed of their dusty pickup. He's doing absolutely nothing to make it easier on them, and I idly wonder if he's going to be the type to try to die rather than talk.

I climb into the front seat with Thompson, Wheeler staying in the back with the Hell Hound. I direct them where to park for easiest access to my building.

Thompson and Wheeler handle my instructions without complaint, getting the pickup into position just outside my door. I hop out of the passenger seat and stretch my arms, feeling a strange sense of calm settle over me. This is what I'm good at—talking and fixing problems.

The deputies get him out of the truck and put him exactly where I direct inside one of my studios.

"Let us know if you need anything," Thompson calls over his shoulder, dusting his hands off on his uniform pants.

Wheeler waves a hand over his shoulder. "Later, Nova. Good luck with the asshole."

The asshole in question stands in the center of my work area, arms bound and raised above him, attached to a hook and pulley system I installed for my brief stint with pendulum painting.

I gesture to his bound hands. "I installed it above the drain for easy paint cleanup, but I guess it works for blood too."

"What do you want from me?" he asks, grimacing as he looks at me.

"Well, see, that's the thing," I murmur, circling around him like a predator does to prey. I reach out and deftly pluck his wallet from his back pocket. My fingers slip inside the worn leather billfold, and slip his driver's license out. "Richard Miller of nine-twenty-eight Cleveland Avenue." I whistle, my brows rising. "Damn, man, you don't look like you're thirty-five. I would've guessed fifty. I guess being the absolute scum of the earth ages you, yeah?"

I let out an exasperated sigh and pull out my phone to snap a photo of his license. With a flick of my finger, I send it to Bane, knowing he'll work his behind-the-scenes magic. I slide his license back inside the wallet and toss it across the room with a flick of my wrist. It skids across the floor, landing just outside the circle of bright white from the overhead spotlights.

"Are you going to kill me?" He doesn't sound scared really, more pitiful. Maybe a little resigned.

I shrug with a smirk. "Do you want me to kill you?"

His beady eyes scan the room we're in and he sniffs. "Isn't that why you brought me here, to your kill room?"

My face twists into a scowl and my neck arches back in surprise. "I don't know what kind of fucked-up club you belong to—"

"The only club worth being in." He bares his teeth, the veins in his neck bulging.

Ah, there he is. I was wondering if he'd show any kind of backbone here. Still, it's hard to take him seriously right now. His face is a mess. Sunburned from baking in Bane's front yard, plus a busted lip and what looks like a blooming black eye courtesy of Rosewood's finest deputies.

"Hmm," I muse, turning around and heading to the cabinets on the far wall.

I'm feeling creative, and while I'm no stranger to the physical methods of getting information, I've found that psychological tactics often work just as well. This is my creative space, after all. If I killed him right now, it'd be a wasted death. And if there's anything Ma taught me, it's to be resourceful.

My chest feels tight just thinking about Ma, and there's no room for that here.

I select one of my favorite palette knives. A wooden eight-sided handle and a rounded point, it's perfect for the small details on a canvas. And for navigating the intricate design of the human psyche.

"It's a bold move, breaking into a man's house," I murmur as I slowly circle him.

"We didn't go inside your house," the man says, blood dripping from the cut on his lip.

I tap the end of my palette knife against my bottom lip before I stop and point it at him. "Except you did."

He shakes his head, his greasy hair sticking to his sweaty forehead. "N-no, not me. I swear. I was outside the whole time."

I nod a few times and continue my stroll around him. My footsteps echo with heavy thuds as I keep an easy pace. "Right. You stayed outside my house, unleashing a maelstrom of bullets at my woman and nephew."

He grunts and looks away, shifting his weight from foot to foot.

"So tell me, Richard, how do you feel about nicknames?"

His head snaps toward me like he's surprised by my question. "Nicknames are good?"

"I've got a few I think we should try out. Little Dicky. One-eyed Dick. Dicky No Hands." I pause in front of him, tilting my head to the side and giving him a good once-over. I let the slumbering menace inside of me unfurl like a jungle cat, all lethal grace. "Now, I know they sound like dick jokes, and see, that's intentional. Who doesn't like a good dick pun, am I right, Richard?"

He nods, his head bobbing quickly in agreement. "Yeah, yeah. I love a good dick joke."

I chuckle, but there's no humor in it. "And how do you feel about your dick?"

"I, uh, like it?" he stammers, his eyes wide as he looks around.

"Good because if you don't start talking, I'm going to fucking cut it off." I waggle the palette knife in front of him, letting the studio lights glint off the metal.

He flinches, his hips jerking back reflexively. But that won't save him. Not when he's tethered to the middle of my studio like a fish on a hook.

He licks his lips. "Fuck, okay, *okay*. Troy, he, uh, he made this deal with Masters."

"Troy Moore, your president made a deal with Deran Masters, the old Savage Souls president?" I say it slowly, trying to puzzle out what the fuck kind of information ol' Richard here will give me and if it's valuable or not.

He nods too quickly. "Yeah. He approached our prez, cashed in on a favor. I don't know what for. We just, uh, we just do what we're told. You know how that goes."

My phone rings, interrupting Richard's rambling. I pull it out of my back pocket, my heart in my throat when I see an unfamiliar number. I'm across the room and into the lobby in a heartbeat.

"Hello?"

"Son?"

"Ma?" Relief takes my knees out, and I have to lock them at the sound of her familiar voice.

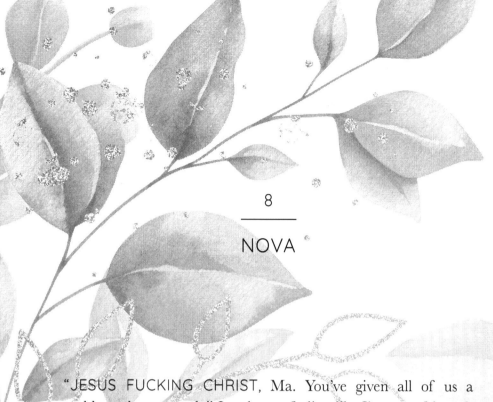

8

NOVA

"JESUS FUCKING CHRIST, Ma. You've given all of us a goddamn heart attack," I rush out, feeling like I'm out of breath with relief.

"Is that any kind of way to talk to your mother, Asher St. James?"

I welcome the reproach in her voice with open fucking arms. I drag my hand down my face and let out an exhale that I feel in my soul.

"Where are you, Ma? Are you guys okay?"

"We're at the safe house, the one on Lincoln. I know protocol says to wait another hour, but I couldn't. I've been worried sick about you boys and Evangeline. Tell me what happened. Are you safe? Where is your brother? And Bane?"

Her words are rapid-fire, like she can't speak fast enough. I'm shaking my head as I try to catch up, my brows crowding my eyes. "Wait an hour, what are you talking about?"

"Our *family evacuation plan*," she stresses, as if those words are going to magically tell me what the hell she's talking about.

"Ma, I don't know—*wait.*" I spin around, facing the wall. My back rounds as I lean over a little, the icy fingers of dread curling around my heart and squeezing. "What did you say?"

"I said this has always been our family evacuation plan if the compound is compromised. Honestly, son, you should know this."

I wave my hand in the air, like I can physically swipe away her words. But it's been so long since I was a civilian, since I had to learn the evacuation plan, that I'd forgotten it I guess. I doubt Silas *or* Bane remembers either, or they would've already been to the Lincoln Street safe house by now, protocol be damned.

"No, no before that. What about Evangeline?" My heartbeat pulses inside my veins, a thudding reminder of the urgency in the situation.

"I said I'm worried about her," she says, pitching her voice louder for a moment. "Honestly, Asher, I'm worried about the quality of service on these burners. Who knows how long they've been here."

"Ma," I bark. "I love you, and I'm so glad you're safe with Hunter, but I need you to focus so I can figure out what the fuck is going on. Where is Evangeline?"

Anxiety felt like a swarm of bees trapped beneath my ribs, buzzing and stinging with frenzied urgency.

"I don't know, son," she says, her voice gentle. "I ran to your house, right when they breached the gate. She grabbed Hunter, and we got on the UTVs. I was going to lead her off the property through the service gate in the back. But the red one, it wouldn't start."

Loathing as thick as tar slides down my throat, filling my stomach with nauseating bitterness. The image of Evangeline's panicked face flashes in my mind, her dark brown eyes wide with fear as she clutches Hunter close on a dead UTV.

I told Silas I was going to fix it, but I've been so distracted lately that I didn't make it a priority.

"Fuck," I breathe out, shame pricking at my eyes.

"I was going to run over to Bane's house, see if his was there. But there just wasn't enough time. She made me take Hunter and get on the blue UTV, so I made her take my gun."

"Since when does anyone *make you* do anything you don't want to?" My words fly past my lips too freely, fueled by anger and self-loathing, and I clamp my mouth shut to stop any more from spilling out.

"Where is she?" The words escape her in a shaken whisper.

"Gone."

She sucks in a sharp breath. "She's dead?"

My jaw tightens as I shake my head. "No, no. We didn't find her here."

"Then she's not gone, Asher," she insists, some of that legendary steel slipping back into her tone. "If she's not on the compound, then she's in trouble. And she needs us, son. She stayed back so Hunter and I could safely get away. If she wasn't already family, that alone would make her part of it."

Determination wars with the overwhelming urge to sink into myself, to let the rot of self-loathing and anger eat me from the inside out.

"So get your shit straight and bring home our girl," Ma says. "By any means necessary."

I jerk my chin up, staring at the wall in front of me unseeing. "I will, Ma."

"I know you will, honey. And for fucks's sake, tell your brother to answer his phone when I call," she says with an exasperated sigh.

I shake my head. "It's a burner. You know how he gets with unknown numbers."

"Yeah, well, he needs to work that shit out too." I can just picture the way she arches her brow and looks down her nose, like she's about to lecture one of her sons.

"Yeah, I'll tell him right now."

"Is he with you? Just hand your phone over."

I glance behind me at the sound of a low groan coming from the studio. I left the door cracked open in my haste to answer the phone, but I'm not worried he can overhear me. Besides, who the fuck is he going to tell?

"Nah, I'm busy having a chat with one of the assholes who stormed the compound. Silas is at the house, trying to figure out where you and Hunter are."

She's quiet for a moment, then she says, "By any means necessary, honey."

She ends the call without waiting for me to reply. I stare at my booted feet on the light-colored floor, trying to figure out what this new information means for my girl now.

Me: Answer your phone next time, asshole

My phone vibrates in my palm, the familiar photo of my brother's face lighting up the screen. I grunt and send it to voicemail, opening up our text thread instead.

Me: I'm busy. Call back the recent unknown number. It's Ma.

I stare at my phone for a full minute, but he doesn't text me back or call me again. I assume he's already on the phone.

I stroll back into the workspace. "Saved by the bell, Richard."

"You're going to let me go?" he asks, hope making his voice high.

"I thought about doing it here, you know. There's something . . . poetic about the way blood splatters. There's no careful precision behind it, no practiced brushstrokes or angles. It's pure instinct. I could do a whole series. I'd call it Hounds and Savages." I chuckle a little, shaking my head at my own pun and pulling myself away from my vision.

A glance at Richard and I notice he's not laughing. If anything, his complexion is paler than it was.

"But then I remembered that my girl likes it in here, and I

think she might have some moral objection to riding my face in the same space where you took your last breath, yeah? See, she's just and moral and so fucking beautiful it makes your teeth ache." I shake my head as the image of her beautiful face flashes before my eyes as clear as if she was standing in front of me.

"I-I—"

I pivot to face him now, feeling a little crazed. "Have you ever had that, Richard? That kind of instant connection with someone that snowballs into something so magnificent that you'll do anything to protect it?"

"W-why are you telling me this?"

"Just making conversation, man. But if you want to skip this part and go right into the—"

"No, no, talking is good. I love talking," he says quickly, a slow smile spreading across his face.

I smile. "So tell me, where the fuck is my girl, Richard?"

His smile falls and he looks around the room like the answer is going to pop out at him. "Your girl?"

"Yeah, see, that was my mother on the phone. Turns out, she made it out of the house with my nephew. But my girl?" I step toward him, angling the knife so it presses on the soft tissue between his ribs. "My girl wasn't with them. Which means you haven't been truthful with me, Richard."

"I swear I didn't take anyone from the house," he says, tripping over his words.

"Well, of course *you* didn't—you're here. I need a name."

"But I-I don't know who took her. They didn't tell me they were taking anyone. It was supposed to be a scare tactic, that's what our president agreed to. But I don't know what Masters told his guys. They seemed . . . I don't know, fucked-up or something."

I cock my head to the side. "Fucked-up how?"

"I don't know, like maybe they were rolling or they were just amped up for violence. Shit's contagious, you know? One thing led to another, and pretty soon, Masters had convinced everyone the only move was to take out your house."

"And my girl? You plucked her from my house like she's a wildflower in a field. When none of you deserve to even breathe the same air as her, let alone touch her."

"I-I don't know anything about that. I swear."

I nod, tapping my phone against my thigh. I open my contacts and scroll to the one saved for our cleanup crew. "Alright Richard. I believe you."

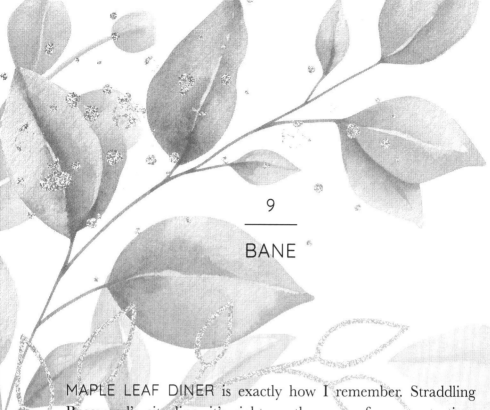

9

BANE

MAPLE LEAF DINER is exactly how I remember. Straddling Rosewood's city line, it's right on the cusp of our protection. Thankfully, the other side of the line is the start of neutral territory. Considering how it went down with Three Crowns Tavern in Silverstone, that's not as reassuring as it used to be.

It's an elevated diner, keeping the classic red vinyl booths and barstools and adding a modern touch with chrome accents and sleek wooden tables. A large counter with swiveling stools and a display case filled with assorted pastries and desserts.

It's kitschy and quirky enough that it's a local favorite, but polished enough to attract tourists and out-of-towners. The bell jingles when I walk inside, and the scents of maple syrup and freshly-brewed coffee waft through the air.

Slipping my sunglasses off and hanging them in the front of my v-neck, I scan the occupied booths for the infamous Carter shade of black hair. The diner is busy, even at this hour, but thankfully not too busy. I'm not sure how this conversation is going to go, and the less eyes on me, the better.

In the far right corner, with her back to the door and her

head on a swivel, I see Elizabeth Carter in a booth. Wearing a pale peach blouse and big black sunglasses, she sticks out far more than she blends in.

The linoleum floor swallows my footsteps as I cross the restaurant, waving at the cook behind the counter. My approach to the booth is deliberate and only mildly confrontational. Given the day I've had, the fact I'm even here right now when I should be out combing the streets of Rosewood is a fucking feat.

I slide into the open side of the booth with my back to the wall, giving me a view of the restaurant. She startles in her seat, her shoulders jerking toward her ears.

"Lincoln St. James?" she hisses, glancing behind her like she expects someone to be with me.

I settle into the vinyl seat, widening my legs in case I need to move quickly. I look her over, immediately realizing my mistake. Upon closer look, Elizabeth looks nothing like her sister. This Carter is all sharp angles, wearing her disdain like a diamond necklace around her neck. Hair brassier than Evangeline's, coarser maybe too.

"You don't recognize me?"

She slides her sunglasses down the bridge of her nose, her narrowed gaze shrewd as she looks me up and down. I jerk my chin up, giving her a minute to get a good look. I'm half tempted to let the mask slip and expose the snarling mass of chaos roaming underneath my skin.

Silas called when I was halfway here, letting me know that Aunt Dixie and Hunter made it to some safe house all of us forgot about. But Evangeline? She's still unaccounted for. And that alone makes me feel untethered to this earth, like the chains I've grown accustomed to have slid down my shoulders.

Every man has a breaking point, and I've only recently realized that mine begins and ends with Evangeline Carter.

So while there's part of me that wants to detail our first

encounter all those years ago, my time and energy is best spent elsewhere for now.

Her upper lip curls. "Should I?"

I shrug casually, rolling my neck from left to right. I don't expect her to remember me, but I haven't forgotten her. It was only a few months after my night on the beach with Evangeline, and I mistakenly thought Elizabeth was her. In my defense, it was late as fuck and we were a state away. None of that is worth getting into now.

I rest my left arm along the top of the booth and smirk. "You're throwing a lot of attitude for someone who called me for help."

"I'm not asking for *help*." She narrows her eyes over her sunglasses, nose wrinkling on the word help like it tastes bad.

I drop my arm, my patience thin. "Where is she?"

She grips her sunglasses between two pointy blue nails and sets them on the table. "Where is who?"

I exhale. "Cut the shit, *Lizzie*. If you have information for me, now's the time to start talking before I walk out the door. Where is your sister?"

She leans forward, her eyes widening so much, I see a whole swath of white. "She's not with you?"

My mind stutters at the genuine display of concern. It goes against everything Evangeline has told me about her sister. And I don't know her well enough to determine if she's playing me or not.

I clench my teeth together hard enough to feel the ache in my neck. "You said *you came for my sister once. Now I need you to do it again*. So here I fucking am, *Lizzie*. Now tell me where the fuck my woman is."

She leans back against the booth, the leather barely creaking under her weight. She glances over her shoulder again. And if I wasn't watching, I would've missed her tells. Her shoulders tighten and her weight shifts, like she's going to spring to her feet any second.

I hear the reason why a moment later.

"Elizabeth Geraldine Carter, you bitch," Coraline Carter seethes, storming to the booth and crowding Lizzie. "You went too far this time. Too fucking far." She points her index finger in Lizzie's face, her mouth twisted into a fierce scowl.

"You follow me, Carter?"

She turns her head to look at me with arched brows, but she doesn't give her cousin an inch, half-bent over her in her seat. "You bet your ass I did. Now scoot over, Lizzie," she snaps, sliding in next to her. She fixes her gaze on me. "My cousin is missing after those slimy fucks stormed the town and opened fire on the compound."

"Who did?" Lizzie interrupts.

Coraline holds her index finger in front of Lizzie's face, effectively shushing her. "We heard it all the way downtown, Bane. It was . . ." She pauses, shaking her head as her gaze turns inward for a moment. "And then you tear outta there like your ass is on fire, so I knew that it had to do with Eve. But what I didn't account for was *you*." She slides her narrowed-eyed gaze on Lizzie, shifting to face her on the bench. "What did you *do*?"

Lizzie raps her nails against the table, pursing her lips and averting her gaze. "I . . . messed up."

"So you mentioned. Elaborate." I catch the approaching waitress's eye and politely wave her away. I don't want any interruptions. The faster she talks, the faster I can get the fuck out of here and start looking for my girl.

"Well, you see, one night on tour, the guys and I were looking for a little fun, and we ended up at this club downtown. It's nothing like The Menagerie in New York City, but it—"

"Oh for fuck's sake, Lizzie, get to the point," Coraline snaps.

"Fine," Lizzie says, baring her teeth at her cousin. "We ended up partying with some guys that night. Had a lot of party favors, parted ways in the morning. It's not unusual, and I didn't think anything of it. Until we saw them at the next city on the tour, and then the next one. I'd lost count of all the times we'd party together after a show or on our off nights. We didn't realize that they were going to charge us for all the party favors we did with them."

"*And?* You tell anyone who will listen how much money you rake in from your tours. And suddenly you're balking at the idea of paying for your own shit?" Cora shakes her head and folds her arms across her chest. "Nah, I don't fucking buy it. Start telling the truth or Bane is going to shoot you."

Lizzie startles in her seat, her head snapping to me with wide eyes.

I won't shoot Evangeline's sister—unless my girl asked me, of course. I'd do anything for her. But Lizzie doesn't know that. So I make sure to maintain my most neutral expression, giving her nothing.

She should be fucking scared, because if we find out she had a hand in this, not even God himself will save her from Coraline Carter. That woman is a fucking menace.

Lizzie sniffs, her gaze darting away. "I've had expenses lately, so my savings are low."

Coraline rolls her eyes and scoffs. "Aunt Ginny is fucking loaded, so spare me your poor orphan Annie routine. And don't for one single second act like you weren't just dying for your moment to take your sister out. You've hated Evangeline from the moment she was born."

"I asked my mother for the money, and she said *no*. In fact, *she's* the one who told me that Evangeline got Nana Jo's house. And all the things inside it," she says, her face red with anger.

Coraline stills. "Tell me you didn't."

Lizzie shifts in her seat, still managing to hold onto her haughty expression.

"Tell me you didn't orchestrate a fucking robbery *on your sister*," Coraline seethes.

10

BANE

LIZZIE HOLDS HER GROUND, her back snapping to a straight line. "She wasn't supposed to even be there. I had someone keep tabs on her to make sure. She'd been spending so much time slumming it with those *bikers* that it would've been fine." The words tumble from her mouth rapidly.

Coraline's mouth moves but no words come out, like her incredulity has stolen her voice.

I don't share in her astonishment. Mostly, I feel fucking sad for my girl. How the fuck she ended up the caring, nurturing woman she is when she was born into a viper's nest is one of the world's biggest mysteries. Newfound appreciation wells up inside of me for her resilience, and I can't help but wonder how she's going to react to this news about her sister.

I let my gaze roam the restaurant, my nerves fried enough that I'm on high alert. "So far, none of this lines up with why you called me."

"Right," Lizzie says, swallowing hard. "So Matty, my friend from tour, well, we got away with a couple of bags worth of stuff, but Owen went rogue, and he, uh, well, *you know*." Her glaze slinks to the side, as if she suddenly remembers who she's sitting across from.

Yeah, I do fucking know. Owen is apparently the name of the motherfucker I shot that night. I have half a mind to dig that piece of shit up just so I can find a couple creative ways to punish him further. He got off too easy. I've overheard enough of Evangeline's true crime podcasts that I have a few ideas to try out.

"Yeah, I guess I do know." I lean back in my seat, my mind reeling with the revelation that Lizzie had orchestrated the robbery on her own fucking sister. I make a mental note to update the guys so they know who to keep away from Evangeline.

Though that feels like a moot point, since I don't plan on letting my girl out of my sight any time soon.

She clears her throat. "By this point, I'd been hanging around these guys a lot. They live a few towns over, and I was mad about the robbery. Like really mad and maybe I was getting a little chatty." She twists a ring around her middle finger, twirling it over and over as she stares at some random spot on the wall next to us. "And I might've mentioned how my sister was hooked up with some motorcycle gang. I didn't know one of the guys at Matty's house was *also* in a motorcycle gang. A rival one, I guess. I had no way of knowing that." She murmurs the last part, more like she's trying to absolve herself by her shitty reassurances.

My gut tightens, dread like sour old milk sending flames of nausea up my throat. If the Savages or Hounds took Evangeline—I can't even let myself go there. Not yet.

"Should I be expecting a ransom call then, is that what you're telling me?"

"No, I don't know anything about a kidnapping. I was warning you about the attack on the compound. I knew they'd go after her. Once they found out who she was to you, I couldn't dissuade them. They were obsessed with getting revenge. And I . . . I was trying to do the right thing."

"The right thing? Are you fucking kidding me, Lizzie?" Coraline scoffs.

"People change, *Cora*," Lizzie says with a sneer.

"My friends and loved ones call me Cora, and you aren't either of those things, Lizzie. So you call me Coraline or Ms. Carter."

My gaze bounces between the women as they volley a few times. And suddenly, it becomes startlingly clear what this is. This is a fucking manipulation.

There's truth behind her *story*, sure, but this isn't an information swap or a cautionary tale on Evangeline. If she was really calling to warn us earlier, she would've called hours before they hit the compound. Shit turned sideways on her, so now she's trying to straddle the line, play both sides. And the shitty thing is, my fucking girl is so good, so kind-hearted, that she'd help Lizzie, even when she doesn't deserve it.

Fortunately she has me, and I'm not bound by the same compulsions.

"And you expect me to do what, fix this for you?"

"You helped my sister," she says, somehow managing to look down her nose at me.

I tap the edge of the sugar packet against the table, rotating it so each side hits the table once. "You're not Evangeline."

She slams her palm down on the table, rattling the silverware next to her untouched coffee. "I am so sick and tired of everyone telling me how I'm not my sister." She expels a breath, her cheeks puffing out like she's trying to find her inner calm. "But she's not better than me, and it's not fair that she gets so much when I get so little."

Coraline shoves to her feet, leaning over and seething in Lizzie's face. "You are such an unbelievably shitty person, and every time I think you can't possibly be as terrible as I remember, you prove me wrong. You don't deserve Eve. You never have."

I push to my feet, hovering next to Coraline's elbow. The energy she's throwing out is volatile and unpredictable, and with the way she's vibrating with anger, I half-expect her to throw a punch at Lizzie. I owe it to my girl to make sure her favorite cousin doesn't get thrown in jail for assault.

I toss a twenty down on the table. We didn't order anything, but we took up space in their diner today. And if the conversation had gone a different way, we might've had service.

Coraline storms out of the diner without another word, and I make it two steps before Lizzie's palm wraps around my forearm. I glare at the offending digits and she removes them immediately.

"Please, help me, Bane."

A wave of forced calm washes over me as I ignore her and follow Coraline out of the diner, making sure she gets into her car safely. I slip my phone out of my pocket and call Diesel, VP of the Blue Knights as I walk across the parking lot, toward where I parked my bike.

"'lo?"

"It's Bane."

He sighs, the sound noisy in my ear. "Look, man, I already apologized for the babysitting detail last week. We got some bad intel, or fuck, I don't know, the girl probably just slipped her tail. She's apparently resourceful as fuck. She's in the wind and—"

"I don't give a fuck about the ride-out we did for you," I interrupt.

He grunts. "Alright. Why don't you tell me why you're calling me then?"

"I need you to keep your ear to the ground."

"What happened?" he asks, the background noise lessening like he moved to a different room.

"First one is five-four, black hair, brown eyes, mid-twenties.

She was last seen wearing jean shorts and a tee. Evangeline Carter."

"This wouldn't happen to be the same Evangeline Carter who's warming the back of your bike and your cousin's bed *and* living with your Prez, hmm?"

I still, like someone pressed pause on my body. I have to forcibly make myself exhale as my gaze scans the horizon. "Where'd you get that information?"

It's not like we're keeping it quiet, but it's not like we're broadcasting it either. We're doing shit our own way, and I find it very fucking interesting to hear that Diesel knows about it. Or fuck, maybe Nova dropped hints to Grizz on the ride-out we did. That asshole is always running his mouth.

"It's not personal, Bane. I make it my business to know things."

My mind rolls over itself, worrying if I have to watch my back from the Blue Knights now. The board is getting full, and in a time where enemies are disguised as allies, I'm worried we can't afford another misstep.

"We've known each other a long time, Marcus." It's a subtle warning.

He laughs. "You tryin' to government name me, man?"

"Do I need to?" I let the threat hang in the air.

"Nah, man, you don't. A favor's a favor. I'll put the word out, and I'll let you know what I hear."

"Use caution, yeah? We don't want to spook him." We don't have any idea who took her, which means we can't predict how he'll act. And the last fucking thing I want to do is push him into doing something permanent. "Seems like the Savage Souls and the Hell Hounds are working together, so it's possible there are other clubs in on this."

"You think it's a personal hit?"

I slide my tongue along the back of my teeth, buying myself a few seconds to respond. "The next Hound or Savage I see gets a bullet first, no question."

He chuckles. "Got it. This ain't my first Rodeo, Bane. I'll be in touch."

Diesel ends the call, and I have to hope that he hears something soon. It's only been a few hours since she was taken, and I can feel the weight of time pressing down on me like a fifty-pound blanket. For as long as I can remember, my world has been shrouded in darkness. But then she came along, a beacon of light that cut through the shades of gray. And I refuse to spend another moment without her.

I will do whatever it takes to find her, and once I do, I'm never letting her go.

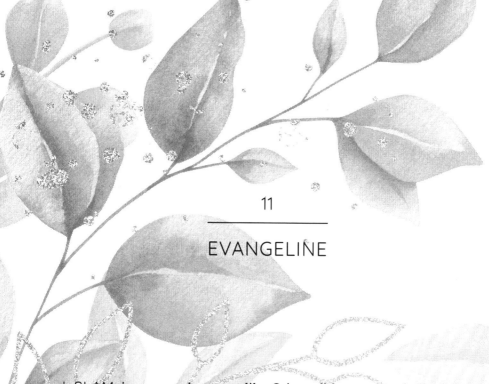

11

EVANGELINE

I SLAM into consciousness like I just did a cannonball in the Rosewood Quarry. And just like that questionable body of water, I swim to the surface confused and scared. Fear holds me immobile while my lashes flutter like the wings of a butterfly, desperate to clear my blurry vision.

Sound filters in next. Quick jazzy riffs dance through the air, accompanied by whistling. It takes me a moment to realize that the whistling isn't coming from the speakers, but rather the person in front of me. It's familiar and jaunty, like some kind of commercial jingle. I don't know why I'm fixated on the sound, as if that will clue me in to what the fuck is happening right now.

My vision clears at the same time my body makes its aches acutely known. They're not as bad as they could be. I don't feel like I've been shot, and nothing seems to be bleeding or broken. It's a small victory I'll take.

It's that moment, on the heels of sweet relief, that realization hits me like a punch to the gut, sharp and sudden.

I'm in a car.

Oh, no. No, no, no, *no*.

A deep-seated panic seizes my body, wringing and squeezing my muscles in a relentless grip. My mother's voice echoes in my mind, haunting me with every syllable.

Never let them take you to a secondary location.

My mother wore her disdain like her favorite lipstick, and Virginia Carter never left the house without it. Except for the time she brought my sister and I to a private self-defense course.

She reasoned that if someone were to snatch me or my sister, it would likely be for ransom. But if they moved us to a different, secondary location, there would be no exchange of money.

Instead, we'd become pawns in a twisted game of survival, with our captors sending back pieces of our broken bodies as either proof of life or threats. She told us we'd wish for death with such calm that I half-wondered if she had firsthand knowledge of such horrors.

Heavy shit to teach a nine-year-old. But I still remember the look on her face when she coached us that day. She'd been more serious than I'd ever seen her. Back then, I didn't understand, and even all these years later, I don't know that I'll ever really understand my mother. But that day, she wasn't Virginia Carter, well-known fixer and boardroom shark.

She was a mother.

Haunted by something no one else could see. And trying to protect her children in the only way she knew how.

I exhale quietly and decide to take stock. I wiggle my fingers and flex my feet as slowly as possible as I try to recall if anyone ever mentioned what the hell to do if you're abducted in a car. I've seen countless videos on what to do if someone slides into your backseat when you're driving. I even had one of those detachable knife keychains that you see advertised on every social media outlet.

But none of that would help me now, even if I did have it. I don't feel the familiar weight of my phone in my pocket or the gun I tucked into the back of my shorts. And when panic tries to sink its icy claws into my skin, I slam down a metal door between us and chop its fingers off.

I don't have time for anxiety right now.

I roll my head to the side, trying to get a better view of my surroundings. I find myself sprawled out on the floor in the backseat of what looks like a minivan. Charcoal upholstered bucket seats pushed as far back as possible, giving my abductor room to toss me in here, I suppose.

It's relatively clean, so he takes pride in his car. If careless enough to snatch someone in his own minivan, then he has an alarming level of confidence.

I glance around the interior, looking for something—*anything*—I can use as a weapon. But there's nothing within reach, certainly nothing that would do damage.

It's just me and the driver in here, and I can't even see him from this angle, but I have to assume that it's the same guy who stormed Silas's house. The timing is entirely too coincidental to be anything other than a coordinated attack. And I have to assume that he's taking me somewhere far, far away to use me as bait or leverage over my men.

A hysterical sort of thought bubbles up my throat and I have to force myself to swallow over the rough boulder of fear lodged there. If this abductor's goal is to get something from Silas, he picked the wrong man. Silas's emotions are unpredictable and tumultuous. A tempestuous sea with fierce waves crashing against the shore one moment, and then calm and placid the next.

I imagine Silas receiving the ransom note for me and sort of sighing, like he can't believe he's being asked to do such a thing.

But no. That's not entirely accurate, is it? my subconscious taunts, plying me with flashes of our time together like some fucked-up video montage.

I close my eyes tight, squeezing them hard enough to see black spots dance across my vision.

Regardless of what Silas would or wouldn't do, I know Lincoln wouldn't let me rot. Neither would Nova. And even in Silas's self-proclaimed black heart, he wouldn't be able to live with himself if he did nothing.

But that doesn't mean he'll give this guy whatever he's asking for. Not if it means sacrificing everyone else.

I'm getting ahead of myself, letting my fears wrap their sharp talons around every thought that flies through my head. The twist and distort every what-if, leaving me momentarily paralyzed with dread. It's a dangerous game, and it does nothing to actually help me.

I exhale and relax the clenched muscles in my face. I do my best to ignore the throbbing on the side of my face and center myself. I give myself five seconds. Five seconds to check in with my senses.

One: The gentle vibration of the car on the road. Which means we're on a paved road and not some backwoods makeshift gravel road. That's good.

Two: The almost cloying new-car scent. Not the actual smell from a newly manufactured car, but the kind they stamp into tree-shaped air fresheners. The kind that used vehicles and rental cars are famous for. Okay, so it's possible he doesn't own this car. I don't know how that helps me or if it even does.

Three: The jazz song has changed but his whistling hasn't. It's the same thirty seconds of music over and over again. There's something familiar about it, but I don't immediately recognize from where. I file that information away for later.

Four: It's still daylight. So hopefully that means I haven't been out too long. Though judging by my lack of restraints, it's also possible that I've been out for an entire day. The thought is sobering and frightening, so I shove it away for now.

Five: The back of my throat feels itchy like the time Cora and I ran through an alfalfa field and my eyes started watering and itching so bad, Nana Jo had to take me to the hospital.

I exhale once more, keeping my breathing even and opening my eyes. I only turn my head, careful not to move any other part of my body in case he's watching me through the rearview mirror. There's nothing underneath the seats I can use, no length of rope or plastic bags or knife. A small blessing, really.

I used to joke that I needed to cut back on my true crime shows, but honestly, if it helps save my life today, I'll never stop watching.

My eyes scanned the backseat pockets until they landed on a noticeable bump protruding from the driver's seat. There's something tucked inside of here, and that stupid little seed of hope takes root once more.

My heart kicks against my ribcage and my palms grow slick as I slowly raise my right hand until my fingertips graze the top of the pocket.

Oh fuck me, I'm too far away. Sweat blooms across the back of my neck, despite the cool air blasting from the vent right in front of me. Okay, I can do this. I *can*.

Each second clicks down like one of those old grandfather clocks, reverberating through my body as I slowly shift my weight and push up onto my elbow. My trembling fingers slip into the seat-back pocket, and I stretch further, my shoulder muscles protesting at the strain.

At the very bottom of the pocket, I grasp my salvation. Extracting it as slowly as I can, praying that he doesn't feel the movement through the seat. Bright pink fabric spills out of my palm as I settle back against the floor.

It's women's underwear.

But not just any underwear.

Seamless high-cut cheeky panties in the color sugar pink.

Confusion cloaks me like a weighted blanket, heavy and unyielding. My lashes flutter as I blink too fast, my mind racing to come up with a reason why one of my favorite pairs of panties are in the seat pocket of this car.

It could be a coincidence, I reason with myself with a shallow nod. One of those things where all the stars aligned and the impossible was made possible. These aren't necessarily *mine.* Just a random pair. I'm sure there are thousands of women who have the same ones in their drawers at home. Yeah, let's just think of it as a strange coincidence.

But more importantly, how am I going to use a scrap of cotton as a weapon?

My mind tumbles over itself, thoughts cycling too quickly for me to fully grasp. Until only one remains. It's incredibly risky and the success rate is undoubtedly low. Panic encircles my throat, squeezing until only a thin stream of air remains.

Make it count, Nana Jo murmurs inside my head.

I let her encouragement and love wash over me, filling in the canyon of fear. The moderate success of my harebrained plan hinges on the element of surprise. And I only have one shot at that. So I better take Nana Jo's advice and make it count.

I let out a long, slow exhale and feel my cheeks puff up with the effort. I ignore the logical part of my brain that reminds me that I'm in a moving vehicle and any attempt to use a weapon on the person who's driving is reckless.

I channel all the superheroes Hunter talks about and will my body to move fast. I curl my legs forward and jump to my feet with a battle cry Nana Jo would clap for. The man in the driver's seat yelps, and the car jerks to the left before he straightens it. But I don't let myself get distracted. I don't think, I just act.

I thrust my arms around the headrest, my fingers looping through the leg openings and gripping the cotton like my life depends on it. In the next breath, I plant my feet on the floor and sink my weight into my back leg. And before he has a chance to pull over or reach for a weapon, I yank the panties toward me as hard as I can. Distantly, I hear him gurgle something, but I block him out. My only focus is keeping my breathing as even as possible so I don't hyperventilate and pass out. And not letting go.

I increase the pressure, and he shouts in earnest. His fingers scramble against the taut fabric against his throat. But I don't let up. I angle my shoulders back, just a little. I don't want to rip the fabric, just cut off his air supply. Death by stolen pink panties, what a fucking way to go.

Nova's going to love the uniqueness of it, I just know it.

The car violently jerks as his panic doubles. He pushes to his feet, the engine revving with newfound intensity a second before the car lurches forward, like he's got the gas pedal pushed to the floor now.

And then I make a mistake. I let a worry slip past my focus, one single thought shrouded in fear. And I glance out the windshield at the sea of green.

We're going to crash.

12

EVANGELINE

DRIP, drip, drip.

My eyes ache as I open them, my lashes heavy as I blink a few times to clear my blurry vision.

"Takin' a nap, are we?"

I recognize the melodic cadence of her voice immediately. I twist to my right to see her, but there's nothing but a grassy meadow. I blink a few more times, the edges of my vision never losing their fuzziness. My head aches like the one time I went out with Cora and some locals convinced us that if we drank only tequila and soda water, we wouldn't get hungover. She lied. Cora and I nursed epic hangovers for nearly three days after that night.

"Nana Jo?" I roll my head to the left, the surface beneath me hard and unforgiving. "Where are you?"

"I'm right here, Eve."

Her voice sounds like it's coming from right next to me now, and I jerk my head back to the right. But the only thing I discover is white-hot pain streaking across my vision. My hand clamps down on my forehead instinctively, and my fingertips are met with warm liquid.

I don't have to look. I already know what I'm going to find coating my fingers: blood.

"I don't understand." Confusion slows my words, drops them into a murmur.

"Yes you do, Eve. My Eve. It's time to get up now," Nana Jo says from everywhere and nowhere.

"Get up?"

"Wake up, Eve. It's time to go," Nana Jo says.

"Go where?" I push to my elbows, and it's only then I realize that I'm laying in the middle of a paved road. But not just any road, it's Main Street in the middle of downtown Rosewood. Only it's nothing like how I remembered it.

I stand up slowly, my lips parting with a surprised exhale as I pivot on my heel to take in the destruction surrounding me. "I don't understand."

Main Street looks unreal. Boarded up windows, garbage rolling around in the breeze, broken signs and crumbled storefronts. Rosewood looks like the set of that apocalyptic film Nova took me to see at the drive-in. Emotion squeezes my lungs, stealing my oxygen as my head spins and my eyes widen. I pivot again, turning in a complete circle to survey the damage of the town. "I don't . . . What is this, Nana Jo?" I crane my neck toward the sky, as if her disembodied voice will float down to me and give me the answers I'm desperate for.

My thoughts are muddled, but there's one that pushes through loud and clear. Where is everyone?

A jolt of fear courses through my veins, skipping my pulse. Without hesitation, I spin on my heels and race toward the Reaper's compound. My feet pound against the ground with each step, and my breaths come out in ragged gasps as I push myself to run faster.

I don't know how I ended up here, but I'm not going to waste time trying to figure it out when my men are *so* close.

Sweat prickles along my brow, and I wipe it away without stopping. My forearm comes away bloody, but I push it to the back of my mind. My head barely hurts and it's nothing compared to the pain in my chest, to the need to find Nova and Bane and Silas *and Hunter*.

My sneakers skid to a stop, broken pieces of concrete spraying everywhere as I look around. My breaths saw in and out of my chest, disbelief coating me like a too-small wool sweater.

"What the fuck?" I murmur.

I should be two blocks away by now, I know I should. But I'm not. I'm . . . back on Main Street.

Right where I started.

"Wake up, Eve," Nana Jo says again, her tone as close to yelling as it gets.

I walk to the middle of Main Street, my anger sparking to life, tangling with fear and producing a devastating cocktail. "I *am* awake," I yell into the stale air.

Anger licks at my heels as I turn around and start running again. This time I take a different side street, one that I know will lead me back to the Reaper compound—to *them*.

Two streets and a left turn later, I'm back in the middle of Main Street again. Desperation claws at my throat and my sinuses sting with frustration. I brace my hands on my thighs, bending over and gulping in oxygen. The air feels different somehow, thin and laced with staticky ozone. It reminds me of the one time Cora and I thought we were going to be the kind of people who hiked on the weekends. We tried a trail up the mountain, only we barely made it fifty feet before neither one of us could catch our breath.

"What do you want?" I ask. The hot breeze pushes discarded plastic bags and crumpled pieces of paper around the deserted street.

I stand up, lacing my fingers and setting them on the top of my head. I turn on the ball of my foot, looking for any signs of life. "What do you want from me?" I yell this time, giving into my quickly rising emotions.

The acidic smell doubles, cloying my sinuses as I breathe it in. It takes me a moment to place it, but then I realize—it's the telltale scent of a looming lightning storm.

Before I can take a step toward shelter, an ear-splitting crack of thunder echoes around me. The sky lights up with bright flashes of lightning.

And then everything goes black once more.

CONSCIOUSNESS ARRIVES with the power of a cannon, overwhelming and almost painful. I suck in a huge breath, curling forward into a sitting position instantly. My heart thunders inside my ears, and it takes me a second to realize that it's not my heart. It's actual thunder.

I blink, my vision clearing immediately as dreamlike memories superimpose themselves onto my vision. But I'm not in the middle of Main Street Rosewood.

I'm in a car.

Fuck. I'm still inside the car.

I have to go—*now*.

My hearing doesn't seem like it's working normal, amplifying my own breaths wheezing inside my chest instead of clueing me into the noises around me. I absently shove my hair off of my face, my hand coming away streaked in blood.

Like a domino reaction, I feel the throbbing along my brow bone a moment later. I do a quick check-in with myself, wiggling my fingers and toes just like I did before I decided to attempt strangulation. And thankfully, my luck holds when I'm able to move the rest of my body without any serious pain. Relief threatens to weigh my shoulders down, but I don't let it. I'm not out of the woods yet. I can't believe my half-assed, crazy plan worked.

Kind of.

I still have to get the hell out of here.

I send a heartfelt *thank you* and *love you so much* to Nana Jo for looking out for me. Because that's the only possible reason that I'm walking away from this relatively unscathed. We crashed into a ditch, and it seems like we rolled onto the roof. You can't convince me she didn't intervene and keep me safe.

I take a deep breath and extract myself from behind the rear passenger seat. I spare the driver a single glance, just to see if he's there. I resist the urge to check his pulse or look at his chest to see if it's moving. I already know I can't win a physical fight against him, I already tried and failed at that. The best thing I can do now is run, find somewhere safe, and call my men.

I scramble out of the broken rear passenger window on my hands and knees, my palms and clothes scraping against the sharp shards of glass. I take a moment to catch my breath before pushing myself up and onto my feet, ignoring the stinging cuts on my skin.

There's a building in the distance, maybe a mile or so away.

My only hope now is to reach it and find help or use someone's phone to call for help. I focus on reaching my destination and ignore the burning pain in my lungs as I dash across the farm field, dodging growing corn stalks and my shoes sinking into the earth with each step.

13

EVANGELINE

I'M RIDING my adrenaline high as I sprint the final few feet across the slippery field. My throat burns and I think my eyes are watering, though it's hard to tell with the rain.

My chest heaves with exertion and cold rain sluices down my face. I hesitate at the edge of the field, staring at the building in front of me.

The gas station stood like a sentinel, its bright spotlights cutting through the overcast and illuminating the cracked blacktop with a hazy glow. The six gas pumps stood underneath the overhang, their age evident but still maintained with care. It wasn't vintage, more like, this place wasn't frequented often.

The gas station buzzes with the faint hum of electricity, the occasional rumble of thunder drowning it out. A lone street lamp flickers a few times on the other side of the parking lot before it goes out.

My stomach churns with fear as the realization dawns on me —I have no idea where I am. How long were we driving? How far had he taken me from home?

My mind races, but I push those anxious questions aside and focus on what little information I do have.

There are three cars parked in the lot, including one at the pump.

I crouch down a little, letting myself catch my breath and figure out my next move. The likelihood of finding someone willing to help me is relatively high. But considering I just ran at least a mile through what I'm pretty sure is an alfalfa field, this might not be a well-traveled area. And I'll be damned if I go through all of this only to end up with some other psychopath. I'm not sure how many chances I have left before my luck runs out completely.

My eyes scan the store until they land on her—a petite woman with a red braid peeking out from under her hood. She pays for her items and makes her way toward the exterior bathroom on the side of the building.

Another glance reveals an older man with a long, gray beard working behind the counter . . . and that's it. I don't see the driver of the third vehicle. Maybe they're in the bathroom or somewhere deeper in the gas station. Though the front exterior is almost entirely windows, I can't really see that far into the building.

I sink my teeth into the corner of my bottom lip, worrying the tender flesh as I decide what to do. Thunder rumbles above me, the rain a steady drizzle. Rocking forward onto the balls of my feet, I make the decision to ask her instead of the employee. Women are more inclined to help other women, right? Isn't that the saying?

I blow out a breath, and as quickly and smoothly as possible, I beeline for the bathroom. I keep my face angled away from the gas station doors and cross my fingers that the woman will help me.

I push open the metal bathroom door, flakes of gray paint

sticking to my fingertips. Musty air greets me like a long-lost lover, smothering me with its acrid scent. Pausing in the threshold, the metal door rests against the side of my sneaker, propping it open. Two stalls—one open and one closed, a rusty sink, and a cloudy mirror. It's not the cleanest restroom I've ever been to, but it's not the worst either.

I take a step forward, letting the door close behind me with a muted clink. "Hello?"

Only the sound of rain answers.

I swipe my hand across my face and exhale. "Look, I-I need help. There was this guy and—"

Something sharp pricks against my neck in a flash of movement, stealing the rest of my words.

"Who sent you?" a feminine voice growls low from behind me.

I feel it then, her presence behind me. Menace and fury roll off her in waves, spilling into every corner of this room. It pulsates with each breath she takes, like a living, breathing entity.

It takes me too long to catch up. I'd convinced myself that she would be my ticket out of here, my way to get back home. I wasn't prepared to be thrust back into the thick of chaos.

My hesitation doesn't go unnoticed. A moment later, she adds pressure to the sharp point against my neck. "Who sent you, bitch?"

My hands fly up into that universal "I'm not going to hurt you" pose, palms facing outward. My shoulders rise with my hands, nearly to my ears as I brace for the pain. I crashed my way out of the frying pan only to unknowingly walk into the fire.

"I said—"

"No one," I answer quickly, letting all my frustration and desperation bleed into my tone.

"Cut the shit. Just tell me who sent you, and maybe I won't

leave you bleeding out in the middle of bumfuck nowhere America."

"No one sent me, I swear. I don't know who you are or *where* we are." I swipe my tongue along my bottom lip, and the taste of summer rain summons nostalgia so thick and potent, I do something reckless. I open my mouth and words tumble out, one after another, before I even give them permission to leave my lips.

"I just strangled a fucking *psychopath* with what could very well be my actual stolen panties. The cheeky, high-cut kind in the color sugar pink. I don't know why the style or color are important, only that it feels like an important detail, ya know? That alone would've been a feat itself, but he was driving at the time. So he crashed into a ditch, and somehow, I miraculously walked away. Which I'm pretty sure is thanks to my grandma. She passed away last year, but she's been, like, appearing to me lately. Like I half-thought I was losing my mind when I could hear her voice inside my head as clearly as I can feel your metal biting into my skin. And I'm a little worried about opening another cut when I'm covered in mud from running through the crop field—*after* I crawled out of a wrecked car. And this asshole who took me from my-my boyfriends' house during this shootout with a bunch of *other psychopaths* on motorcycles and—"

"Jesus, fuck, stop talking." The words are spat out through gritted teeth, her voice low and sharp.

I roll my lips together tightly, my shoulders flying toward my ears once more.

"Tell me about the guys on motorcycles." Her command is harsh, amping up the rising tension in this tiny restroom.

I nod a couple times, keeping my movements shallow. "Sure, sure, can you, uh, move the knife though? It's kind of hard to think with it against my neck like that."

"Bullshit," she grunts, angling the blade up until a quick,

sharp pain lances through me. "You just told me your life story without blinking. Start talking."

I swallow, my Adam's apple pushing against the sharp blade. "Right, okay. Well, I'm not exactly sure who they are. Just that they came to send a message to my men."

"Who are your men?"

I try to glance at her from the corner of my eye, but all I can see is her black hoodie. "Ever heard of a town called Rosewood?"

"Should I have?"

I lift a shoulder and glance in the mirror across the room. The angles are all wrong, and even if they weren't, it's too cloudy to see much of anything clearly. "It's where I was, when that asshole took me. The same asshole who's probably looking for me right now." I pause to inhale, the ever-present internal clock ticking faster inside my head. It feels like a warning, like I'm running out of time. I clear my throat and switch angles. "I thought I could, I don't know, appeal to your sense of sisterhood to help me, but I can see that was a miscalculation on my part. I'll take my chances with the guy behind the counter."

"I'm pretty sure that old fuck has illegal shit happening in the back room of this shithole gas station. He's not going to let you call the cops on your panty-snatcher," she grumbles.

"I'm not going to call the cops. And the guy out there is a *person* snatcher." My brows furrow together, frustration thinning my lips.

"Jesus Christ, he'll take one look at you and lock you up in his backroom, moron. He's not going to give you his phone once you tell him your sob story about being abducted," she says with a scoff, her tone telling me exactly what she thinks of me.

Alarm blazes through me. I don't like the finality of her tone. Like I'm already a tragic footnote in her story. I shift my weight to my back foot, my muscles tensing, just waiting for the right moment. I will myself to think. What would Lincoln do if he were in this situation? Nova or Silas? What would any of them do if they were in such a precarious position?

Anything, I imagine Nova saying.

Everything. I would do everything, imaginary Bane vows.

There are no limits to what I would do to come back to you, fictitious Silas says.

My brows furrow when it occurs to me that I might very well have a concussion if I'm imagining Silas of all people waxing on about his devotion to me.

The woman behind me digs her fingers into my shoulder, jostling me. The cold steel of the knife presses harder against my throat. "Don't faint on me. If you go dead-weight, you're gonna cut your own throat, and then no one will find you because that asshole won't call the cops, remember?"

I jerk my shoulder forward, wincing at the bite of the knife against my skin. "Jesus. I'm not—" I exhale sharply. "I just want to make one phone call. And then I'm gone, I swear."

"So you can signal to whoever the fuck sent you? I don't fucking think so," she snaps, turning us around so I'm facing the doorway. She nudges me forward with a hand in the middle of my back. "Let's go." She pushes me forward with more force than I expected, and I reluctantly take a step toward the door.

"Go? Go *where*?"

"We're leaving. If I walk outside into an ambush, I'll drag this blade across your throat and your flailing limbs will still supply me with the distraction I need to get away from those motherfuckers."

14

EVANGELINE

"*WHAT THE FUCK,*" I drag the words out on a breath. "Is wrong with you." It's not a question. "I don't know who you are or who you're running from, but I swear I have nothing to do with it."

"We'll see, pretty girl. We'll see," she mutters. "Open the door."

I shake my head, the edge of the knife dragging across my skin sharply. The metal is cold under my palm as I wrap my hand around the door handle. "I thought you were going to be my salvation."

"Didn't you know?" she asks with a tsk. "I'm everyone's ruination."

I don't even know what to make of her cryptic words, but my heart races with anticipation as I try to imagine who or what could be waiting for us on the other side of the door. Will it be the guy I left in the ditch, or the gas station employee? Or maybe whoever she's running from is waiting to ambush us.

With a heavy breath soured with dread, I open the door and brace myself. But only the deafening sound of thunder greets me.

The loud crack explodes across the sky, rippling outward like the tide and rattling the walls of the bathroom.

She nudges me with her hand on my back, guiding me around the corner and never easing the sharp pressure at my neck. "Over here."

Rain sluices down my face, icy droplets stinging my eyes as I stumble forward. The wind howls like a wild animal, the violent force of it whipping against my clothes, tugging at my hair.

We stop next to the driver's side door of an older model luxury car. Panic pricks against the back of my scalp when she shuffles me to the side. It's hard to see much with the rain in my eyes, but I can almost feel someone's gaze on us—on me. It's intrusive and unyielding.

"Wait," I blurt. "Take me with you."

"No shit, Hollywood. Get in, you're driving," she grits out as she finally removes the knife at my throat. She opens the driver's side door and shoves me into the seat in the next breath.

I sink into the cream-colored leather bucket seats with a grunt. I manage to swing my legs inside before she slams the door closed and runs around the front of the car.

The interior of the car is dark, only lit by the occasional flash of lightning outside. A couple partially-folded paper maps line the dashboard, but otherwise, it's devoid of any personal touches. Before I have a chance to think about it further, she's sliding into the passenger seat next to me.

"Before you think about driving *me* into a ditch, know that I'm the one saving your ass. Plus." She opens the glove compartment, pulls out a handgun, and places it on her lap, finger resting next to the trigger. "I have this. And I promise you I can shoot you faster than you can crash my car."

I swallow roughly as I look from the gun to the windshield. "Alright."

She makes a noise in the back of her throat. "What are you waiting for? Let's go."

"You didn't give me the keys."

She leans forward, and my back snaps ramrod straight. I don't know what's wrong with me exactly, almost like my well of fear is nearly depleted or something. Because while I'm definitely afraid of her and what she's capable of, I'm not nearly as fearful as I think I should be. Or maybe it's because I'm behind the wheel, and there's inherent control there.

She taps the end of the gun on the ignition. "It's already in. Now move your ass, Hollywood. We've got a long drive ahead of us."

I lean over and reach out to turn the key, but instead of a plastic fob, my fingers wrap around the smooth handle of a screwdriver. My gaze slides to the woman in the passenger seat, surprise raising my brows.

"Problem?"

"Nah, no problem." I twist the screwdriver handle, and the car sputters to life. I wait a second before I shift it into drive. "Where are we going?"

"East," she grunts. "We're going east."

As I begin to drive, the rain continues to pelt against the windshield in a rhythmic pattern that matches the uneasy beating of my heart. The woman beside me remains silent, her steely gaze fixed on the passenger side mirror, as if she's making sure we're not followed.

With each passing minute that we're alone on the road, my adrenaline recedes. My fingers tremble and my goosebumps have goosebumps. I cautiously fiddle with the heat settings, adjusting it to a warmer temperature and angling one of the vents toward my face.

I clear my throat and steal a glance at her. "Why did you hot-wire your own car?"

I think she might ignore me, but she sighs. "Because some asshole wouldn't give me my keys."

"But this *is* your car, right?" I press, turning left where she indicated.

She looks over her shoulder at me. "Would it matter?"

I sink my teeth into my bottom lip and weigh my response. "Not really, I guess."

I feel her gaze roam over my face, like she's trying to peer inside of me or something equally intense. My knuckles grip the steering wheel a little too tightly at her silence. The road stretches out ahead of us, winding through dense woods that seem to swallow us up as we drive deeper into the night.

After what feels like an eternity, she finally speaks. "Pull over."

Alarm zips through me, sparking the dredges of adrenaline to life. There's nothing here though, not even one of those paltry rest stops you see on the side of the roads.

"Why?"

She gestures to me with the gun. "Because your eyes have been drooping for the last thirty minutes, and I don't feel like dying because you're too tired to drive safely."

My mouth falls open, surprise swallowing any reply. "Oh." I ease the car onto the shoulder of the road, shifting it into park.

She pushes open her door and walks around the car, and I don't give her an opportunity to leave me on the side of the road like some unwanted fast food bag, so I crawl over the center console.

She slides into the driver's seat and smirks. "You've got two hours, then you're driving again."

My brows shoot up in surprise. It's the most I've gotten out of her since we first got into the car. I can't figure out a good enough reason not to stay in this car, and it seems safe enough.

Definitely safer than the middle of nowhere, on the side of the road at night.

My eyelids feel heavy, and my body aches in places I didn't know it could. So I give in to temptation, sinking into the seat and allowing myself to drift to sleep.

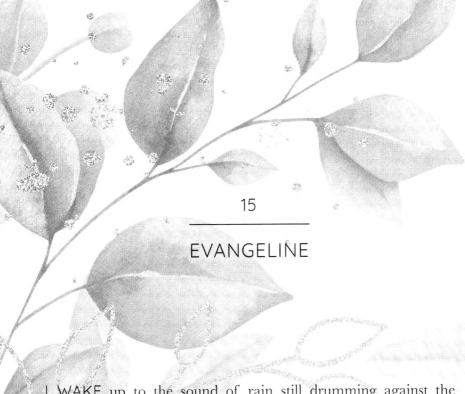

15

EVANGELINE

I WAKE up to the sound of rain still drumming against the windshield, but the car is no longer in motion. Rubbing the sleep from my eyes, I glance over to see the woman leaning against the driver's side door, facing me and eating a protein bar.

She tosses me one without a word and gets out of the car once more. Guess my disco nap is done. My body protests any movement as I crawl over the center console with a yawn.

I keep looking for anything recognizable—a city or town or landmark. Hell, I don't even know what state I'm in. My quiet companion tells me where to turn and when, keeping us on the backroads. She's not looking at a map or her phone, and I can't even begin to guess how the hell she knows where we're going.

The rain has subsided, leaving a dewy mist hovering in the air as I drive us back onto the road. I open the protein bar with my teeth, wincing a little bit when I catch my reflection in the rearview mirror. My mother would be horrified by it. Even in this, she'd expect me to maintain a certain level of *decorum*, as she liked to say.

I look at the woman next to me, trying to piece together who she might be. What her story is. And maybe where the hell we're going.

Locks of unruly red waves of hair frame her face, freed from the loose braid tossed over her shoulder. Dark lashes and darker eyes, high cheekbones and full lips pursed into a scowl. I can see it though, the softness that used to be there. She wasn't always the knife-wielding type, I'd bet my house on it.

"What?" she snaps without looking at me.

"Nothing," I murmur, looking at her and then at the road one more time. "You're just not how I imagined you'd be."

"You're not the only pretty girl around here," she drawls.

My brows furrow. "Why do you keep calling me that? Pretty girl or Hollywood."

She tips her head back against the headrest. "That's our worth, isn't it? Our value lies in our ability to decorate. Arms, events. Families."

My mind turns over on itself, spooling together like a ball of yarn and trying to piece together the things she's not saying. "Is that who you're running from?"

Her fingernail taps an unsteady rhythm against the barrel of the gun. I honestly don't know how she's maintained her vigilance. Though I guess she didn't crash a car into a ditch or escape through a hidden tunnel or get tossed into a literal gunfight. For all I know, she could've just woken up before I saw her at the gas station. Somehow, I doubt it. There's exhaustion carved into every line of her posture, weighing her down.

"Don't try to psychoanalyze me, pretty girl. A wall of degrees couldn't help me, so it's not really worth your time," she says.

I clear my throat. "Evangeline."

"What?" she asks, but it's a slow drawl of the word. Like she's unwilling to further this conversation.

"My name is Evangeline."

She laughs then, this low, raspy bark of humorless laughter. "Of fucking course it is."

"Are you going to tell me yours?" I hedge.

"Not a chance in hell. This isn't a sleepover and we're not braiding each other's hair. This is a one-way ticket away from your panty-snatcher. That's it."

I shift a little in my seat, my jean shorts stiff and stuck to my skin like damp papier-mâché. The seat warmer has been great for warmth but not for drying clothes. Either my skin feels irritated from sitting in wet clothes for hours or the bush I squatted over when I peed an hour ago was really poison ivy.

I nod a few times. "You ever had poison ivy before?"

She gives me a long look. "Do I look like the outdoorsy type to you?"

I lift a shoulder. "I don't really know you, so it's hard to say."

"No one does," she murmurs. "Slow down a little. Your stop is almost here."

Hope leaps into my throat, quick and heavy as it lands on my tongue. I lean forward in my seat as I peer out of the windshield. "Are we close to Rosewood?"

"I wouldn't know. But this is your stop," she says, gesturing toward a green sign on the side of the road for a rest stop in five miles.

I flex my fingers on the steering wheel, my hands clammy with nerves. My gaze bounces from her to the rearview mirror to the windshield to her to the side mirror and back to the windshield. "Can I please use your phone? What if that guy followed us from the gas station?"

"Nah, we would've seen his headlights during the night," she says, her red hair swishing when she shakes her head.

Dawn's first rays grip the edges of the horizon, painting the sky in hues of pink and orange, the colors bleeding into the darkness like watercolors on a wet canvas.

I marvel at the beauty of it all, even in the thick of this fucked-up situation. Even as anxiety gnaws at me from the inside out.

How am I going to get back home?

"Please," I whisper.

She lifts a shoulder in a lazy shrug. "I did my good deed, yeah? For the *sisterhood*."

I squeeze my fingers around the steering wheel, tightening them to the point of pain. "*Please*. Just let me call someone to come get me. To let them know where I am at least."

She shakes her head and another piece of hair falls free from behind her ear. "I can't risk it. Sorry." Except she doesn't sound sorry at all. She sounds indifferent really.

I nod a few times. "What about if you called them then? Or put them on speakerphone? Or just tell them where we are? I don't even have to talk at all."

Her silence hangs heavy in the hair, and I can't tell if she's reverting back to her silent treatment or if she's wavering in her resolve. But I have four miles to plead my case, so I decide I don't have a hell of a lot to lose at this point. The thought of who might be at the rest stop lingers in my mind, a terrifying unknown. Given my recent luck, it's likely there's another unhinged psychopath just waiting in the wings.

"Hunter."

She side-eyes me, but doesn't say anything.

"He's, uh, five." I glance at her, finding her eyes on me already. So I keep going. "And I sent him away with his grandma, the moment we knew something bad was about to happen. But the assholes on motorcycles came so quickly, and there were so many of them." I pause, my mind flashing back to those moments. I can't believe that was only today. Or yesterday, I guess. My stomach sinks as I realize that it could've been *days* ago.

I don't know what was in that syringe or how long it knocked me out for.

I can't let myself think about it too much, or I'll fall into a tailspin. And I don't have the luxury of being vulnerable right now. Not until I'm back in Rosewood.

Until I'm home. With *them*.

I swallow over the heartbreak of it all and continue, my voice quiet. "There were dozens of them, and they opened fire on the house like it was nothing. Like they were playing a video game. The violence they unleashed was . . . it was *devastating*. And all I kept thinking was how not even five minutes earlier, I was teaching Hunter how to tap dance and catch butterflies in the backyard. How twenty minutes before that we were eating dinosaur-shaped chicken nuggets in the living room fort we'd made the day before. And I-I have no idea if he made it out safely. Or if they found him somehow."

Tears fill my vision, and I blink reflexively, sending them cascading down my cheeks in twin rivers of heartache.

The woman next to me clears her throat, and I look over at her in time to see her pull out a phone from somewhere.

Gratitude ripples through my limbs, flowing all the way to my fingertips. I wiggle them to disperse the pins and needles feeling. "Thank you."

"I'll call. You stay quiet. And if I suspect for one second that this is a trap somehow, I'll kill you faster than you can blink."

I blink a few times reflexively, my lashes fluttering like they're scared they'll never be able to move again. "Alright. Thank you."

"What's your boyfriend's number?"

"Uh." My mind blanks. Totally and completely empties out. "*Shit*. I don't have it memorized."

She rolls her head along the headrest to deliver a glare so sharp and potent, I actually wince.

I roll my head from right to left, working out some of the

tension tightening my shoulders. "But I know Cora's phone number by heart. Coraline Carter. She's my cousin and my best friend and she lives in Rosewood. She's probably with my boyfriends right now." My lips twist to the side as I imagine her giving the Reapers hell because that's what she does when she's scared: she lashes out.

"Fine," she snaps.

I rattle off the number and she puts the phone to her ear. I can faintly hear the ringing through the silence of the car.

Once, twice.

C'mon, Cora. Answer your phone.

Like she heard me, she answers on the third ring.

"Hello?"

The familiar sound of her voice steals my breath. I have to clamp down every instinct inside of me that's screaming at me to just yell something to her—anything—to let her know I'm here. But I'm not going to gamble my life like that, not when there's a gun pointed at me by my ambivalent companion.

"Coraline Carter?"

"Yes," Cora hedges. "Who's this?"

"I found something that you might be interested in. The rest stop by mile marker seventy-nine." The woman ends the call, pops the sim card out of the side of her phone, and tosses it out of the open window without a word.

I nod my thanks and swallow hard, my mouth suddenly dry.

A minute later, I exit the road to the right, pulling into a rest stop. There aren't any other cars or trucks here, just an octagon-shaped brick building with one side made entirely of glass. An array of vending machines in the little lobby area and signs for restrooms. As far as rest stops go, this one isn't bad. I just hope that it stays empty.

I shift into park and get out of her car without a word. This time, she crawls over the middle console instead of getting out and walking around the hood of the car.

"Mary." She pauses with her hand on the door handle.

"What?" I ask distractedly, my gaze straying to the corners of the parking lot.

"My name is Mary," she grits out through clenched teeth.

My brows lift at her admission. I nod in acknowledgement. "Pretty name."

She smirks but it's all hard lines and thinly veiled violence. "'Pretty name for a pretty girl.' That was the last thing he said before I cut out his tongue."

My eyes widen at her confession. Her gaze crawls over my face, her smirk growing like she enjoys my shock.

"See you around, pretty girl," she murmurs with a flash of her teeth. She slams the door closed, and she's gone in a cloud of gravel dust.

16

BANE

"YOU HAVE SOMETHING FOR ME?" I glance over my shoulder at Duffy, one of the Reapers who was lucky enough to walk away unscathed after the attack on us.

"Fuck, Bane, I . . ." Duffy drags his hand across the back of his neck. "It's like they vanished into thin air. No one has seen or heard anything, not since they fled here."

I nod my head a few times, looking at Duffy without really seeing him. It's been three days since someone snatched our girl right from underneath our noses. Broad daylight in the one place we told her she was safest.

For fuck's sake, we had her move to the compound so she was safer than being alone at Magnolia Lane. Though she was never really alone. I slid into her bed most nights, and I had eyes on her all the time.

And still, she was stolen from me just like that.

There must be something I'm missing. There's pieces here I didn't anticipate. Too many fucking pieces. There's a whole goddamn playing board I didn't even know about.

"The warehouse in Silverstone?"

"It's abandoned."

"And what about Crestview? Have the Hell Hounds been seen around town yet?"

Duffy shakes his head. "Our contacts in Crestview said the Hounds haven't left their clubhouse in three days. No sign of any other kuttes, Savages or otherwise."

I cut him a look, my eyes going into focus. "Has something happened with any of the other MCs? What about the Outlaws?"

The Outlaws mostly keep to their claimed strip of desert in the west. It's full of all kinds of shit to fuck someone up. They've never waded into anything before, and not for lack of manpower. But for lack of fucks. They literally couldn't be fucked to get involved with anything. And now I hope they don't change their philosophy.

If the Outlaws align with the Savages, we might be well and truly fucked. I don't even know if all of our alliances and favors could get us through a war if they join in.

Duffy leans his shoulder against the wall, propping his foot up. "No, no sign of the Outlaws leaving their territory. But you thought there could've been prospects here too, yeah? The number of guys they rolled up with doesn't match what we thought they had. So either they're pulling in other clubs or they're adding bodies."

"With the intent to let them drop," I murmur. It's the same shit Masters did when he ran the Savages.

How that motherfucker inspires enough loyalty to grow his fucked-up club is beyond me. Those poor bastards don't understand that wearing the Savage patch means they're fodder for Masters's twisted agenda. If I had to guess, I'd say he entices them with shit that he never has to follow-through on because they're already dead before they can collect.

Duffy frowns, running his hand through his messy hair. "Seems like it."

"And Gunner?" Gunner took a bullet to the shoulder in a valiant attempt to close the compound gate. But one man is no match for dozens of bikes.

"He's fine," Duffy says with a shrug. "Discharged later today and ready for revenge, I think."

"Good. Make sure someone stays with him until they get to the compound. If we can't find these motherfuckers, that leads me to believe they're lying in wait."

"On it, VP." Duffy dips his head and pushes off the wall, leaving me to wallow in my misery alone.

It's fucking wild to me that they left the clubhouse virtually untouched. The garages took minimal damage too. Nah, they inflicted the most amount of damage on our homes. Mine and Silas's. What kind of fucking monster goes after a man's home? And I don't mean a fucking house, though I do think that adds insult to fucking injury.

I mean a man's *home*.

His mom, his son, his woman.

My fucking woman.

I slip my right hand into my pocket, rubbing the syringe cap between my thumb and index finger. The small piece of plastic walks the fine line of grounding me and stoking my rage. I probably *shouldn't* have kept it, but I couldn't bring myself to throw it away. It felt too much like defeat.

So instead I find myself rubbing the plastic like it's some faux rabbit's foot keychain or something equally superstitious.

I grew up on stories of the Reapers. Tales of hostile takeovers were my bedtime stories, legends of turf wars were my nursery rhymes, and the code was our commandment. Guidelines that were ours alone and just two cardinal rules. Universal agreements made between friends and enemies alike.

Back when my old man was a kid and his dad ruled the Reapers, they endured the worst bout of violence this area had ever seen. It wasn't just in the Diamond either. It was every club, gang, and crime syndicate in a three-hundred-mile radius. The way Dad tells it, Grandpa changed when a few of the gangs started stealing the kids of their enemies. Some of those kids made it home, but not all. He claimed Grandpa made alliances with the Diamond, agreeing that they didn't have to agree to shit except one thing. A cardinal rule.

No women and children. Ever.

Grandpa rolled it into Reapers code, second only to brotherhood above all else.

And Uncle Ray and Dad stuck to that order of operation their whole goddamn lives. But not me. If I'm ever fortunate enough to have a child, then you can fucking count on Reapers taking a back-burner. Because there is nothing—absolutely nothing—I wouldn't do to get to my kid.

Or my woman.

Which is why sitting at the bar inside the clubhouse, nursing two fingers of whiskey feels exceptionally painful. It's not the stillness or even the day drinking that fucks me up. It's the inaction.

The indecision that plagues me. The cloying fingers of fear shoved down my throat, a persistent gag.

For the first time in my life, I don't have the answers. I don't have contingency plans and variables laid out.

I don't know what to do.

And the very act of silence after such a brutal incitement of war is maybe the most unsettling aspect. They didn't stick around to watch their havoc. They didn't parade around town and gloat. They vanished.

They slunk back into the shadowed corners of the world,

content to do whatever the fuck soulless men without honor do. Until something or someone forces them out.

My blood starts to boil inside my veins, a hot river of ire trapped underneath my skin. I sigh and spin my glass around on the bartop. Maybe if I stare at the worn and knotted surface hard enough, I'll connect the dots and a brilliant idea will magically come to me.

Yelling from outside the clubhouse pierces my thoughts. My nerves are fried enough that even the slightest raise in volume pulls my attention. I slam my glass down and storm outside, ready to unleash my wrath on whatever asshole decided to try me today.

Bright sunlight sears my eyes as I step out into the daylight, letting the clubhouse door slam closed behind me. The air is thick with tension and the scent of ozone, and I half wonder if we're going to get another storm today soon. I have to shield my eyes with my palm, squinting as I stroll closer to the small crowd gathered in the courtyard.

"I swear to god, Jagger, if you don't get out of my way, I'm going to—"

"What, baby?" Jagger goads. His back is to me, blocking whoever he's arguing with. "What are you going to do, hm?"

"I'm going to chop off your balls with my favorite bread knife, asshole," the woman in front of him seethes. I recognize the venom as easily as the voice. Evangeline's cousin is here.

I haven't seen Coraline since the diner showdown with Lizzie. She sounds just as angry now as she did then.

Jagger leans in close to her, arms folded across his chest and a smirk plastered on his face. "You know I like it when you talk dirty to me, baby."

Coraline's face turns ten shades of red, anger seeping from her pores and evaporating into the air like steam. "If you don't let me by, I'm not going to be the only one dealing with you."

Jagger rocks back on his heels, shaking his head. "I already told you, Cora. Prez told me Bane's not to be disturbed for at least three hours. Which means"—he glances down at the watch wrapped around his wrist—"you can't go in there for another fifty-two minutes."

Fucking Silas, always sticking his nose in my shit, telling me to take a fucking nap like I'm a goddamn toddler. I should've expected it, and if I wasn't so goddamn tired, I would've noticed that only Duffy came into the clubhouse during the last couple of hours.

Silas and Nova ganged up on me about sleeping, as if I could just lie down when Evangeline is god-knows-where.

As a general rule, I don't give a shit who is in anyone's bed. The only reason I even keep general tabs on it is for the safety of the club.

But I'd be lying if I said I wasn't surprised when Jagger brought Cora around. The Carter family has been in Rosewood as long as we have. And despite Aunt Dixie saying numerous times that Josephine Carter was a friend of the club, the Carters weren't regulars on the Compound.

But looking at these two now, I kind of see it. It's that sort of opposites attract type of chemistry.

Coraline is five and a half feet of outspoken moxie, and Jagger is nearly a foot taller and almost criminally chill.

But if I had to guess, I'd say he finds her charming.

"I need to talk to Bane. Right fucking now, Jagger," Coraline snaps.

I take an involuntary step forward when I hear my name. And I curse my cousin under my breath when I realize that Jagger is running interference.

I knew I shouldn't have told Silas how little I've slept. But I can't take it anymore. Every time I closed my eyes, I saw her face. Only it wasn't the smiling, happy, laughing woman that I have fallen in love with. Tears filled her eyes, her mouth opened in a silent scream, and pain etched in her face. So, yeah, I guess I haven't slept much in the nearly three days she's been gone.

I decided to put Jagger out of his misery. Though judging from the smirk tugging at his mouth, I don't think he considers his current predicament *misery*. The asshole looks like he's enjoying having his hands all over Coraline Carter. Even if it's just to keep her at arm's length so she doesn't actually go for his balls. And knowing her, she has the determination to do it.

"I'm right here," I say, pitching my voice louder. "What do you need?"

Cora spins on the ball of her foot, pivoting to face me. Worry pinches the skin around her eyes, and she practically runs toward me. She huffs a few deep breaths like she just ran around the block.

"Oh my god, Bane, thank god you're here. You have to go, right now. That asshole wouldn't let me see you, even though *I told him* I had something so important to tell you." She's talking too fast, tripping over her words, and not bothering to stop as she throws Jagger a dirty look over her shoulder. "I told him you'd want to hear this, but that—"

"Stop," I bark out.

Her wide eyes come face me once more.

"Slow down and start from the beginning."

She takes a breath and blows it out slowly, defiance blazing in her eyes. I wonder if she's going to stop talking altogether just out of spite. But then her shoulders sink an inch, like she's forcing herself to relax.

"I got a call, okay?"

"From who," I ask. My pulse quickening as if my body knows something's coming before my brain does.

"I—I don't know who, okay? It was just some seemingly random woman. But that doesn't matter. What matters is that she said she has something important for me. And I just—I just know it's Evangeline."

It takes effort I didn't know I was capable of to lock every single muscle down. Planting my feet into the cement beneath me, I force myself to stay still and let her finish whatever else she has to say. The urge to jump on my bike and find her, go to her is so strong it nearly takes my knees out.

"How do you know it was her?"

"Evangeline didn't call me, some woman did, but the way she said it, it's just—I . . . I don't know, why else would she call me, you know? There's no one else it could be."

I lean toward her, intensity vibrating underneath my skin. "What did she say exactly?"

"She said, 'I found something that you might be interested in. The rest stop by mile marker seventy-nine.'"

As far as proof goes, it's slim. But I'll take fucking anything at this point. "Okay, give me your phone." I hold out one hand, palm up, and pull open my maps app with the other.

She drops her phone in my waiting hand. "Why?"

"What's your passcode?" I murmur distractedly, my attention on the highlighted route from here to the rest stop by mile marker seventy-nine. "Jesus fuck."

"What? What's wrong?" Coraline steps closer to me, peering at my phone.

"She's in Silver Lake." A shiver of shock rolls down my spine. That's two states away. My muscles tense, my mind already plotting how I'm going to get there faster than the proposed time on the app. I gesture to Coraline with her phone gripped in my hand. "Passcode. In case they call this number back."

She rattles off some numbers, and I type them into my notes app so I don't forget them.

I walk backward toward my SUV and look at Jagger. "Don't

let her out of your sight, yeah? And you call me if you hear anything."

"Bane," Coraline yells. "Bring our girl home."

I nod, my mouth curling into a feral sort of grin before I spin around and jog toward my SUV.

17

SILAS

I DRAG my hand over the scruff along my jaw, scratching the length. Exhaustion settles into my heels like I'm the one wearing cement boots and not this motherfucker in front of us. One of the Savage Souls bloodied and bound to the pier piling at the end of the dock. Hands zip-tied behind his back, standing in a white five-gallon bucket filled with drying cement.

I fold my arms across my chest and look at the mismatched grain of the wood beneath my boots. I let my gaze trail the length of a particularly noisy plank, the dark brown color pitted in some places. I make a mental note to replace it.

I don't pull my attention from the pier, keeping my voice even. "Where is she?"

"I already told you," he says with a weary sigh.

I lift my head, spearing him with my gaze and look at him dead in the eye. I let him see the swirling pool of rage that's quietly banked, just waiting for the green light from me. "Tell me again."

The outer corners of his eyes sag as his face falls with acceptance, like he's resigned himself to his face.

"I've told you everything I know. A couple months ago, Masters found me in Pewaukee, told me he had a way to get us back again. The Savage Souls. Told me he'd buddied up with some other club from the Diamond. I told him I wasn't interested, you have to believe me. Leaving here—leaving the Savage Souls was a blessing for me."

"Really?" Nova drawls from behind me, the kind of deadly humor warping his tone. "It was a blessing to have your club torn to shreds and scattered in the wind?"

The Savage lets his head fall forward. "Yeah. Rocker was a fucking tyrant, and the only reason I stayed was because Masters promised shit would change when he became Prez. But then he had us pulling jobs we didn't agree to, and I wanted out."

"But the Savages don't let guys out," I muse, tilting my head to the side and looking at him.

His head bobbles in some macabre agreement. "Exactly. So you, uh, dispersing us like that? A fucking *blessing*."

"So that's it? Masters asked, you said no, and he just . . . left?" Nova asks, pushing off his perch on the little bench at the end of the pier. "Why did I find you skulking around Crestview then?"

Whispering Pines Lake is surprisingly deep. Environmentally protected and shielded from any law enforcement. Too many traitors and enemies meet their watery ends fifty feet deep, further tormented by the walleye and muskie in this lake. They have an appetite for traitors.

I haven't been up here for years, but I'll never forget the first time I saw a small school of walleye and a lone muskie converge on the Whispering Pines's newest addition like it was a buffet.

The Savage sniffs, rubbing his nose on his shoulder. "Well, I was curious, I guess, but I don't know anything about a girl being taken."

Nova puts his phone up to his ear without a word. His eyes

narrow as he faces the horizon, and I find myself bracing. I can't see him answering his phone for anything less than important. And these days, *important* usually means bad news. My mind plays tricks on me, imagining the worst possible scenarios unfolding as I check my own phone, even though I have it on vibrate *and* sound. The worry that I'll miss an important call from Ma about Hunter eats at me slowly. But even that tastes bitter, a little bit like a half-truth.

No missed calls.

Okay, so probably nothing with Ma or Hunter. That's a relief. I've never been away from my son this long, and it feels like a piece of me is missing. But it's a necessary separation. As much as it pains me to admit it, the safest place for Hunter is far, far away from me.

I met them at the safe house on Lincoln Street before they went to stay with a trusted friend of Ma's just over the state line. She lives in an area untouched by anyone who could even remotely consider us an enemy.

Hunter's smile as he raced toward me a few days ago flashes before my eyes. The way he jumped into my arms and squeezed me as tight as he could. The relief I experienced was so goddamn potent, I still feel little ripples even now.

I've never really considered myself a nihilist, but I had somehow convinced myself that I'm not worthy of good things. And *this*, this felt like a deserving punishment, too harsh for me to bear.

Because if I don't have Hunter—I shake my head, scattering those thoughts away. It doesn't do me any good to dwell on them now. The fact is that Hunter's safe.

So I've spent the last several days keeping busy. Idle hands and all that.

But if it's not Ma, then it's probably Reaper-related. Which, fine, a lot of the guys go to Nova for shit because he's always been the mouthpiece. It's never bothered me much before, so I don't know why I'm annoyed by it right now.

The air around him shifts, and I'm walking toward him before I even give myself permission to. I stop in front of him, straining my hearing to discern who's on the call or what they're saying. But that asshole has his volume too low for me to make out anything.

"We're on the way."

"What's going on?"

"Well, you know what they say: curiosity killed the cat." He slips his phone back into his pocket and stalks toward the end of the pier.

It happens so quickly, I don't even have time to protest before Nova shoves the zip-tied Savage. Gravity and momentum are on my brother's side, and the asshole flops into the lake. He yelps, but it's quickly drowned out by the splash and gurgle of the lake swallowing him whole.

"What the fuck, Nova?" I stalk toward him, wrath circling my wrists like shackles. "We fucking needed him."

"He doesn't know shit. And if he did, he wasn't going to give us anything. We're done with him." He dismisses my worry with a wave of his hand and starts walking toward the shore.

I throw my arm out wide and stare at my brother's back. "The fuck we are! He was our only lead!"

"Today," he calls over his shoulder.

"What?" My brows furrow and my hands curl into fists as irritation prickles across the back of my head.

"He was our only lead for *today*." He emphasizes the word like I don't already fucking know he's been slowly and methodically taking out every Savage and Hound he can get his hands on. And all with a fucking cheery disposition too.

I look over the side of the pier, willing my eyes to see beyond the murky depths. But Whispering Pines is an efficient partner, and there's no sign of the Savage Soul.

"We don't need him. Let's go." The wooden pier groans as my brother jogs toward the shore, jumping over the rotten planks and skirting around the missing ones.

I grind my teeth and remind myself for the millionth time not to snap on him. It's not really him, anyways. It's everyone. It's this day and yesterday and the day before that, and every person and every thing. It's this fucking town. And it's this fucking sunshine that just won't quit.

I don't know why, but I had some misguided notion that the weather should be as turbulent as I feel inside.

And then a healthy dose of guilt washes all of my self-indignation away, as if I have any right to these foreign emotions swirling inside me like a storm.

The rollercoaster of emotions that I've experienced in the last several days makes me feel like I'm actually losing my mind, like I'm trapped in some alternate version of the movie *Groundhog Day*. Only instead of waking up to the same day over and over, I'm experiencing the same cycle of emotions, just tumbling one after the other in an endless repetition.

Fear, sadness, shame, so much fucking shame. I don't feel deserving of Evangeline's sacrifice. I hate myself a little every time I feel relief that Hunter and Ma are safe, because that means in this situation Evangeline is not.

I was a fool to ever think that we didn't live in a world of mutual exclusions.

I jog after my brother, watching my steps, and once again, adding the pier to my mental to-do list. I'll probably come back out here tomorrow just to give myself something to do.

The three of us are doing our best to protect the club and each other while exorcizing our demons and planning for what's to come. There's no part of me that believes this is the last we'll see of the Hounds or Savages, especially not when Evangeline is still gone.

"Jesus, would you slow down already?" I pitch my voice loud enough for Nova to hear. He's halfway up the lopsided cement staircase built into the side of the sloped hill.

"Hurry up, asshole," he shouts over his shoulder. "Or I'm leaving without you."

I grind my teeth at his back and remind myself that it's not personal, he's just dealing with his shit the only way he knows how.

Methodically snatching enemies off the streets, interrogating them, and eliminating them while acting like this is a normal fucking Tuesday.

I reach the top of the staircase with a huff, glaring at the fifty steps I just ran up.

Nova smirks. "Maybe you should add cardio to your workouts, yeah?"

And it's like I've forgotten

Anger bubbles out of me like an over-carbonated soda. "Something to say, little brother?"

He sneers at the moniker. "Little brother, really?"

I plant my hands on my hips and glower at him. "Yeah, yeah. Trust me, no one fucking cares you've got two inches on me. Big fucking deal."

Nova sucks his teeth and smiles, but it feels all wrong. It's sharp and almost cruel. "I don't know, man, I can think of at least one person who rather enjoys my extra two inches."

"Don't," I warn, my voice low. "Don't act like this is normal. You've dropped more bodies in the last two days than you have in the previous five years. Evangeline isn't going to even *recognize* you—"

He's in my face in an instant, fist curling into the fabric of my tee. His green eyes are muted, washed out with torment. "You don't get to talk about her."

I step into him, anger rolling off of me in waves. "You think you're the only one worried about her? Get in fucking line, *brother*."

"Brother, hm? So fucking curious you use such a term for me." He jostles me as he lets go of my shirt, taking a large step back.

My brows crash low over my forehead. "What the fuck does that mean?"

He turns around and starts walking around the cabin at the top of the hill. "It means get your ass in the car. Jagger called. Bane went to get our girl."

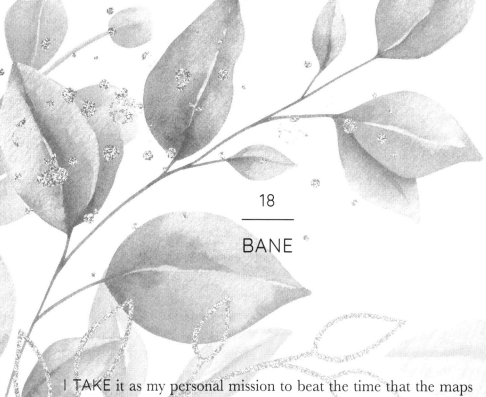

18

BANE

I TAKE it as my personal mission to beat the time that the maps app predicts. And thank fuck there's a more direct route that cuts through the corner of one state, even if it costs me more money in tolls. I'll pay it a hundred times over if it gets me to her quicker.

I find the rest stop by the mile marker that Coraline told me easily enough. I've spent enough time in this car to come up with a million different scenarios, and some of them were far-fetched and ridiculous.

Coraline's phone remained blissfully silent, and I'm not sure if that's a good thing or not.

My fingers tremble slightly as I ease the SUV into the parking lot. Anxiety tightens her rope around my throat, and I swallow hard, trying to ignore it.

I slam on the brakes hard enough to send gravel flying as I swing into a parking spot. There are no other cars here, which trips a few internal wires. Methodically, I turn the car off, snag the keys, and get out. The air carries a thick scent of incoming rain, but the ground is dry and the sun's still out. Birds chirp from one of the few trees next to the parking lot, and I glance around once more.

My unease grows when I don't see any movement, and I remind myself that's a *good* thing. I didn't really expect to see Evangeline just sitting outside on the wheel stop of a random parking space.

I don't have that overwhelming feeling of eyes on my back, but I can't rely on my senses alone today. My instincts feel frayed and fucked. So over-preparedness is what we're going with today.

I grab my gun from the back of my jeans and shake my muscles out as I jog toward the little lobby inside this rest stop. Floor-to-ceiling window walls make up nearly two sides of the building, giving me an unobstructed view of the empty lobby.

A knot formed inside my gut since the moment I realized this whole fucking thing with the Savages was a setup, and it's only grown with every hour she's been gone. It feels like an ulcer, a painful burning spot that reminds me of her absence every time I move. And now, she's within my grasp and that sore spot pulses, like the quiet hope I've been harboring is splashing acid against its tender edges.

I'm a fucking mess without her.

I exhale and note the thicket of woods to the right, slightly behind the building. If she's not inside the building, it's possible she's hiding in there.

There's also a chance that this is entirely unrelated. Or it's some bullshit trap. It's one of the reasons that I didn't tell Silas or Nova before I left. If this is another trap, then at least only one of us goes down instead of all three of us. Learning from our mistakes and all that.

The back of my neck prickles with perspiration, and I make a quick plan to clear the lobby first, then the bathrooms. I pause just outside the double doors, peering inside the glass. Forcing myself to wait those fifteen seconds feels a little bit like torture when my blood is thumping a staccato rhythm.

I pull open the door and pause just inside the threshold, tilting my head to the side to listen. The low hum of electricity greets me. It's coming from the vending machines in the little alcove in the middle of the wall, next to a wire stand of pamphlets full of things to do in the area. Looks like random nature excursions and summer attractions.

I ignore all of it.

"Evangeline," I call out. The hair on my arm stands up, and I raise my gun on instinct.

I press my back against the cool window-wall. My gaze darts around the lobby, turning my head slightly to make sure I'm still alone. The parking lot remains empty, but I can't shake the feeling that something is very wrong here.

Think, I command myself. If I was Evangeline, where would I go? What would I do?

My brain feels muddled and sleep-deprived. I shake my head a few times, the movement small and quick, my eyelashes blinking too fast as if that will simply clear the cobwebs and fog from my brain.

Think.

It's been *days* since she was taken, so If I was her, I would find somewhere relatively safe. A space where I could lay low and defend myself if I had to.

I squint, scanning the lobby for any blind spots or out-of-the-way spaces. My gaze snags on the large fake potted plants in the corners and the little alcove with three vending machines. Otherwise, the lobby is a big open, empty space.

Which leaves the restrooms.

The soles of my boots crunch over shattered glass from the corner of the last vending machine. I idly wonder if Evangeline busted it open to snag some food. My gut clenches at the idea of her being hungry and scared.

My senses are on high alert as I listen for even the smallest, the most minute noise. I shoulder open the door to the women's restroom and the hinges creak so loudly I have to suppress my own flinch.

"Evangeline?" I keep my voice nice and even. I don't know if she's in here, but I have to imagine if she is, she's scared. Possibly not thinking straight. And the last thing I want to do is be the cause of more fear.

"It's me, sugar. Are you in here? You can come on out now, you're safe."

Silence echoes off the walls, the only sound a faint drip of a leaky faucet. The fluorescent lights flicker, casting shadows around the room.

I tuck my gun back into the waistband of my pants and take a step forward. Every beat of my heart pounds against my ribcage and adrenaline courses through my body, making me feel weightless.

Two stalls stand open and empty, their metal doors gleaming under the harsh lights. I approach the last stall and push against the door, but it doesn't budge.

It's locked from the inside.

Hope zips down my spine, sparking along each vertebrae as I realize that maybe, just maybe, she's in there.

"Evangeline," I murmur. "Come on out now, baby girl. It's alright." I try the handle again, giving it a gentle shake, but it stays firm.

A sniffle breaks the silence, and then the lock spins and the door swings open with a low creak. And in the dimly lit public restroom of a rest stop, in the middle of nowhere, I lay eyes on the love of my life for the first time in three days.

Evangeline Carter looks like an avenging angel.

Dirt-stained clothes, dried blood on her forehead, and wild eyes.

And still, she's the most breathtaking creature I've ever seen.

I find myself thanking god or whoever is listening for giving her back to me.

"Lincoln," she says on a hopeful gasp, dropping something to the floor and rushing toward me.

I barely have enough time to open my arms before she jumps. She wraps herself around me with a sob, burying her face in my neck. One hand instinctively goes under her ass to hold her up while the other slides up her back and hugs her to me.

Her soft gasp catches in her throat. "Lincoln, you're here."

Relief and gratitude become a tempest of storms inside of me, swirling around and around until I feel my sinuses tingle. It's a foreign feeling, and it takes me an embarrassing amount of time to realize what's happening. I squeeze my eyes shut and pull her in even tighter. I worry for a second that I'm hurting her, but when I try to lessen my hold, she makes a low noise in protest.

"Are you okay? Hurt anywhere?" I run my hand up her spine, palming the base of her hairline and sinking my fingers into her locks.

She shakes her head, her lips skimming against my skin. Hot tears seeping through the fabric of my tee and soaking into my skin. The words she mumbles are incoherent, but I can feel the heavy weight of her emotion.

As she presses her face into my neck, I feel the sharp edges of heartbreak splintering within me. My palm settles against the back of her head, silently giving her permission to take whatever she needs from me. I don't know the right words to say, but instinct compels me to say something, to comfort her.

"It's alright, sugar. I'll take care of you. You're alright."

Time ceases to have meaning as we stay wrapped around one

another. It could be a minute or an hour. The soft touch of her body against mine is a soothing salve to my overflowing anxiety.

For the first time in days, I feel a sense of peace wash over me. Part of me knows I'm undeserving of such a gift, but I'm going to take it all the same. I vow then and there to do whatever I have to in order to make sure she stays safe.

Falling in love with someone isn't as black and white as I thought it was. It's a speeding freight train barreling toward a cliff until you're suspended in air for that one perfect moment of clarity. And it's a slow trickle of happiness that you don't realize is filling your hollowed soul until one day you wake up with a smile and a show tune stuck in your head.

Evangeline Carter is the answer to every single question. Even all the ones that haven't been asked yet.

"I can't believe you're here, that you came." She leans back, tilting her head up so our lips are an inch apart. "My white knight."

"I'll always come for you, Evangeline," I murmur.

"I love you," she whispers as tears fill her eyes once more. She leans in and brushes her lips against mine. It's a soft kiss, tender with the weight of emotion.

As much as I welcome any chance to kiss my girl, this isn't really the time, and it's definitely not the place. I slow our kiss, drawing back slightly and tucking a strand of her hair behind her ear. Her lashes sweep open, and the light gold flecks in her eyes seem to glow in this light.

"I've missed you, sugar. Let's get you home, yeah?"

The corner of her mouth ticks up and her eyes look a little glassy. She wiggles her legs, her arms loosening their hold around my shoulders.

A grimace tightens my forehead. "I can't put you down yet, sugar. I just—" I sigh, running my palms over her back to reassure myself that she's really here. "I'm going to be so fucking mad if I wake up and realize that Silas fucking drugged me to sleep."

I see it the moment it happens. Panic and fear crowd together in her eyes, blowing her pupils wide. "Oh my god, Lincoln. Where's Silas? And Nova?" she asks, pushing against my chest with both hands.

I release her, reaching out to steady her. "They're—"

"*Oh my god, where's Hunter?!*" Her voice takes on a thread of hysteria as she spins out of my grip, stumbling slightly in her haste to scan the bathroom. Like Hunter is going to appear behind me.

"Hey, it's alright, they're alright." I cup her face in my hands, tracing the curve of her cheekbone with my thumbs.

Her wide eyes hold mine, and it almost feels like she's asking to look into my very soul. I fucking welcome the invitation. "All of them? Are you sure?"

I nod and keep my voice low and soothing. "We're all okay, sugar, I promise. It's you we're worried about."

I thought it would alleviate her worries, but she blinks, and a fresh wave of tears falls from her eyes. "I'm fine."

I let my gaze roam over her, looking for visible signs of her time away from me. She looks relatively unharmed, but I know from personal experience that sometimes the deepest wounds are the cuts on the inside.

19

EVANGELINE

THE PLUSH SEATS enveloped me in a cocoon of warmth as I settle into Bane's car, but despite the comfort, I can't shake off the unease that gnaws at my stomach. I feel unsettled, anxious and jittery like I've had too much caffeine on an empty stomach.

The gentle hum of the engine and soft music playing from the speakers should have put me at ease, not to mention the company. I *know* I'm safe with Bane. And yet, I'm still anxious.

Nothing some sleep and food and time at home won't help. Like the thought alone summoned it, my stomach grumbles. A few hours ago, desperation and hunger twisted my insides up enough that I found myself breaking the glass on one of the vending machines. I snagged just a few snacks, enough to stave off the hunger pains.

"I grabbed a few things on my way out town." Bane nods to the drinks in the cupholders and opens the middle console.

I flash him a small smile and lean over, spotting a couple of protein bars, some pretzels, and a pastry bag. I recognize the logo immediately. Sugar and Spice Bakery, the place Cora works at. My stomach pitches and my smile falls from my mouth at the thought of my cousin. I can only imagine how worried she's been.

"What's wrong? You feeling okay?" Concern wraps around Bane's voice as he eyes my forehead. I did my best to wash it off in the restroom, but I was limited to scratchy brown paper towels and watered-down soap.

I clear my throat and waggle the pastry bag. "Be honest, how much has Cora been around, giving everyone a hard time?"

He grunts with a smirk. "She's been up Jagger's ass the entire time you've been away."

Away, I think, looking out the window at the passing trees. Like I was gone for an extended weekend. I blow out a breath, letting it puff up my cheeks for a moment.

"I bet he loved that." I snort at the image of my cousin becoming Jagger's shadow.

He chuckles quietly. "He does alright. She nearly took his head off when he wouldn't let her come into the clubhouse to tell me about the phone call."

Silence settles between us. It's a little uncomfortable, like suddenly we don't know how to act around one another. Or how to process the whole situation, which feels like some kind of hallucination.

Part of me wishes I could just bulldoze right past it, move on with life as if it never happened. And maybe I'll be able to in some capacity, but there's still so much that needs to be said about it.

And I've never been more grateful than I was when he asked for details on what happened but didn't push me when I told him I wanted to wait until we're all together. So I don't have to recount it over and over again.

I swipe my tongue along my bottom lip and blindly reach for a can of caffeinated water. I pull the tab and take a drink, letting the carbonated bubbles dance on my tongue for one blissful moment.

He nods toward the untouched bag in my lap. "Why don't you eat too, yeah?"

I unroll the bag and pull out a blueberry muffin. I take my time peeling the muffin paper down, my mind exhausted but not quiet. "What happens now? Do we just go back to the way life was before?"

Bane nods slowly, stealing a sidelong glance at me. He still looks at me with the same soft eyes and quiet intensity as before.

And I wonder if that's how my life is going to be now. A *before* and an *after*. Like this will be another defining moment in my life. And maybe five years from now, I'll look back on this and see the fork in the road for what it is and not just a traumatic event.

I think the scariest revelation I've had this last week is rooted in fear but not in the way I would've thought. Sure, I was scared. But more than that, I felt scar*y*. Like I was something to be fearful of.

And the wildest part? I *liked* it.

I liked the way I felt powerful when I was defending our house, when I was buying time. A fearsome distraction to make sure Hunter and Dixie got out okay.

And I don't know how they're going to look at me once they realize that. I worry that I'm going to catch them looking at me sideways, like they're unsure of who I am or what I've become. My stomach twists with discomfort as I imagine the scene they must've found at the compound.

"Are you sure they're all okay?"

He dips his head. "I'm sure, sugar. The family is fine."

Warmth spreads inside my chest at the word *family*. "What about everyone else? Did any Reapers get hurt?"

He shakes his head. "Nah, they're fine. Just a couple of minor things."

I clear my throat and focus on breaking off a small piece of the muffin, my fingertips running over the coarse sugar crystals. "I suppose you saw the, uh, mess"—I wince at my word choice—"around the house."

"You mean the bodies you dropped?" he says, a smirk tugging up the corner of his mouth.

My face feels hot, and a warm prickly wave of embarrassment rolls over me. "Yeah, about that."

He reaches over and places his palm on my leg. His fingertips graze the bare skin of my inner thigh, and a flutter of an entirely different kind of warmth unfurls slowly.

"Don't be embarrassed, sugar. You did what you had to do, and there's no shame in that. It was a game of survival."

"And I didn't." Shame curdles inside my stomach as images roll over my vision. Following the unnamed man into the secret tunnel, him jabbing me with the syringe, waking up in a car in god knows where. My hand drifts up to my neck, my fingers brushing over the smooth skin.

"You're here, aren't you?"

I swallow hard and nod, the blueberries and sugar turning to cement inside my stomach. "Yeah, I am."

"You protected yourself, Evangeline. And make no mistake, as much as it pains me to say this: they would've taken you out in a heartbeat. They didn't care if you've never fired a gun before, or if you were an innocent bystander. Those men didn't give your life a single second thought, so I don't want you to give theirs another one, yeah? It's a game of survival now, baby girl. And we always play to win."

"Survival," I whisper, nodding and toying with my wrapper in my lap. "What does that mean for now?"

He blows out a breath. "I don't want to lie to you, okay? So you tell me if you want to be kept in the dark. And I'll respect your wishes. I'll do everything I can to shield you from Reaper business."

I run my tongue along the back of my teeth and look out the windshield. I let my head roll across the headrest and look at him.

My white knight who calls himself a Reaper. The juxtaposition isn't lost on me, and in fact, it makes me feel better about how I'm going to move forward in this life.

Because I can be both Evangeline Carter, nanny to Hunter and lover of baked goods and show tunes.

And Eve, a secret badass who protects her family and doesn't shy away in the face of danger.

Okay, so maybe the last one is a bit of a stretch, but I'm going to roll with it for now.

"I think it's a little late for being kept in the shadows, don't you?"

"I think what happened to you was unacceptable. But it's not normal for Rosewood or for the Reapers, not anymore. And I love you enough to make sure you're protected, in whatever facet that means. Remember my offer stands, sugar. If you want out, we're out in a heartbeat, yeah?"

My lips curl into a smile as I impulsively lean over and plant my lips on his cheek. The love and affection I have for this man feels like an effortless, nurturing sort of thing. "You really do love me."

He turns his head, his gaze flashing to mine briefly before returning to the road. "I don't ever say things I don't mean."

"I'm learning that," I murmur, letting my lips drag against the corner of his mouth. I sit back in my seat, looking out the window to hide my small smile. "I think it's a little late to leave too."

I want to say more, but I don't think I really need to. He knows how I feel about him *and* his cousins. I've spelled it out for him before, and Lincoln St. James is nothing if not observant.

Goosebumps flow down my legs, and I snuggle into the seat further. Without a word, he adjusts the vent so the heat is aimed directly at my legs. I miss the warmth of his palm instantly.

"Ironic, isn't it?" I jerk my chin toward the heat vent in question. "Middle of the summer, and here we are, cranking the heat up like it's December. You must be sweating like crazy." I eye the leather jacket, jeans, and boots he's wearing, which is basically his signature look. Only today, he's wearing a pale blue tee instead of his usual black.

"Don't worry about me, sugar. I'm fine."

My lips twist to the side as I let myself really look at him. He really is so handsome it hurts sometimes.

Gratitude inflates like a balloon inside of me, expanding until it reaches every hidden nook and cranny. I don't know how the fuck I ever got so lucky as to end up with him or Nova or even Silas, but I half-wonder if Nana Jo is somewhere in the universe pulling strings. She always did seem to know things about the town and its people.

I loved the woman, but she fancied herself a matchmaker on more than one occasion. And I don't think it ever worked out quite so nicely for her though.

Until now.

"Okay, then deal me in, Lincoln. Give me the full report. Or whatever it is you guys say when you're at 'church.'" I use air-quotes around the word.

Bane chuckles. "You really do watch too much of that TV show. It's not really like that."

I arch a brow. "So you don't vote on stuff?"

A muscle in his cheek twitches and he smiles, but it's a little more self-deprecating than joyful. "Nah, we do. But it's not usually life-or-death things. It's more like when do we want to have the family barbecue? Or what should we do about refurnishing the common rooms? But lately . . ." He trails off with a sigh.

"Lately?" I prod.

"Lately, it's more like the TV show, I guess."

There's a screech of tires that sends my heart thundering inside my chest. I pull my gaze from Bane to the other side of the two-lane highway and see a car do an illegal u-turn.

"Oh my god, is that him?" Fear coats my voice like thick syrup.

Bane's head whips toward me. "Him who?"

I turn around in my seat and look out the rear windshield as the dark SUV gains on us. "*Him*. The guy who abducted me from the house."

20

EVANGELINE

BANE EASES the car to the side of the road, pulling over on the small gravel shoulder. "What guy are you talking about?"

Confusion wrinkles my brow, and I look from the car to Bane. "What? Why are you stopping?"

"It's alright, Evangeline. It's just Nova and Silas behind us. But this conversation isn't done, yeah? We're going to have some serious words about everything that happened."

I nod because I have my own questions that need answers. Some long overdue ones too. But I don't have time to say anything more because the passenger door is yanked open in the next instant.

I spin around, the muffin falling from my lap to land on the floorboard. Nova St. James stands in the space between the open door and the car, lips parted and eyes wide. His hair looks wild, like he's had his hands raking through it for days, and his usual charming smile is absent.

His hands rest on the top of the car, gripping the frame like he might fall over if he lets go.

"Evangeline," he breathes, voice shaky with emotion. There's a breathlessness to him that I haven't seen before.

I unbuckle my seatbelt and twist to face him, but he sinks to his knees on the gravel shoulder before I can stand up. He rests his forearms against the seat, caging my hips in, and rests his forehead against the top of my thighs. A squeak of surprise slips out of me, but I swallow any words I was going to say when I feel his breath warming my skin in small puffs.

"Sweetheart," he murmurs, rolling his forehead back and forth once. He lets out a deep sigh, like he hasn't taken a full breath in days, and something inside of my chest cracks open.

I thought I'd cried all my tears up, but it seems I'm not quite done. I curl over him, my vision going watery. I trace the hard muscles of his back as I try to press myself closer to him and offer whatever comfort I can. Nova shudders against me, his hands trembling where they grip the sides of my hips. His shoulders rise and fall with uneven breaths, each one a ragged hitch that tugs at something deep within me.

"Nova," I whisper, running my fingers through the hair at the nape of his neck.

"Jesus fucking Christ, sweetheart. You scared the shit out of me," he says, his voice muffled.

I cringe, acutely remembering just how many days it's been since I showered, how long I've been wearing this outfit, and how many events I've gone through in it. A shootout, a secret tunnel, a drugging, a car crash, a muddy field, a stolen car.

Exhaustion tugs at my limbs, a special blend of physical and emotional, and it takes effort to hold strong for him.

"I'm sorry," I murmur. "But I'm okay. I'm alright." It feels like some kind of role reversal. Not even an hour ago, Bane was comforting me like this. And now I'm doing the same to Nova. I glance to my right, where Nova came from, and wonder if Silas is here too. Or is he with Hunter somewhere?

I worry my bottom lip with my teeth and wonder how that conversation with him will go. Will we comfort each other, or will he ice me out again?

Nova grunts and scoots closer to me still.

"Are you okay?" I whisper, running my palm in a wide circle over his back.

He lifts his head, giving me an incredulous look with wide, red-rimmed eyes. "Am I okay? Baby, you've been gone for three days. Three of the most miserable days in my whole fucking life. And I mean this with all the respect in my body, but you are never allowed to leave me again, yeah? I don't fucking care if you want to travel to Alaska and live in one of those snow hut things we saw on that documentary."

A laugh bubbles out of me without hesitation. "But you hate the cold."

"Aye," he says with a slow nod. His face is devoid of any of his usual humor or charm. "I go where you go, yeah?"

I run my fingers through his hair, watching his eyelids sink lower with pleasure. I half expect him to start purring like some kind of domesticated jungle cat. "I hear you. Did you and Bane coordinate your speeches or something? I'm getting a lot of grand gestures lately. Not that I'm complaining." The smile escapes me as a soft exhale, a gentle burst of happiness.

Nova hums under his breath, letting his eyes close fully. "Nah, Bane's just trying to hitch his wagon to my train."

My smile grows wider at his mismatched idiom.

"I think you have that backwards, man," Bane says with humor in his voice.

"You're trying to hitch your train to my wagon?" Nova asks, arching a brow. He flashes me a wink, the side of his mouth curling into a smirk. Trust Nova to break his emotional moment with some humor.

Bane huffs a laugh. "Where's your brother?"

Nova's smile falls a little. "In the car."

My chest pinches with something dark, and I look back toward the car parked behind us. But the angle is all wrong, and even if it wasn't, they have a special tint on all their SUVs.

I bite the inside of my cheek. "Oh. Why isn't he out here? Is everything okay?"

The corner of his mouth lifts up a little. "He's giving me some privacy."

My brow furrows as I trace the slope of his nose with my gaze. "We're on the side of the road."

"And I'm right here," Bane drawls.

Nova lifts a shoulder, and I see the familiar sparkle flicker in his eyes as he holds my gaze. "I may or may not have told him in explicit detail all the ways I'm going to enjoy my reunion with my girl."

"Our girl," Bane grunts.

I don't fucking care that they're both being possessive and a little ridiculous because it's exactly the thing I needed. Only instead of laughing like I normally would, a watery sort of laugh falls from my lips.

Regret etches into Nova's features as his smile fades. "Fuck, I'm sorry, sweetheart, don't cry. I was just fucking around—*not* that I don't want to do unspeakable things to you, but I was just fucking with Silas. Because he definitely deserves a little shit."

Nova's gaze sails over my shoulder, and I'm sure he's exchanging a loaded look with Bane.

"I know," I say with a hiccup, my tears slowing. "It's just . . . I didn't know if I'd ever see you again, and I—" I stop, flicking away the tears as they leave my lash line. "I don't even know why I'm crying, except that I can't seem to stop now that I've started."

"It's alright, sweetheart. You can cry as much as you need to. You can do *whatever* you need to. Just tell me what I can do to help." As he inches closer, my knees part to make room for him.

His torso presses against my inner thighs, lining our bodies up perfectly. I can feel the heat radiating from his skin as he settles between my legs.

In this position, our faces are only inches apart. I can see the light dusting of freckles along his cheekbones, and the amber-colored constellations embedded in the rich mossy green of his eyes. My breath hitches, and I know the situation feels a little weird, but I think I'm going to have to embrace the weird and just go for it.

"I just need you," I whisper with a sniff. It's all too easy to fall into Nova's gaze. Where Bane makes me feel safe and protected, Nova makes me feel playful and brave.

His hands land on my hips, a gentle yet possessive reminder. "I'm here, Evangeline. Take whatever you need from me. It's yours, yeah?"

I lean forward and take what I need from him, regardless of where I am or who else is here. There are plenty of little hiccups we're going to have to smooth out if we're going to make this unconventional relationship work between all of us. And there's no time like the present.

There's a spark when our lips connect, electricity zipping through my body at the contact. His lips are soft against mine, moving with familiarity that stirs something deep inside of me. Like my soul is exhaling, and my body is perking up and paying attention. It feels like coming home in a different way than kissing Bane.

Or Silas, my mind helpfully adds.

I can taste the saltiness from the dried tears on my lips, and when he swipes his tongue against the seam of my lips, I'm more than happy to let him in. Our tongues tangle together in a familiar dance that sets my blood on fire. He lets me lead, content to be an active participant. I sink my hands into his hair and let myself fall into his kiss.

A throat clearing from above has me pulling back and blinking my eyes open. Silas stands behind Nova, his hands shoved into his pockets and his trademark scowl gracing his full lips.

I pull away from Nova with a gasp, and I try to, I don't know, stand up or something. But Nova isn't moving away from me anytime soon. In fact, I'm pretty sure his palms just slid over the curve of my hips and dipped underneath, so he's halfway palming my ass.

I'm flustered and surprised, and okay, a little bit turned on from that kiss. But mostly, I'm so fucking happy to see them all here, in one piece.

I let my mouth curl into a genuine smile, and I eye the eldest St. James. "Fancy seeing you here, Silas."

It seems it's the day for miracles because Silas's mouth twitches like he's going to full-on smile at me. He nods, but it seems more like to himself than to me. His gaze roams over me like a physical caress, sloping down my exposed neck, gliding over my breasts, and tucking into my jean shorts. It's so potent that if I close my eyes, I can feel his lips ghosting across my skin instead of his gaze.

Silas's gaze has always felt good on me, among other things.

He blows out a breath before looking to the left and right, along the road. "We shouldn't stay here like this. It's not safe, and we need to get you to the hospital to get checked out."

Disappointment sinks like a stone inside of me, popping the hopeful balloon all too easily. "Oh, um, I'm fine. I don't need to go to the hospital. Really. Besides, I want to see Hunter. And Dixie," I add as a bit of an afterthought. It's not malicious, it's just that the last time I saw him—I shake my head, scattering those thoughts like seeds in the wind. No good will come of reliving that right now.

"We need to debrief, remember, sugar?" Bane says, not unkindly.

I nod once, decisively. "Right. So we should probably head straight home to go over all that stuff, right? I don't want to have to repeat it three times."

"We don't know what was in that syringe Bane found, Evie," Silas says, shaking his head slowly. "There could be lasting side effects or complications. We need to get you checked out." There's intensity in his words, an underlying concern that tightens his jaw and darkens his eyes.

I shake my head and hold in my cringe when a lock of my stiff hair scrapes against the side of my neck. I'm pretty sure it's dried mud. But it's the shock of awareness that I needed, and suddenly I want nothing more than to go home and spend thirty minutes inside a shower before snuggling with Hunter on the couch. Maybe we could watch his current favorite movie.

"I'll make an appointment and go tomorrow instead. I'm fine, honestly."

Silas glances behind me, and I fight the urge to grind my teeth together. Bane is not my keeper, and I'm not sure how I feel about both Silas and Nova looking to him when it comes to something about me. If it were any other day, I'm sure it would annoy me, but it probably wouldn't irritate me as much as it is right now.

I expel a breath and square my shoulders. I look at Nova first, hoping that I'll be able to convince him the easiest since I just had my tongue in his mouth less than five minutes ago.

"I want to go home, Nova."

Nova nods, his lips pressed into a straight line. "You heard her. She wants to go home, yeah? So let's take our girl home."

Nova stands up and extends his hand toward me, palm up. I hesitantly slide my hand into his, my brows low over my eyes. His fingers curl around my hand, giving me a gentle squeeze and he tugging me to my feet. "You're with me in the back."

My shoulder grazes Silas's chest, and I hear him inhale at the contact. I glance up at him from underneath my lashes, wearing longing on my face like my favorite blush.

His hands shoot out of his pockets, reaching for me in an instant. I blink and his palms curl around my shoulders as he turns me toward him. I exhale and his hands are on either side of my neck, tilting my face toward him.

My lips part, a question on the tip of my tongue. But Silas bends down and steals the words right out of my mouth. A hard, brutal sort of pairing of lips. It's intense and packed with more emotion than I think Silas knows what to do with. It's over before it really starts. He pulls back, resting his forehead against mine, his warm breath fanning against my lips.

We stay like that for a precious few seconds, my heart pounding so hard against my chest, like even that part of me wants to be close to this man. I'm conflicted when it comes to him, and I wish he would get out of his own way sometimes. But if this is how he greets me, then maybe there's hope for us yet.

As quickly as he was in my space, he's out of it. He kisses the corner of my mouth, his eyes closed with reverence, before he steps back. His fingers are slow to leave my neck, and when my eyes slowly open, the pained, tortured look on his face sends an echoing pulse inside my chest.

He doesn't say a word as he stalks toward the SUV.

It's not until he's out of sight do I realize that I never let go of Nova's hand.

21

EVANGELINE

"TIME TO WAKE UP, SWEETHEART," Nova murmurs, smoothing a lock of hair off my face.

"Mm?" My eyelids feel heavy and it takes considerable effort to open them.

"We're home, sugar." Bane's low voice floats from the driver's seat and wraps around me like a soft caress.

I sit up, belatedly realizing that I was sprawled all over Nova's lap. My cheeks warm at the realization and I quickly straighten up, trying to shake off the drowsiness that still clung to my mind. "Oh, sorry about that."

"You can lay in my lap anytime, sweetheart," Nova muses, trailing his fingertips down my arm.

Looking out the window, I recognize the street right away. We're almost to Magnolia Lane. I turn toward Nova, nerves and something darker swirling inside of me. "What's going on? Am I . . . am I not welcome at your house anymore?"

"Of course you are, sweetheart. It's just—" He pauses and blows out a breath of air, his gaze sliding out the window for a moment. "We've all been staying here."

My brows leap toward my hairline. "You have? Why?" I roll my lips inward, wishing I could shove those words back inside my mouth. "It's not that you're not welcome, I'm just surprised."

Nova nods a few times, his smile lazy and effortless as he looks at me. "Our houses, they need some serious renovation and cleaning before we can stay there again."

Bane grunts from the front seat, pulling into my driveway. "*If* we stay there again."

I lean forward and scoot to the end of the seat in alarm. "What do you mean? Are you leaving?"

Bane meets my gaze in the rearview mirror. "It's just a house, sugar. One that I'm not especially attached to."

"So, you're not leaving then," I say with an exhale, relief flooding me.

"Nah, I'm not leaving you." There's a teasing tone in his voice, but his face remains serious, like he knows I had a quick spike of panic.

"Good. So you're going to just, what, tear it down then?" My brows arch high over my eyes.

"I might," Bane says, dipping his chin and putting the car into park in front of my garage. "That bother you?"

His question catches me off-guard. As if I have any reason to have an opinion on his house—*his parents'* house. "I mean, it's your house. You can do whatever you want to do, including not having it anymore."

Bane grins, and the sight sends a flutter in my lower stomach. I feel like I passed some kind of test I didn't know I was taking. "And what about your house, sugar?" He jerks his chin toward the front door of Magnolia Lane.

"What about my house?"

"How do you feel about having us there with you? I'm not offering to leave, but Nova and Silas can—"

Nova leans forward, across me, and shoves Bane's shoulder. Bane just grunts with a low chuckle.

"It's fine. It's too big for just one person anyway." I wave my hand in the air, toward the house in question.

I'm not sure how Nana Jo survived living alone all those years. I imagine I'd get lonely. Though I guess I did come stay with her every summer for nearly all of my childhood. But it's been years and years since I was able to do that. Mostly, I would pop over for a visit, maybe stay for a week or two if I had time off of work.

Besides, it's not like the five of us weren't all living together in Silas and Nova's house this past month. This isn't really any different.

And okay, so there isn't a sauna or a secret tunnel, and generally, it's an entirely different layout. But otherwise, it's virtually the same thing.

Though now that I think about it, I wouldn't be surprised if there are some secrets in Magnolia Lane I haven't discovered yet. I haven't forgotten Nana Jo's mysterious book of town gossip and secrets. For all I know, she buried gold in her backyard and I'll find the treasure map hidden in a loose brick in the foundation or something. I don't think she did hide her money in her yard, but she was quirky enough to color outside the box. And I vaguely remember her telling me stories of her parents hiding their money in random places around their house. So I guess anything is possible.

I push open the rear passenger door, and welcome the sunshine on my face. Nana Jo used to tell me that there was nothing in this world a day spent in the sunshine couldn't fix. And I don't know if it's going to actually *fix* anything, but feeling the soft caress of warmth does help. Like the very universe is comforting me.

I exhale and skip toward the front door. I know I should get myself cleaned up, and I desperately want to, but I'm too anxious to see Hunter. Both Bane and Nova assured me he and Dixie are both okay, but it's almost like I can't relax until I see him with my own eyes.

I raise my hand to shield my eyes from the sunlight as I peer into the SUV parked behind ours, but it's empty. Silas must've gone inside when I was daydreaming about hidden treasure in the backyard.

"Hunter?" I call the moment I open my front door. I hear soft rustling and the sharp sounds of pots and pans coming from the kitchen. My heart leaps into my throat and I rush toward the sound, my footsteps echoing in the empty hallway.

I stop at the threshold of the kitchen, momentarily speechless. It's not Hunter in my kitchen, but Silas. He's looking inside my refrigerator while tying a half-apron around his waist. It was one of Nana Jo's favorites, pale peach with white lace scalloped along the edges.

My breath catches in my throat at the unexpected sight. There are so many unexpected things, I think my brain kind of short-circuits for a moment. The way the refrigerator light seems to bathe him in golden hour light. His broad back takes up so much space in this room. How he makes Nana Jo's apron work for him. The fact that he beelined to the kitchen at all, really.

"What are you doing?" The question leaves me on a breathless exhale.

He doesn't answer me right away as he grabs some bell peppers from the crisper, walks around the island, and starts dicing them on the black cutting board. "You need to eat for this conversation."

He says it so matter-of-factly, like of course he's in here cooking for me because I need to eat. I feel like I woke up in an alternate reality.

"Oh. Okay, thanks." I shift my weight to my other foot and

glance at the spread of food around him. "Where's Hunter? I don't want him to see me like this." I half-heartedly gesture to the expanse of my body.

If I wasn't already looking, I would've missed it. The pause in his chopping motion. "I don't think he should hear the details, do you?"

My face flushes with embarrassment. "Right, of course. Yeah, I don't want to scare him." I step inside the kitchen, propping my forearms on the island. I don't know what I expected but I certainly didn't expect to feel like I'm the interloper inside my own house. "I should probably get cleaned up before I see him anyway." I rap my knuckles on the countertop and push off of it.

He makes this noise that's somewhere between a grunt and clearing his throat. He doesn't look at me as he tosses a pat of butter in a pan on the stove. "Eat, debrief, then you can clean up."

I tilt my head to the side and watch the way his forearms flex as he finishes chopping up all the veggies he got from the refrigerator. "You like this look on me, hm? What should I call it: disheveled duchess?" I offer his back a ridiculous half-hearted curtsey.

He looks over his shoulder at me, his forearms flexing as he rotates the pan so the butter melts evenly over the bottom. God, what is my fascination with his forearms?.

"I much prefer those little sleep shorts you wear at night." The smallest smirk curls up the corner of his mouth, showing just a whisper of his sense of humor.

My own smile stretches across my face. "Did you just make a joke?"

His smile grows, his dark eyes locking on mine. And for a single moment, I forget all the confusing back and forth between us. He's slow to pull his gaze from mine as he returns his focus to the stove once more.

"What are you making?" I don't even know if I'm that hungry, but I'm curious enough to see this through.

"An omelet. You could use the protein, I'm sure."

"I love bell peppers in my omelets," I murmur. A surge of warmth courses through my veins as the realization hits me: he's making my favorite.

"I know," he grunts. "Sit down, Evangeline."

There's no real heat in his voice, more like gruff affection. Like he's trying to mother-hen me. In my own home. There's irony in there somewhere, I'm sure of it.

The stool screeches on the floor as I drag it out from under the island and collapse into it, feeling the weight of the day finally catching up to me. I watch as Silas moves with practiced ease around my kitchen, the clinking of pans and sizzling of butter filling the air.

"You seem quite at home here," I muse.

"Is that a problem?" With a flick of his wrist, he flips the omelet over and slides it onto a waiting plate. He sets the plate in front of me, his hands steady as he braces them on the island across from me.

"No, no problem." I hum under my breath, a noise of appreciation as I eye the fluffy eggs and colorful veggies. "Thank you, Silas. This looks amazing." I pick up the fork and cut off a corner of the omelet.

There's a beat of silence, and I glance up at him from underneath my lashes. He looks more serious than I've ever seen him, and that's saying something considering I would describe his usual demeanor as *stoic*.

"What?" I whisper, dropping the fork to the plate with a clink. I smooth my hair back off my face, wincing a little when I graze a tender spot on my head.

"Thank you, Evangeline," he murmurs with sincere intensity, his gaze holding mine. He jerks his chin to the food between us. "This is just a small token of my appreciation for what you did."

I swallow over the lump of emotion in my throat. Sincere Silas is uncharted territory for me, and I don't know what to do or say that won't spook him. I drop my hand to my lap, glancing to the side for a second.

"Oh, it was nothing."

He leans forward, his biceps flexing against their cotton confines. "It was everything."

Nova sinks into the stool next to me, and Bane walks around the island to lean against the counter. I'm not sure if I'm grateful or frustrated by their interruption. I feel like there's a lot of unsaid things between Silas and I, and the only way we can all work is by going through it. And that might mean having a couple of uncomfortable conversations.

The four of us look at one another, as if we're all mentally preparing ourselves for the conversation we're about to have.

"Where should I start?"

"At the beginning, sugar."

I nod and blow out a breath. "Alright, here we go."

22

BANE

I HAD an idea of what went down. I think we all thought about all the different possibilities of what transpired there that day. Not that we talked about it together, at least nothing more than strategic questions. I didn't realize it until now, but all three of us were careful not to bring up her too much.

You would think that this type of thing would bond me and my cousins, and maybe in a roundabout way it did. But as I look around the kitchen—*her* kitchen—I find myself conscious of the way we're all standing. Like we're on a trip wire, waiting for the one word that's going to set each of us off. I idly wonder if it would be the same word.

I find myself holding my breath, dread and anger circling each other's tails like a macabre game of cat and mouse.

All the hope and prayers in the world couldn't have saved her that day, and yet, here she is. Relatively unscathed. How the fuck that happened is a goddamn mystery. A miracle really.

We didn't have a spoken agreement, but it seems we're all on the same page, content to let Evangeline pour her story out uninterrupted. I don't want to interject any kind of questions right now, fearful that she'll lose her train of thought, or get sucked into a whirlpool of emotions. Not that she's not entitled to them, but they can be so derailing.

But surprisingly, she's delivering the facts and details she remembers with a stoic sort of clarity. Almost like she's reading transcripts of a movie—because that's how absolutely wild this whole thing is.

If this wasn't my life, I'd be worried that I'm in some alternate reality, on one of those eye-in-the-sky shows. Entertainment for the masses. Because that's the only reason I can make sense of what the fuck happened.

Evangeline blows out a breath and slumps against the back of the stool. Nova recovers first. He throws his arm around her shoulders and pulls her into his side, dragging his lips across the top of her head. "I'm so glad you're okay, sweetheart. So fucking glad."

"You did good," I murmur, catching her eye.

"Better than anyone else could have," Silas says, his arms folded tightly across his chest.

"Better than you?" She smirks, a small smile playing at the corner of her mouth. But there's exhaustion there too, and she leans into Nova's embrace.

Silas lifts his shoulders. "Probably."

She smiles then, a low chuckle, and shakes her head slightly. "I don't believe you, but I'm going to take the compliment anyway." She shifts her gaze to me, pausing as if to communicate something. "So what happens now?"

I dip my head in understanding. "Evangeline and I came to an agreement on the way home."

Nova arches a brow, but he doesn't release his hold on her. "Oh yeah? What's that?"

I look from Nova to Silas, pausing to hold his gaze for a second. He's the wild card in this situation. He's the one I need to worry about when it comes to this development in our . . . whatever the fuck this relationship is called.

"She's all-in."

Predictably, Silas reacts. He narrows his eyes, a flicker of something unreadable passing through them before he schools his expression into neutrality. "What does that mean?"

"It's not safe for her to be with us and not be *with us*. You know that as much as anyone." It's a subtle reminder of what happened when Hunter's biological mom was in the picture, however fleeting it was. She didn't want to be involved in the life, despite living in the clubhouse while she was pregnant, and it almost cost him everything.

He shifts his gaze to Evangeline, wary acceptance painted on his face. "What do you want to know?"

She sighs. "I honestly don't know. I don't think I can take any more tonight, but maybe tomorrow you guys can explain to me who those guys were and why they were here. Help me understand what happened."

Silas nods, his demeanor shifting slightly, though still rigid. "I can do that for you, Evie. I owe you that much, at least."

"I just think . . . that more information is always good, ya know? I don't want to be caught off-guard like that ever again." Her teeth drag over her chapped bottom lip, her gaze roaming around the kitchen. Her brows sink low over her tired eyes.

"We're with you twenty-four seven now, yeah? We won't let anything happen to you."

"And we'll find him," Silas assures her quietly.

The guy who abducted her and somehow knew about our tunnel system. I catch Silas's eye, a silent request for a conversation. He blinks his agreement.

"I'll make him pay for what he did," Nova says, pulling her into him further.

"I know," she mumbles, but she's distracted. She looks up at

Nova and nods her head, dipping her chin a few times absentmindedly. Like she's stuck somewhere inside her head, not really paying attention. And I just fucking know whatever happened has left a mark on her that she hasn't even begun to process yet.

"What is it, sugar?" It's a quiet demand.

Her lips twist to the side and she moves out from underneath Nova's arm and slides off the stool. She spins slowly, looking around the large kitchen and attached dining room. "There are little pieces of you three here. Even though it's only been a few days. Nova's sweatshirt hanging over the chair, your espresso maker on the counter, and Silas's familiarity in my kitchen." She faces us and pauses. "But I don't see any sign of Hunter."

She stares at Silas, questions and confusion written in every curve of her face.

"He's not here right now," Silas says, shoving his hands into his pockets.

She tilts her head to the side. "When will he be here?"

Silas shakes his head, his lips pinched into a firm line.

I don't know what sets her off, and I don't know if she even realizes it, but the air around her stills. There's a sharpness to her that wasn't there a week ago.

"You said Hunter was here. That he was waiting for me. Where is he, Silas?" Her voice is low and even. A carefully-laid trap.

But I meant what I said last month, if we're going to make this work, really fucking work, then we can't be stepping on each other's toes all the fucking time. We don't encroach on our time with her unless she asks for it. And that means we let each other sink when she lures them into tumultuous waters.

I know I sure as hell won't be invited to the makeup portion of their rift when they work through their shit, so why the fuck would I wade into the deep end now.

Besides, I told Silas it was a bad idea not to tell her about Hunter right away. This woman stood between a literal fucking firing squad to protect him, if that's not a bond, I don't know what is.

I grab Nova's attention and jerk my head to the side, letting him know that I'm staying out of it and so should he.

Silas folds his arms across his chest and looks to the side. A muscle in his jaw pops and I imagine the asshole is grinding his molars hard as hell right now. He's probably realizing just how badly he fucked up, but what the fuck did he expect? He was intentionally vague about his kid to get her to spill the details right away. I get the need and usefulness of gathering intel while it's fresh, but he should've told her the truth.

Nova clears his throat. "I'm gonna go be *not here* while you two work this shit out."

Evangeline's head whips over her shoulder and pins Nova with a glare. "No, you stay. The two of you didn't step in when Silas lied."

23

BANE

EVANGELINE PAUSES LONG ENOUGH to send me the same dark look. I don't like the implication that I lied, and right now, I don't like that she's lumping me in with those two. That doesn't bode well for me, considering my cousin's most dependable personality trait is grumpy.

So I tip my chin up and hold her gaze, resting my shoulder blades against the wall, and let her look her fill.

I'm not like them, I tell her with my gaze.

Prove it, her dark brown eyes accuse.

"I'd prefer my punishment in the bedroom, sweetheart," Nova drawls, breaking our little conversation.

Or maybe I'm sleep-deprived enough to start hallucinating. Weirder shit has happened.

Evangeline pulls her gaze from me to send Nova the sort of smile that would make grown men stumble. "What a great idea, Nova. As soon as you three start talking, I'll head straight to my bedroom. *Alone*."

"C'mon, sugar. You know that's not a deterrent."

She answers my soft reminder of our nighttime arrangements

with a fierce glare. But I notice the cracks like lightning strikes bisecting the mask she's desperately clinging to. And the steel mask of indignation is melting, forged in the pits of survival, hastily adhered with desperation. But looking at my girl now, I realize how ill-fitted it is. The shape and emotion is all wrong.

She's tougher than she'll ever give herself credit for, but she's not infallible. And right now, she's trying so, so hard to remain a pillar. Unmoved, unfeeling. But my girl is spent.

Tears shine in her eyes as she looks at me, and my heart aches inside my chest, like it echoes hers.

"I didn't lie. He's not here, Evangeline. I had to send him away," Silas says.

"What?" she whispers, keeping her gaze locked on me.

"I sent him away. He's with Ma, somewhere far away from here," Silas says.

She turns to look at Silas finally, her jaw clenched and neck arched defiantly. "Well what are we waiting for? Let's go see him."

She stalks toward him, skirting around the side of the island, and heading toward the front of the house. When she gets close enough, he reaches out and stops her with a hand around her bicep. It's not forceful or tight, just a gentle grip to get her attention.

Silas shakes his head, his jaw clenched tight, like he's physically stopping words from falling free.

"I want to see him, Silas. I need to make sure he's okay," she says, her voice trembling.

"He's fine," he says, voice low.

"You lied about this, maybe you're lying now." She lifts her right hand and sweeps it out in a general motion.

Silas shakes his head. "I didn't lie, Evie."

She flinches at the nickname, tugging her arm free from his grip. "It was an intentional omission then. Why even bother?"

Silas's fingers curl into fists, like he's holding himself back from reaching out toward her again. "Because I wanted you to come home. I wanted you to tell us what happened. And I wanted you to see a doctor."

Evangeline starts shaking her head halfway through his half-assed reasoning. "What about me? What about what I want?"

Unease churns in my gut as I watch the two of them face each other. The red haze of anger and something darker, deeper swirls between the two of them.

Silas clenches his jaw and glances away. "If this is about what happened in the garage, I think we should—"

"Don't be ridiculous, Silas. This has nothing to do with that," she snaps.

"Then what's the problem?" he asks with a low glare.

"You have no idea all the horrible things that have played out in my head for days. *Days*, Silas. I've been worried sick about him."

"I understand, but he's not yours to worry about, Evangeline," Silas murmurs, not unkindly.

"Of course he is! I'm his . . ." She falters, like a realization has stolen her breath. "He's my . . ." She clears her throat and shakes her head, straightening her shoulders. "I care about him, and you—you just let me sit there"—she flings her arm behind her, toward the stools at the island—"thinking he's going to walk in any second when you knew he wasn't."

"It's not safe for him, okay? You're not safe for him to be around," Silas says quickly, like the words exploded from his mouth without his permission.

Evangeline gasps, her face falling so dramatically that I can almost feel her devastation from across the room.

"Fuck," Nova curses under his breath.

Her eyes are too wide, and her chest rises and falls quickly.

"What are you talking about? I protected him. I made sure he was safe with Dixie! How am I—"

"You were taken, Evie. *You.* Not Ma or Hunter or anyone else. But someone came into my house and snatched you like that," Silas says, snapping his fingers. "How did he know to be there? About the tunnel?"

Okay, I guess we aren't going to have this conversation privately first.

She stumbles back a few steps, her hand flying to her chest. "Are you suggesting that I had something to do with this?"

My pulse thunders louder in my veins, and I'm this close to breaking my own self-imposed rule and stepping in.

Silas shakes his head. "No. No, of course not. But we have to find out who did. And until we do, it's not safe for him to be here."

"Around me, you mean." Her voice is barely louder than a whisper, but I feel it like an arrow to the chest. Her eyes brim with unshed tears as she looks at Silas, a mix of hurt and betrayal evident on her face. "I would never do anything to hurt him, Silas."

Silas's expression softens, his eyes flickering with a mix of regret and understanding. He takes a step closer to her, but not close enough to touch. "I know you wouldn't ever do anything to hurt him, Evie. But I'm his father, and it's my responsibility to protect him."

Silas's words hung heavy in the air like a thick fog. He's not wrong, and I know he's only doing what he thinks he has to. He's always been the first to fall on his sword, and as his best friend, I feel for him. But Evangeline's pain is palpable, like a sharp knife twisting in my gut. And for the first time, I start to wonder if we can make this relationship work between us. Maybe I was wrong about keeping shit separate.

Evangeline swallows roughly, her gaze darting around the

room without stopping on anything for too long. "Right, of course. I'm really tired, so I'm going to go."

She pivots on her heels, and her hair flutters around her shoulders with the sharp movement. She's out of the kitchen without another word, leaving the three of us stranded as we watch her leave.

"Before either of you start, I don't like it either. But I can't risk it. Not when it comes to him," Silas says, his voice heavy with regret.

"Yeah, well what about her well-being? When are you going to start worrying about that?" Nova reprimands quietly before he follows after her.

24

EVANGELINE

THERE'S a knock on the door that I promptly ignore. It feels weird being here. It's my house, but it still very much feels like Nana Jo's house, and nothing about having them here feels normal. It's not a bad feeling, more like a sweater that's five sizes too big. I don't know how to appreciate its cozy comfort yet.

I don't know why I expected to go back to Silas's house. If I would've been thinking clearly, I would've realized my mistake earlier. I never made it back downstairs that day, but I saw firsthand just how many bullets those assholes unloaded into their houses. There's no possible way the entire first floor isn't torn up. There's a perverse part of me that wants to see the damage in the daylight. To get a good look at the destruction and practice gratitude to the universe and Nana Jo for helping me find my way back home in one piece.

I exhale a deep breath and let my head hang forward. "I don't want to talk right now." I make sure to pitch my voice loud enough so whoever is on the other side can hear me. It's not a lie really. I *don't* want to talk right now. I'm all talked out now that

I've recounted everything. I'm not sure if I even have any words left.

"Open up, sweetheart."

"I don't want to talk, Nova." I cringe at the despondence wrapped around my voice.

"I know, baby, but we need to get those cuts cleaned. We don't have to talk, I promise."

I slide off the edge of the bed with a grimace and shuffle toward the door. I twist the handle, and there he is, filling up the entire doorway. I reach over and grab his hand, pulling him into the room and then closing the door behind him softly.

"It wasn't locked," I murmur, arching my neck and looking up at him.

"I know, but for this to work, we have to respect each other's privacy, yeah?"

I arch a brow. "Really? Weren't you the one who watched me sleep through those security cameras everyone thinks I didn't know about?"

There's a faint pink that tints the apples of his cheeks, but the smile on his face is the epitome of shit-eating grin. "If you want me to apologize, I'm afraid you're going to be left wanting, sweetheart."

There's that charm again. That sort of subtle cockiness that I find absolutely irresistible. It makes it hard to stay mad at him if I'm being honest. Which obviously I can never tell him that. He's exactly the type of person to use it to his advantage.

"Let's get you taken care of," he murmurs, nudging me further into the room.

"Okay, where do you want me?"

The side of his mouth hooks into a grin and he drags his palm over his mouth like he's trying to hide it. "You could tempt a saint, Evangeline. Head to the bathroom. There's better lighting in there."

I nod and shuffle into the bathroom. I look longingly at the clawfoot tub in the little alcove that runs on the side of the house. I've been back in Rosewood for months, and still, I haven't had a chance to dip so much as a toe into the bathtub. I sigh, and head toward the linen closet next to the shower.

"I got it," Nova says, stopping me with a gentle touch at my elbow. "You go sit on the counter."

I nod and step to the side. It feels good letting someone else take care of me. It's not like I've never had it before, because I have. By several different people, in fact. But it just feels different coming from him. It's different with any of them taking care of me.

I hop onto the counter and Nova brings over the small first aid kit. It's a white tin box with a red cross painted on the top, and it's been here for my entire life. I'm pretty sure Grandpa Dalton won it as some carnival prize a few decades ago. But when Nova flips open the lid, I'm surprised to see it's been recently refilled. I'd expected a few random bandages and some antiseptic cream, but this thing is fully stocked with all kinds of things.

Rows of bandages organized by size, gauze pads, and a small pair of scissors. Rolls of medical tape, small bottles of hydrogen peroxide, and alcohol swabs. There's even an emergency suture kit.

"Is this your doing?"

Nova drags his hand across the back of his neck, his gaze darting to the side. "As much as I'd like to take credit, this is courtesy of my brother. He takes this kind of thing seriously, yeah? Not that I don't agree with him, given recent events. But we're not trying to overstep, and I think he did leave the three old bandages you had—"

I place my hand on his wrist, halting his almost rambling explanation. It's not like him to be so nervous around me, but I find it a little endearing. "It's alright. I want you to make yourself at home, all of you."

"He didn't mean it like that, you know," he murmurs. His hands move with practiced ease as he cleans the wound on my arm, his touch gentle and soothing. "Years ago, before we became what we are now, we were in the middle of some serious shit. Hunter was a baby, like brand-fuckin'-new baby, and Pops, he told us we were goin' on lockdown. The kind of lockdown that means to brace for impact, yeah?" He shakes his head, his hair sliding across his forehead. "And my brother damn near lost his mind."

My brows lift with surprise as Nova's words paint a different version of the Reapers than I know.

"My brother isn't perfect, sweetheart, but it wasn't as personal as I know it felt, yeah?" His voice grows slow, his tone measured. I watch his expression smooth into something contemplative, lips pursed and eyes serious.

"Why are you telling me this?" I ask softly, feeling a sense of vulnerability in his confession.

Nova shrugs a shoulder. "It feels like the right thing to do."

I tsk under my breath, a little surprised by his answer.

"Besides, I want you in my bed tonight and not just because I'm the default when you're angry with my brother," he drawls with a smirk.

A soft laugh spills free. That's the kind of answer I expect of him. Quiet settles around us, but it's the good kind. A welcome reprieve to the intensity from downstairs.

I don't begrudge them for their emotions, but sometimes it's hard to bear the weight of their emotions and mine at the same time. Especially when everyone is heightened. Or maybe that's just me.

The warmth of his fingers against my skin relaxes me enough that my eyelids start to droop.

"Tired, sweetheart?"

"Hm." It's a humming sort of acknowledgment.

"I'm almost done, then you can lay down and get some rest. Most of these are superficial, and nothing needs stitches."

I shake my head a little bit, careful not to dislodge his hands as he finishes cleaning the last scrape. "I'm not getting into bed like this. I need to take a shower, but I need to muster up the energy first."

"Alright. Wait here a second, sweetheart."

I lean back until my shoulders hit the mirror behind me and rest my eyes. I'm so tired that I actually think I might be able to fall asleep just like this. I startle awake when I hear the water running. My head snaps forward, and I see Nova on his knees, bent over the bathtub.

"What are you doing?"

"You're too tired to stand, so you're gonna take a bath. And I'm going to help you."

25

EVANGELINE

MY MOUTH PARTS on an exhaled breath. "But—"

"No buts. C'mon, Evangeline. I know you're not worried about a little thing like nudity." He shakes his head with a rueful sort of smile. "Damn, I already miss that sauna though."

I don't know how it's possible, but this man never fails to bring a blush to my cheeks. The sauna memories live rent-free in my head, that's for sure.

He adds some bubble bath underneath the faucet and drops a tie-dye bath bomb in the water.

"Don't be shy on me now, sweetheart. Let me help you in?"

"Alright." I slide off the counter and shimmy out of my clothes in record time. Despite my objections, Nova really does take it seriously. He doesn't so much as ogle me when I'm standing in front of him in nothing but my birthday suit. Honestly, I can't say I would be as chivalrous if I were in his situation.

He holds out his hand, palm up, and I settle mine into his. I use his hand for support and step into the pink water. Fragrant bubbles hit my senses, and I close my eyes as I sink into the water's warm embrace. It smells like sugared lemons.

"Good?"

"Mmm," I groan and lean back, letting my head fall on the natural curved headrest in the tub.

The slow drag of a loofah against my leg has me cracking an eyelid open. I peer between my half-open lids to see Nova sitting on the side of the bathtub, his arm fully submerged into the water. My breath hitches when he slowly pulls the soapy loofah from my ankle to my knee and back down again. He sinks his other hand inside the water and gently grasps my ankle, lifting my leg out of the water. He cradles my heel like it's something precious, dragging the loofah all the way down my leg so every single inch of skin is covered in suds.

He shifts his hold, dropping the loofah into the water so he can run his thumb down the middle of my arch. It's a delicious amount of pressure, and I feel something releasing inside my chest. Like I've been coiled so tight, spun even tighter and tighter with every passing hour the last few days. And with every pass of his thumb on my arch, and every drag of the loofah down my skin, it unwinds one rotation.

Nova replaces my leg back in the water and picks up the loofah once more. He repeats the process with my other leg, dragging his thumb down the arch of my right foot, and eliciting more groans from me.

I settle back against the tub, content to let him pamper me like this. I might've expected something like this from Bane, but not him.

I quickly realize my mistake the moment the thought floats across my head. I shouldn't put any of them into any boxes. They're all multi-dimensional men, and to place them into these stereotypes is a disservice to our relationship.

Nova's fingertips graze my inner thigh as he drags the loofah upward, pulling me from my musings. My breath stutters inside my chest when he gets close to the apex of my thighs, but he doesn't attempt to take it there. I think I'm both grateful and disappointed.

Grateful because I don't think I have the energy to be any sort of active partner to him right now, but disappointed because nothing feels better than his touch. I might've made a noise of protest, and Nova might've smirked at me, but he kept his movements even as he diligently washes my legs.

He moves on to my arms, taking the time to apply pressure to every single finger, releasing tension in other parts of my body. I have half a mind to ask him if he has some kind of training, because he seems entirely too good at this. But I also don't really want to open my mouth and ruin this magic little oasis he's created in here.

I'm not sure if talking would ruin it, but I don't want to chance it. And besides, I'm enjoying myself too much. I'm drowsy, one step away from actually falling asleep when he curls his hand around my shoulder and guides me forward.

I sit up and pull my knees toward my chest, resting my cheek on them.

"Head back, sweetheart."

I arch my neck, tipping my face toward the ceiling. Warm water runs down the length of my hair. It feels heavenly, like a mini waterfall cascading over me.

I hear the pop and snick of a bottle and imagine him getting more body wash. But it seems he still has more surprises for me. His hands are in my hair in the next breath, his fingers digging into my hair and massaging my scalp. I was wrong, *this* is the best feeling ever.

"Are you washing my hair." I meant it to be a question, but instead, it comes out as some kind of awed statement.

"Mhmm. Does it feel good, sweetheart?"

I nod, a few small dips of my chin. "This is always my favorite part when I go to the salon. The head massage when they're washing your hair. It feels . . . I don't know, magical I guess."

"Magical," he says with a small chuckle. His fingers work against the especially tension-filled spots on my scalp before he rinses the shampoo out.

"Are you shampooing again?" My brows lift toward my hairline when I smell the strawberry scent of my shampoo.

"I've heard Ma talk about double-washing your hair enough to know that it's supposed to be good for you, especially if you need pampering. And sweetheart, you definitely need some pampering."

I hum under my breath, biting the inside of my cheek to stop the smile from blooming across my face. I didn't know I'd find this kind of thing so appealing: a man washing my hair. "You're spoiling me."

"You deserve it, sweetheart. And if you want me to wash your hair for you every day, I will."

A low laugh leaves me. "Maybe not every day, but once in a while, it might be nice." I open my eyes and look at the wall in front of me. "Maybe you could even join me sometime."

His fingers sink deeper into my scalp, his hands big enough that he can nearly cover my entire head, thumbs working close to my ears. "I'm free tomorrow."

Nova rinses out the shampoo and starts on the conditioner. The vanilla scent permeates the air, mixing with the strawberry-scented shampoo and the lemon-scented bubble bath. It smells like a dessert in here, and if I wasn't so tired, I'd make a strawberry lemon shortcake.

I zone out for a little bit when Nova massages my scalp.

"I was scared," I whisper, breaking the silence.

His fingers still, but he doesn't say anything.

I close my eyes and pull my legs tighter to me. "I was really scared. And then, it was like this flip switched, and I wasn't as afraid anymore. And I . . ." I swipe my tongue along the corner of my mouth. "I'm a little nervous about what that says about me."

"There's nothing wrong with you, Evangeline. You did what you had to and no one is going to judge you for it. All that says is that you're an incredible woman."

I feel the press of his lips against my neck as his fingers leave my hair.

"Brave." Another kiss on my shoulder blade. "Loyal." A kiss on the ball of my shoulder. "Strong." A kiss on the top of my spine.

My sinuses tingle and my eyes fill with tears.

"Kind and nurturing." A kiss behind my ear. "And so fucking beautiful. Inside and out." A kiss on the edge of my jaw. "And so fucking *mine*."

I lift my head and meet him halfway. Our mouths brush once, twice, three times for the most tender kiss we've ever shared. My heart swells with warmth, and I revel in the softness of his lips against mine. All too soon, our kiss slows, and Nova pulls back enough to drag his mouth along the edge of my jaw once more.

He resumes his work, and I let myself enjoy the sensation of Nova's hands on me, rinsing out my hair.

He pushes to his feet and holds out a hand to help me up. I hold his gaze as I place my hand in his, letting him wrap a fluffy towel around me. I try to take the towel from him, but he gently pushes my hands aside.

"I got it, sweetheart. Let me take care of you." I look into his eyes and what he means is that he *needs* to take care of me.

I nod and release my grip on the fabric. He bends down, dragging the towel over every inch of me, paying especially close attention to the juncture of my thighs.

He grabs my silky bathrobe off the hook on the back of the door. "C'mon, sweetheart. Let's get you into bed."

I let him help me into my bathrobe, biting the inside of my cheek when I want to tell him that I don't usually sleep in it. But it's not like it's going to hurt anything if I do. He towel-dries my hair, and then tries his best to wrap a towel around it.

I let him guide me into my bedroom and tuck me into bed, both of us quiet. He steps back, like he's going to leave, and my heart pitches at the thought.

"Won't you stay?" I murmur, snuggling down underneath the blankets, my eyes doing that thing where they act like they're made of lead.

He hesitates next to the bed. "You want me to stay with you?"

I slip my hand free from the sheets and reach out toward him. "I always want you to stay."

He nods, his mouth set in an uncharacteristic straight line. "Alright sweetheart. I'll stay. Let me take care of the bathroom first."

I shake my head, my damp hair dragging against the pillow. "It'll keep. Just get in."

26

EVANGELINE

I WAKE UP SLOWLY, blinking a few times to figure out where I am. It takes me a few moments to realize that I'm in my bedroom at Magnolia Lane, with a furnace of a man wrapped around me. The towel has fallen off my hair, and my bathrobe ties have loosened, exposing the upper swells of my breasts.

I wiggle a little bit, a half-hearted attempt to get a little space between me and the space heater behind me. But it's a little hard to do when Nova is spooning me. Leg wedged between both of mine, hand under my arm and palm splayed over my heart.

I shift again, twisting a little bit to the side and like I planned it, my breast falls directly into his palm. I swallow the gasp at the sensation of the pads of his calloused fingertips grazing my nipple.

"Stop moving, sweetheart. We're sleeping," Nova mumbles from behind me, his voice all raspy with sleep.

I glance around the room, trying to discern how long I was asleep. I feel rested, if not a little groggy, but I don't have any concept of day or time.

I try to roll over to face him, but he tightens his hold on me with a grunt. I swallow down the laugh. He buries his head in the space between my neck and shoulder.

"What if I have to go to the bathroom?"

I feel his lips curl up against my skin. "Do you?"

I shift my legs a little, sending the fabric sliding off of my thigh. "Well, no."

"Then there ya go," he mumbles, scooting impossibly closer to me.

"How long have I been sleeping?" The gentle whoosh of the air conditioning kicking in through the vents fills the room. I've always found that noise to be soothing.

"Not long enough," he says with a grunt.

I chuckle, tracing my fingertip along the length of his forearm, swirling over his tattoos.

"I don't want to sleep anymore, Nova."

"No?"

I shake my head, my hair dragging across the satin pillowcases. "No, I woke up with something else in mind." The last wisps of a dream lie just out of my reach, but I still have the feeling. A newfound gratitude.

The world seems brighter, like a veil has been lifted, and now I can truly *see*. The feeling is like standing outside, the sun beating against your skin and the grass soft on your feet. It's the life-affirming feeling of contentment and pure appreciation.

And it makes me feel bold.

"You hungry, sweetheart? I'll go grab you something to eat, but you have to stay in bed. That's the agreement we made, remember?"

I roll my eyes at his highhandedness. I made a couple of comments about being tired earlier, and he acts like I'm on bed rest. It didn't help that Bane and Silas backed him up during our little debrief.

I tsk a little bit and shuffle my ass closer to him. "Well, what if I told you I had something else in mind? Something that doesn't require me leaving this bed."

He hums under his breath, his fingers tracing small circles around my nipple. "I'm listening."

"What if I told you that I woke up this morning—"

"It's ten p.m." he interrupts with a laugh.

I tsk, this impatient noise from the back of my throat. "Do you want to mess around, or do you want to talk about semantics?"

His head pops up behind me and he drags his mouth along the exposed curve of my neck. "Is that even a question?"

I tilt my head so I can catch his eye and arch a single brow. "I don't know. Are you going to tell me that I need to rest, or are you going to let me play?"

His mouth curls into a sinful smile. "Oh, sweetheart, you definitely need to rest. Doctor's orders, remember?"

"What doctor?" I laugh.

"Me, baby," he says, nipping at my skin. "So you're going to be a good girl and sit back and relax while I do all the work. How's that for compromise?"

I grin and tilt my neck so I can capture his lips in a kiss. It starts off slow and sweet, a tentative hello. He swipes his tongue along my bottom lip at the same time his fingertips gently pluck at my nipple. It hardens immediately, and there's a pulse all the way down in my clit. It's as if there's an invisible string connecting the two, and it's being pulled tighter with every soft caress.

I pull away from his mouth with a gasp, my eyes falling closed as the sensation sends a corresponding wave in my clit. "Jesus, Nova."

He kisses his way down my neck as he slides his free hand underneath my pillow, curving it around my shoulder to hold me close. I shiver as his lips drag across my skin, leaving a trail of goosebumps in their wake.

His palm smooths down my torso, parting my bathrobe and letting the fabric pool open. Cool air wafts over my heated skin, and I'm nearly trembling with anticipation.

He ghosts his fingertips along my inner thigh, teasing me with his fleeting touch on my pussy.

"Nova," I whimper, tilting my hips toward him in a wordless demand.

He chuckles softly, his breath fan-like against the skin behind my ear. "Patience, sweetheart," he murmurs.

"I don't want to be patient today," I grumble, rocking my hips against his hand once more. "I thought you wanted to take care of me?"

"I'll always take care of you, Evangeline," he murmurs, nipping my earlobe.

He doesn't make me wait any longer before his fingers finally slide inside of me, sinking deep, crooking to find that sweet spot. I moan when he presses against that sensitive spot inside of me.

"Yes," I whisper with a gasp, my hand flying to his wrist to hold him there.

His finger thrusts inside of me at a slow, torturous pace, and I rock my hips against his hand with a whimper. One finger becomes two, and then he swipes his thumb across my clit with a feather-light touch, sending an electric current of sensation coursing through me.

I reach behind me and tangle my fingers in his soft hair, pulling him closer to me. Our bodies intertwine as we lose ourselves to each other.

He drags the edges of his teeth across my neck. "You trust me?"

"You know I do," I reply, breathless with lust.

"Then turn over for me, baby. I want to try something I think you'll like."

With his hands on my hips, he guides me until I'm halfway on my stomach. My right arm is trapped beneath my torso, but it's not uncomfortable. It gives the illusion of being pinned down, and I'm already dripping wet with excitement.

"Tell me if it's too much." It's not a question.

I nod, mumbling my agreement into the pillow.

Anticipation sings in my blood, sending pinpricks of awareness throughout my body. It spreads like goosebumps. First, it's at the base of my neck, and then, it cascades down my back like a river.

Like this, I can't see him. I can't read his body language or his intention in his gaze. But I'd be lying if I said I don't enjoy the thrill that comes with this.

I don't have that much experience when it comes to sex, but I'm slowly realizing as I spend time with each of my men that there's a lot of things that I might like to explore.

His palms smooth over my ass cheeks in big broad strokes, like he's committing the shape to memory. And then when I expect to feel the calloused palm, I feel his lips. He sweeps his tongue over the swell of my ass, dragging it down to the underside curve.

His hands don't stop just because his mouth is busy. They continue their exploration, smoothing up and over the flare of my hips, dipping to tease my clit with light strokes.

I sigh and wiggle my legs apart, giving him more room to *explore*. He lifts my hips up a little, so I'm not quite on my knees, but my back is arched enough that he can see *everything*.

His fingers play in my arousal, dragging it up and down, stopping to dip inside of me and swirl around my clit. I can feel the heat of his breath on the back of my thighs, and the anticipation is almost too much to bear.

I moan softly, my body trembling with need. His lips trail up the backs of my thighs in open-mouth kisses, his tongue playful and delightfully teasing.

I'm captivated, lost in a sea of sensation. My heart races as he draws closer to where I want him most. And then, he stills.

"Ready, baby?" he says, never taking his lips from me.

I tilt my hips even further, arching toward him. "Yes," I hiss out on a breath.

He palms my ass cheeks, spreading them a little and buries his laugh inside my pussy. His tongue delves between my folds, licking and sucking with abandon.

"Oh my god," I groan, my face squished against the pillow.

Nova St. James is eating my pussy like it's his favorite meal. Like it's his last meal, and the man is leaving no crumbs left behind.

"Oh shit," I groan. It quickly turns into a ragged gasp of ecstasy as he sucks my clit with a delicious intensity. Shockwaves of pleasure course through me at lightning speed. My legs quiver, my toes start to curl, and my whole body seems to shudder with each rotation of his tongue.

Just when I think I'm racing toward the cliff of oblivion, he retreats. His tongue dances away from my pussy, tracing lazy lines up my inner thighs, leaving a trail of lust in its wake.

"Nova," I whimper in frustration, my hips rocking toward his face.

"Yes, Evangeline?" There's mirth in his voice.

"I want to come." At this point, I don't even care if I sound whiny. I'm too turned on to care.

"On it, sweetheart," he says.

I shudder as his tongue traces a delicate path over the uncharted territory of my body. I freeze for a moment, the sensation foreign but not unpleasant.

His left hand comes up to grasp mine, and he twines our

fingers together. That little bit of connectedness relaxes me faster than anything else could. Besides, I know he would stop if I asked him to, that's not even a question.

But I don't want him to stop. I want to see where this is going. And I want to see what he wants to do next.

I get my answer a moment later when he uses his free hand to spread my ass cheeks open, giving his mouth more room to tongue my asshole.

I squeak in surprise. "Oh. *Oh,*" I breathe out a second later.

I feel his chuckle against my skin more than I hear it. As I relax into him, I can feel my body respond. With every swipe of his tongue and press of his lips, my breathing grows shallow and uneven, and bright-white sparks of pleasure dance across my skin.

He continues his exploration, teasing me with soft little flicks. And I realize so very quickly that it's not just *not unpleasant*, it's *incredible*.

I maneuver my free hand that's pseudo-trapped between me and the bed until I'm close enough to flutter my fingers against my clit.

I'm so close to coming, that it only takes two swipes before I'm flying high. Higher than I've ever flown before.

Stars explode behind my eyes, and I lose myself in a cacophony of bliss. My muscles tense and I sink further into his embrace on instinct, riding out the waves.

27

EVANGELINE

"I THOUGHT I'd find you here."

I look over my shoulder to see Lincoln standing in the open sliding glass door. My lips curl into a smile before I even think about it.

"What are you doing here?"

He arches a brow and then takes a slow, deliberate step toward me. It's an intentional move, one to give me plenty of time to tell him I don't want his company, I'm sure. But what he doesn't seem to understand—what none of my men understand, is that I don't ever see myself *not* wanting their company. Except maybe when Silas is in one of his exceptionally grumpy moods.

Past me calls myself a liar when the memory of The Garage flashes before my mind's eye. And yes, I've now taken to referring to Silas fucking me like he would die if he didn't as an event in my mind. Just thinking about the way he palmed my throat makes a slow flush roll over my nervous system. The man was most definitely grumpy that night, and before he turned it to shit with his callous remarks, it was decidedly one of the hottest moments in my life.

I pat the cushion next to me. "Want to join me?"

"Always." He closes the door and crosses the cement patio in a few steps.

"I've thought about changing this, you know, making it my own."

"What's that, sugar?" he asks, settling next to me on the wicker loveseat Nana Jo loved.

Hunter and I were working on color theory and painting this set, but the rest is still at Silas's house. I smooth my palm over the tropical-patterned cushions with fondness.

Lincoln extends his right arm along the back of the loveseat, widening his legs as he gets comfortable. I kind of hate how lowkey attractive I find that little move. But maybe I just find everything about him attractive.

I let my gaze dance along his body, follow his torso and up the corded muscles of his chest, trail over the sharp line of his jaw, and linger over his lips. The bottom one fuller than the top, and his five o'clock shadow looks more like a beard than I've ever seen him with. My gaze connects with his, the gray flecks in his dark brown eyes seem to dance with mirth as he holds my stare. My cheeks flush, but I'm not embarrassed to be caught, not really.

I bite the inside of my cheek and pull my gaze from my man. My *boyfriend?*

He feels like so much more than a boyfriend, but I don't know what else to call him. Mine, I guess.

I incline my head toward the backyard. "This patio. I thought I might extend it, add a little pergola or something so I can spend more time out here during the day. Right now, the best time of day is during golden hour when the sun doesn't feel like it's trying its best to turn you into a kabob."

His fingers toy with the ends of my hair, and I can feel his gaze on me. Everyone always says he's so hard to read, but I don't get it. He seems like an open book to me. Like right now, I can feel his quiet amusement.

"What's stopping you?"

"I was thinking Nana Jo might actually have buried stuff in her backyard."

He chuckles, this smooth low sound that floats around me and settles into my skin. "She was . . . eclectic."

I roll my lips inward and look at him. "You're thinking of her phallic vase collection, aren't you?"

He slides his hand underneath my hair to palm the back of my neck with a laugh. "Well I am now."

I lean into his touch, amusement making me feel weightless. "I think I'm going to get one of those metal detector things and use it in the backyard just to make sure she didn't bury anything important. I'd hate for them to pour concrete over something that she buried. I'd never find it then."

The pads of his fingertips press against my neck in a gentle sort of pulsing massage. "We'll get one then, sugar."

"I thought it would be something that Hunter and I could do together. I know he'd love it, ya know?" There's a pang in my chest when I think about him too long. I'm sure there's some trauma I need to work through from everything.

His fingers thread through the hair at the nape of my neck. "He'll be home soon, sugar."

I look at him across my shoulder through the watery haze of my eyes. "Are you sure he's safe?"

His gaze roams my face, his mouth curved in a sympathetic sort of smile. "I promise you he is."

I exhale audibly and look out into the backyard once more. "Good. That's good. That's what matters, right?" I reach over and snag my iced coffee from the little side table next to me, holding it up in a salute. "Thank you for this by the way."

He lifts a brow. "How do you know it was me?"

I take a sip from the straw and smirk. "You've been handling my coffee needs since I got here, Lincoln. If you're not bringing me daily coffee, then you're paying for it at the coffee shop downtown."

His fingers still on my scalp. "I didn't pay for your coffee at the shop downtown."

My brows crowd together over my eyes, and I lower my iced latte. "What?" I shake my head a little. "Of course you did, the guy behind the counter said you took care of it."

He stares at me with the kind of intensity you see on a predator before he lunges at his prey. Not that I think I'm the prey here, but it sends a shiver of awareness down my spine all the same.

"Think, sugar. What did the barista say exactly?"

I sink my teeth into my bottom lip and spin the glass around on the top of my thigh. "Well, he started acting cagey when I told him my name, then he wouldn't let me pay for my drink, and said 'please don't tell him' and something about 'he's gonna kill me.' And I guess I assumed it was from you. Like he was worried you were gonna get mad or something?" My gaze ping-pongs between his eyes. "Did I do something wrong?"

"Nah, sugar," he says, his fingers gently massaging my scalp again. "Just thinking."

Quiet settles around us, but it's heavy with anxiety, at least from my end. I think back, trying to remember anything else the barista said, or anything else that seemed weird.

"You sleep okay?" he asks, pulling me from my spiral.

I nod with my lips around the straw, enjoying the way the spiced chai melts on my tongue with the perfect consistency. "Yeah. I'm a little off, and I felt like I could keep sleeping, but I'm tired of being in bed. Besides, it's lonely in there alone." I send him a sly look, hiding my smirk.

"C'mon, sugar, we both know you weren't alone last night."

I tsk. "That was two nights ago. *Last night,* I was alone. I really thought you were going to come and join me." I'm teasing him. I'm perfectly capable of spending my nights alone, even if I do prefer to be sleeping with one of them. I can't get over how warm they are, how good it feels to snuggle something. Or *not snuggle*, in some cases I think with a proverbial brow waggle.

His fingers flex against the sides of my neck, a wordless request for my attention. "I'm sorry, sugar. I was trying to give you space, especially after Nova basically super glued himself to your side the first day you got back."

My mouth curls into a small grin and I look at him. "I'm not mad, Lincoln. Just giving you a hard time."

He nods, his expression pensive. "It's okay to not be okay, you know. You're safe here, with me. With all of us. To feel whatever you're feeling."

My smile slips free. "I know, and I appreciate that. But I . . ." I trail off as I try to find the right words. "I don't know. I'm not going to dwell on it. I just want to move on. I want to find that asshole who took me, and then I want you guys to do whatever you have to do to get Hunter home. And then I want to move on."

"We're trying, Evangeline. You have no idea how much we want all of that too. But that guy's a fucking ghost. We don't have any footage of him entering the compound, and Dixie didn't see anyone on her way out through the backend of the property. So it's taking longer than I'd hoped."

I shake my head, sinking my teeth into the soft fleshy part of my cheek. "It's too bad I didn't steal his driver's license when I left him in that ditch."

He chuckles. "I doubt he had any kind of identification on him, sugar. If he was smart enough to evade all kinds of security and traffic cams, then he would've known better. But it's a good thought. You sure there's nothing distinguishable about him?"

My face scrunches up as I try to remember the emblem on the back of his jacket. "There was something, some kind of logo or artwork on the back of his jacket. But it was faded, like it was worn and aged. Not one of those artfully distressed jackets they sell for hundreds of dollars."

He shifts to attention next to me. "Describe it. Colors, shapes, anything you can think of."

I close my eyes and try to picture it. I do my best to block everything else out, not letting myself get swept into the anxiety thinking about that day brings. "I think it was kind of a circle shape, maybe oval. And the design was kind of light, like a yellow or gray maybe. It was too dark to make out much else."

His thumb sweeps over my pulse in my neck. "That's good, sugar, real good."

"Yeah?" I ask, a hopeful smile ticking up the side of my mouth.

He pulls out his phone with his free hand, his fingers flying over the screen. "Just adding a few things to my search parameters." He clears his throat and slips his phone back into his pocket. "There's something I want to tell you."

Alarm races up my back. "Okay."

"It's about your sister."

I swallow hard, my heart thumping inside my chest. My feelings about my sister are complicated on the best of days. She's a sibling in name only, but the idea of her—of what she could've been—is what eats away at me sometimes.

"What about her?"

He hesitates a moment, his gaze locked on mine. "She called me. The day they came to the compound."

I suck in a sharp breath. "What? *Why?*"

He drags his hand along his jaw. "Shit, sugar, I don't know how to tell you this."

I swipe my tongue across my bottom lip, my skin starting to

feel prickly with awareness. "Just tell me. Whatever it is, I can handle it."

He nods, his lips pursed as he looks at me. "She was involved in the robbery. And maybe the compound thing, at least indirectly."

Shock reaches down my throat and yanks all the air out of my lungs.

"She didn't tell me much, seemed real skittish when she met me at the diner on the outskirts of town. Seemed kind of remorseful, but I don't know, sugar, she seemed off, ya know?"

I close my mouth, belatedly realizing that it's been hanging open in genuine surprise. "Wow." I shake my head a few times, looking out into the backyard. "I, uh, I don't even know what to do with that information."

His fingers pulse around my neck, a wordless reminder that he's here. "You don't have to do anything with it. But I wanted you to have it."

I nod a few times, letting my mind wander and shoving that little development into a small box inside my chest, tucking it away for later.

The warm breeze rolls over us, lifting a few stray pieces of my hair. "If you could go on vacation right now, where would you go?"

He chuckles, but if he's surprised by my topic change, he doesn't show it. "Right now?"

"Yeah." I nod and take another sip, despite it being close to eight o'clock at night. One of the perks I was born with: I can drink caffeine literally five minutes before I go to bed. It doesn't really keep me awake at night, despite it giving me a nice little boost. "If everything was normal, and there were no fires or worries or anything bad, where would you go? Or top two places if you can't narrow it down."

"I'd go wherever you are."

I roll my eyes playfully, but I can't deny my insides feel squishy and warm. "You can't say that. You have to say an actual destination."

"Okay, sugar. You first, give me your top two."

"That's easy: Disney World." There's a beat of silence, and I turn to take in his expression. I don't think I've ever seen him look so surprised. "Not what you were expecting, hm?"

He drags his teeth over his bottom lip, but I see the smile behind it. He shakes his head slowly. "Gotta be honest, I for sure thought you'd say somewhere tropical. Where you can lay on a beach and order Silas to bring you fruity drinks in pineapples and coconuts."

The image blares across my consciousness, and I laugh. "Oh that'd be good but no. I've always wanted to go to Disney World. I even asked for it for Christmas and my birthday for two years straight when I was in elementary school. And for five years, every time I blew out a single candle in whatever fancy dessert at whatever fancy restaurant my parents dragged us to, I wished for a trip. Every time I asked my parents why we couldn't go, Mom said something disparaging about theme parks. How she wouldn't be caught dead in them."

"Sugar." He says it like he's apologizing.

"I know I could've gone when I was an adult. I had money and I wasn't under my parents thumb quite as much as when I was a kid, ya know. But I don't know, going there solo felt too daunting. Too humiliating." I add the last two words quietly. I didn't realize how lonely my life was until I came back to Rosewood, until I found them. "It's stupid, isn't it?" I force a shaky chuckle.

"It's not stupid. I've never looked into that place that much, but if you want to go there, then we're going to take a fucking trip to the mouse house."

"Maybe one day," I murmur with a chuckle, letting my head

rest on his shoulder. "I think Hunter would like all the rides and the characters. Plus, there's some amazing food there too. And I've heard they do a fireworks show every single night. Can you imagine how fun that would be?"

"The most fun," he murmurs, planting a kiss on the top of my head.

28

EVANGELINE

IT'S late and I'm tired, but I feel like all I've done is sleep and lay around. It's a weird paradox because my body is tired but my mind isn't. It's in a constant state of spinning, trying to dig into the recesses of my mind and uncover things. At this point, there are so many different things that could stress me out, I'm worried my newfound gratitude for life and my general commitment to living life without regrets is going to slough off like dead skin.

So instead of sleeping next to one of my very attractive, very warm and safe boyfriends, I'm in my kitchen. Overlooking my backyard and the new security lights someone installed and wondering where the fuck I'm supposed to go from here. How long must we live in this sort of suspended state?

My mind drifts to Hunter, as I've found it doing often lately. Sometimes I feel guilty about it, too. Like I'm not allowed to think of him so often. The humbling and painful realization I had the day I came home still pricks at me like an embedded thorn.

I'm Hunter's nanny. That's it.

It's a position I cherish, and there's absolutely nothing shameful about it.

But it's temporary. And it serves to make me *feel* temporary. It's an uncomfortable place to be inside my body, like I don't belong. The most ridiculous thing is that I don't even blame Silas for opening my eyes to the facts. His son *should be* his number one priority, and I would never begrudge him of that. In fact, I think I might side-eye him if Hunter wasn't his number one.

But I know better than anyone how foolish it is to wish for circumstances to be different. No amount of blown-out birthday candles or loose eyelashes or shooting stars will end all of this.

Hesitant footfalls pad across the house, and I tilt my head to hear them. It's entirely possible that Lincoln came looking for me if he rolled over and realized I was gone. I wait for him to wrap his arms around me or tease me.

"I'm sorry." The voice is low, barely more than a murmur, as if it's weighted down by emotion.

Surprise tightens my shoulders, my hands curling over the edge of the counter in response. It's not Lincoln behind me or even Nova. It's the one person who's all but avoided me for days. And I don't trust myself to turn around.

I don't know what version of Silas stands behind me. The man who was so consumed by his lust for me, the man who's tortured by the fact that he desires me. The frosty mask he wears when he wants to establish the lines he's drawn in the sand, boxes around us labeled employee and employer.

I think . . . I think that might push me over the edge. I've been balancing on a tightrope of emotion since I got home. My lids sink in a slow, labored blink at the word *home*. It's such an inconsequential word, only four letters long. And yet, it houses the biggest pool of emotion. Love, longing, acceptance, and joy are all wrapped around the concept of home. And without conscious thought, I'd foolishly started to think of this as home. Not Magnolia Lane. *Them.*

"Evie," he murmurs.

He squeezes my heart with his fist when he says my name like that. Like it's a prayer falling from his perfect mouth. But in between his fingers is barbed wire, and it sinks deeply into the softness inside of me. It shreds and sears every inch that it touches.

And I realize with heartbreaking clarity that *I* have been irrevocably changed in the last week. And I . . . I don't know how to go back to who I was before. There's been another rift in my timeline, another event that signals *before* and *after*.

But perhaps I'm not the only one changed. This could be yet another new version of Silas, and perhaps, it's the most deadly of all. I don't understand it, and I don't trust it.

More importantly, I don't trust myself with him.

Restlessness hums underneath my skin, the pulsating energy that grows with each moment I'm still. And yet, I can't bring myself to move.

I clear my throat and keep my gaze firmly on the backyard. It's the middle of the night, so it should be pitch black. But the spotlights make it look like a park playground, bright yellow circles of light shining strategically all over the property.

"It's late, Silas."

"What are you doing awake?" There's no reproach in his tone. It's soft and almost tender. It's disarming.

I swallow roughly. "I couldn't sleep."

I feel him then, like he's parting the very molecules of air as he crosses the kitchen. The space between us heats up, charged and churning by the constant push and pull. His breath ghosts along the back of my neck, stirring the hair that's fallen from my messy bun.

"I'm sorry, Evie. I shouldn't have been so harsh with you before," he murmurs.

My shoulders tense at his proximity, but I barely breathe, afraid I'm going to spook him into leaving. "It's fine."

"It's not fine, baby. I—" He exhales sharply, cutting himself off and stepping into me. "What you did, getting Hunter and Ma out of here like that, I just . . . thank you."

"I didn't do it for you." Uncertainty keeps my voice low, weighing it down like a lead balloon.

"I know—I know that." He exhales and places his palms on the counter on either side of me. "But that should've been the first thing I said. I should've said it a hundred times. I can't—I don't know how—I'm ill-equipped, Evie. I don't know how to thank you properly. I should've gotten on my knees in gratitude."

My traitorous heart skips inside my chest as he cages me against the sink. Citrus and bergamot surround me, and I hate the way my body seems to sigh with relief. Like the very scent of him is enough to ease something restless inside of me.

He rests his forehead against the place where the top of my spine meets the bottom of my neck, like his head is too heavy to hold up. There's something so intimate about the move, like I am his pillar to lean on when he's weary. It's such a tender gesture, so unlike the versions of him I've encountered before.

"And I am so fucking grateful, Evie," he murmurs, his breath warming my spine. "I'm forever indebted to you for shielding my boy. For protecting him the way you did." He pauses, swallowing audibly. "The way a mother protects her child."

I suck in a sharp breath, his words a direct hit. Tears fill my eyes and my fingertips press tightly against the counter, grounding me.

He inhales, like he's preparing himself for something. "I'm an idiot and an asshole, and I don't fucking deserve your forgiveness.

But I'm asking for it all the same. In five days or five years from now. However long it takes for me to earn it, I'll do it willingly."

"What am I forgiving? The way you treated me in the garage? The way you stretched the truth about where Hunter is? Or how about your tendency to decide you want me one day and want nothing to with me the next? What do you even want from me, Silas?" By the end, I'm nearly pleading.

His nose skims the line from my shoulder to my ear, his lips halting beside my earlobe. "Everything, Evie. I want everything from you."

My heart stutters inside my chest. "And what about you? What do I get from you?"

He traces the edge of my ear with his tongue. "You can have every inch of my shriveled black heart, baby. Whatever's left of my soul, every good thing about me is yours."

I spin around then, the urge to see his expression too much for me to bear. My heart feels like it's floating somewhere in my throat. "What are you saying?"

"I'm saying *I'm fucking yours*. I have been since the moment I saw you in those ridiculous pink cowboy boots."

"Those were Nana Jo's boots," I mumble.

"They looked amazing on you, Evie. Everything looks amazing on you."

My gaze flies to his, widening at the intensity I see. "You're laying it on a little thick. It makes me nervous that you're going to do another one-eighty, and Silas, I don't think I can do this if you're going to keep changing your mind."

He swallows, his hands sliding up my biceps, rounding over my shoulder, and settling against either side of my neck. "I'm going to mess up, and sometimes, I'm going to be an asshole. But I promise you." He pauses, using his thumbs to tilt my face toward him. "I promise you I'll always come back to you with an apology and a promise to get better, to be better. I'm not perfect, Evangeline, but I'll try. For you, I'll try.

I place my hand over his heart, feeling the fast rhythm as if his heart is trying to communicate with me. "I don't want you to be perfect, Silas. I just want you to want to be with me. And then not having immediate regrets and saying things like *this was a mistake*. I deserve more than that, more than the constant reminder of my temporary place here."

His eyes close, his lashes a dark smudge against his cheekbones. "I'm sorry, Evie. I'm so fucking sorry." He opens his eyes, pinning me with his brown eyes. They look nearly black in this light, with this level of emotion behind them. "And I'll spend every day showing you just how much. Starting now."

And then Silas St. James sinks to his knees.

29

SILAS

THE TILE FLOOR bites into my kneecaps, but it's a small price to pay to be this close to Evangeline. She's wearing one of those lounge sets, thin cotton sleep shorts and an oversized shirt that keeps falling off of her shoulder.

I lean my forehead against her stomach, my hands curling around the backs of her bare thighs. Her skin feels warm and smooth, a stark contrast to the cool tile beneath me.

"I'm so sorry, Evie," I murmur, letting my lips brush against the fabric of her shirt with every word. "I'm sorry, and I'll keep telling you every single day until you believe me."

"I don't want your words, Silas," she murmurs with a small shake of her head.

I look up at her, my body sinking back on my heels as I position myself at eye-level with her pussy. I curl my fingers around the edges of her sleep shorts from behind, tugging the material until it's taut against her. I drink in the sight of her, the way the fabric clings to the outline of her perfect cunt.

My mouth fucking waters as anticipation sinks its fangs into my bloodstream. "Then how about I apologize with my tongue."

I press my lips against the fabric of her shorts in a chaste kiss, and she inhales sharply. The electricity between us buzzes, an audible feeling that skates down my spine. It drowns out all sound and rational thought, and I feel a little unhinged.

And I haven't even gotten my mouth on her yet. Not properly, really.

The fabric is soft against my lips, but I feel the tension in her body as my tongue presses against it. I pull the fabric tighter, swirling my tongue around her clit as she lets out a low groan. Her hand flies to my shoulder, her fingers flexing against me with every swirl of my tongue.

"Mm, fuck me," I mutter against her, feeling lightheaded with arousal already. It feels like a current passing between us, a fucking live wire of unbridled desire.

"Jesus, Silas. What are you doing?" she says with a gasp.

"Having a midnight snack, baby." I suck her clit through the fabric of her shorts, feeling it swell under my mouth as she arches her neck back and moans.

I hook my thumb around one leg opening, tugging it to the side and exposing her perfect pussy. Pink and soft and so wet already. I drag the tip of my tongue through her arousal, swirling it around her entrance, and savoring the taste of her.

Her breath hitches, and I can feel her trembling underneath my touch.

"Silas," she groans my name.

"Yeah, Evie?" I look up at her, sliding my tongue inside her cunt.

"Fuck," she curses low, her hand sliding into my hair.

"Yeah, baby," I murmur before I drag the edge of my teeth over her clit.

"Oh fuck," she breathes.

I smirk against her soft flesh, pride fizzing inside my veins like that popping candy.

"Someone could see us," she protests, but it's weak.

"You want an audience, Evie? You want them to see how you come all over my tongue, yeah?" I drag my tongue through her folds, savoring the taste of her. I'm careful not to rush, enjoying myself entirely too much. The way she squirms backward and shifts forward in the same breath, grinding her cunt against my face.

"I want to fuck you, Silas," she breathes.

My name sounds like a prayer on her perfect lips, and who am I to deny her anything?

I slide my hands over the swell of her hips to settle on her waist. Instead of standing up, I pull her down to the floor until she's kneeling, our faces nose-to-nose.

"Here?" she asks, eyes dark with lust.

"Here, baby," I murmur, dragging my lips along her jaw. "So be a good girl, and ride my face, yeah?"

She laughs, this breathy sound that vibrates through her entire body. She presses her palm to my chest, right over my heart and gently nudges me until I fall back onto my ass. My shoulders crash against the cabinets, and I can feel the almost silly grin spreading across my face. I don't even care that I probably look ridiculous.

"How about I ride your cock instead?" she murmurs against my mouth. She gently sinks her teeth into my lower lip before swiping her tongue along the sting.

It's a distraction, and it's fucking working.

"Fuck," I growl, my hand sliding down her waist to grip her perfect ass.

Her fingertips dig into my shoulder, her nails biting through the material of my shirt. I fucking relish the idea of wearing her marks. I hope she leaves dozens of them all over me, proof that she's mine.

I slide my palm up her back, reveling in the softness of her skin. And I get a little lost in the way she handles me.

The way she grips my cock in her hand and slides it free from my jeans. The hunger in her gaze as he looks at it like she's dying for a fucking taste. I imagine her on her knees for me then, taking as much of my cock as she can handle, and then taking another inch.

My dick throbs in anticipation, nearly painful with desire.

As she positions herself above me, her gaze never leaves mine. I watch the moment she lowers herself onto my cock, her lips parting in awe. Her tongue snakes out to wet her lust-swollen lips, and a low growl rumbles in my chest.

She's the most perfect thing I've ever seen, and I was a fool to keep her at arm's length for as long as I did. She was never just the nanny, but she was always mine. I just didn't know how to accept it.

I don't know what I love more: the taste of her cunt on my tongue or the way it squeezes the life from my cock. All I know is that I would happily spend the rest of the night, fuck it, the rest of my whole goddamn life tangled up in this woman.

I fear she may not realize what she's done though, because now that I've had her—really fucking had her—I'm never letting her go.

In the labyrinth of my tangled life, she's the map to my salvation. And I'll follow her to the ends of the earth, offering her every tattered piece of my soul.

30

NOVA

I JOG DOWN THE STAIRS, my mind already focused on all the shit I need to get done today. I've spent the last couple of days playing catch-up with work. As much as I want to spend all of my time with my girl, the excuse "sorry, I'm busy either fucking my girl or fucking up the assholes who might've been involved in the kidnapping of my girl" just doesn't really roll off the tongue that well.

I beeline for the coffee pot, nodding my hello to both my brothers. God that's fucking weird to think. I side-eye both of them as I pull a mug from the cabinet, wondering if today is the day I finally confront them. There's no way they both don't know about our *sibling bond*, and that's the shit that eats me up more than anything.

The design on the mug catches my eye, sky blue with a giant sunflower aesthetic hand-painted. And I'd bet one of my asshole brothers' lives that Evangeline's grandma painted this. I hesitate for a moment, scanning the rest of the mugs on the shelf for a different one. But they all seem to look like they're hand-painted, so I keep it.

"Where's my girl?" I ask the room. It's a double-edged sword, asking them about her. Because I have to ask them where she is, I can't stop myself from wondering if they've been with her today when I haven't.

Jealousy is a real bitch.

"Our girl," Silas grunts from in front of the stove. He's making an omelet, and I wonder if it's for Evangeline.

I had to stifle my disappointment when I didn't see her in bed. I woke up with the intense urge to eat *her* for breakfast. I can't fucking help it. Her skin is a flawless canvas, one I ache to explore fully. Every single fucking day.

"She's around here somewhere with Coraline. Garage, I think," Bane mutters distractedly.

I knew she wanted to continue going through Nana Jo's things in the house, and she keeps mentioning something about buried treasure. I can't quite tell if she's joking, or if I'm going to walk downstairs one day and find her in the backyard with a shovel.

I raise my brows at my brother and pour some pumpkin spice creamer in my coffee, because sometimes I'm basic as fuck like that. "*Our girl*, hm? Strange hearing you say that."

Silas makes some low noise in the back of his throat and I take it as he doesn't want to tell me. I shift my focus to Bane and arch a brow. That asshole always knows more than he lets on.

Bane takes a sip from his own colorfully-painted mug, smirking at me over the rim. "Strangest thing happened last night. I heard our girl in the kitchen, but I was still in her bed. That you, Nova?"

I pretend to think it over, really hamming it up with an exaggerated brow wrinkle. "Hm, me? Nah, I wasn't in the kitchen last night."

Bane tsks with a faux-frown. "Strange because I heard her, and you know how loud our girl is, yeah?"

"Oh, I'm well aware." I grin, the salacious quirk of my mouth as my mind instantly supplies me with the pitch-perfect sound of Evangeline coming on my tongue and then on my cock. It's the sweetest noise I've ever heard, and I have half a mind to make it my new ringtone. Except then everyone else would get to hear her, and those are for my ears alone.

Well, mine and theirs, I guess. Nah, the sounds I elicit from our girl are different from what she gives them, I just fucking know it.

"So if it wasn't me, and it wasn't you, that leaves"—Bane pauses because apparently I'm not the only one who loves a good dramatic pause—"you," he says, using his coffee mug to gesture to Silas.

He glances over his shoulder at Bane first, then me, his trademark scowl deepening the V between his eyes. But there's a little something in his eye. Vulnerability, maybe.

"Glad to see you got your head outta your ass, brother." I'm surprised to find that I actually mean it. I'm mad as hell that he didn't tell me about Ma, but I'm not so far gone that I don't appreciate how fucking good Evangeline is for him. For all of us.

He turns around with a noncommittal grunt and continues cooking. Something about it feels disrespectful, even if he doesn't mean it that way. I suppose I'm just looking for an excuse at this point.

"Nothing to say, hm? How very diplomatic of you. I thought you were always the type to kiss and tell." I snag an apple from the fruit basket on the island and sink my teeth into the tart fruit.

"It's too fucking early for this shit," Bane says from the table. He's drinking his coffee with one hand while his other flies over the keyboard on his laptop. He's been running some kind of program, scouring the intel he's being sent by whoever the fuck he activated when all the shit went down.

"Hey, you started it," I say around a mouthful of the red

apple. "And you know what? I don't ever think it's too early to give your brothers some shit, yeah?"

That gets his attention. Bane's head rises slowly, his gaze shifting to me. But I'm playing my own game now, so I keep my gaze on my apple in front of me, taking a nice slow bite.

Every once in a while I have a fleeting thought that I'm not addicted to chaos, but maybe more so justifying my need to stir the chaos pot. As if I'm owed a little havoc simply because my world has been flipped on its head. And if all that shit didn't go down, if we didn't walk into a fucking trap, and if we didn't come home to find our girl missing, then I might've brought this shit up earlier. But as it stands, I'm just brimming with untapped rage.

"You got something to say, Nova?" Bane asks.

I can sense the tension in the air, seeing the flexing of his arms as he grips his coffee mug.

I'm nodding before he finishes his question. "Yeah, man, I do. I'm going to take Evangeline to visit Hunter."

Silas spins around, spatula in the air and the same frilly half-apron tied around his hips. "The fuck you are."

I glare at him. "You really think she's a danger to him?"

"Of course not," Silas says with a scoff. "I told you I didn't mean it like that. But we don't know who took her yet, which means someone could follow her. She'd unknowingly lead them right to Hunter, and she'd never forgive herself for it." Silas shakes his head, more to himself than to us. "No. No, I'm not doing that to her or us."

"We've been down this road before, man. We know how dark it can get—"

"You're proving my point, Nova," Silas snaps.

I sigh and glare at him. "My point is that we've done this song and dance before. And I've been tap dancing my way across the city for the better part of a week. And by tap dancing, I definitely mean—"

"We know what you mean," Silas interrupts me. Again.

"Tossing bodies in Whispering Pines, delivering a couple to the cleaners, and even returning one to sender," I finish with a smirk. I'm fucking proud of that last one. "My point is, I've been all over and I haven't seen a single thing out of place. Not even a glimpse of a Savage *or* a Hell Hound."

Bane takes a slow drink of his coffee, and I can practically see the wheels turning inside his head. "That's because you take out every one you set your sights on."

I snap my fingers and point at Bane. "Exactly. So it stands to reason that I'm the most well-equipped one to take our girl for a visit to my favorite nephew."

"At some point, they're going to hit us back, you know."

I shake my head. "Not if we take them all out beforehand. Hard to retaliate when you have no more men to use as cannon fodder."

"We need a better plan than that, Nova. We can't do it your way forever," Silas says.

I shrug quickly, glancing outside and idly wondering what Evangeline is doing in the garage. "Call a meeting, Silas, and come up with something else."

Silence falls over the room, but it's not oppressive or demanding.

Bane clears his throat and locks eyes with Silas. "It's not the worst idea he's ever had. And I think it'll be good for Evangeline to see him."

Silas drags his hand across the back of his neck, indecision warring with his need to protect his son clear on his face. "You're asking me to trust you with my son's life. With her life."

It's not an accusation or dripping in indignation. For the first time in a long time, I feel like I'm *seeing* my brother. Not the gruff persona he wraps around himself like a light-tight shelter. Or the reluctant president of the Reapers. Or the overbearing older brother who has a penchant for getting his way.

The man before me is vulnerable, tentative and unsure in a way I'm not sure he's ever been before.

"God damn, she's fucking magic," I murmur on a gasp. I'd bet *my* life that this change is because of whatever went down in this kitchen last night. I clear my throat and set my coffee mug down, giving him my full attention. "I'll make sure they're safe, Silas. And I'll protect them with my life. You have my word."

Silas nods slowly, his brow pinched with concern. "Two hours, yeah? I don't want to push our luck."

"Three hours. Let 'em watch a movie and bake something together."

Silas narrows his gaze at me. "Did you already talk to her about it?"

My mouth curves into a sly grin. "Nah, I'm gonna surprise her. But Ma and I might have already talked about it. Don't worry, brother, she didn't mention it to Hunter yet."

"You're an asshole sometimes, you know that?" Silas grumbles, but it lacks any real frustration.

I lift a shoulder and lean back against the counter. "Learned from the best, big brother."

Silas nods, his gaze faraway as he murmurs, "I'm trusting you, Asher. Don't make me regret it."

31

EVANGELINE

"JESUS, Eve. I can't believe you went through all of that. It sounds like the kind of shit you see in a movie. That stuff isn't supposed to happen in real life," Cora says.

"Tell me about it," I mutter, leaning back in a lawn chair.

We're sitting in the middle of the closed garage. Cora came over to help me go through Nana Jo's things in the garage, but as soon as she saw me, she burst into tears. And then I burst into tears. And soon enough, we were a weepy, tangled mess of hugging and crying and declarations of love. But eventually, we dusted off the backs of our jean shorts and got off the concrete floor.

I snagged two of the crocheted lawn chairs hanging on hooks on the far wall of the garage. Nana Jo had these for as long as I can remember. I wouldn't be surprised if she either made them or picked them up from someone in town at one of the festivals. They're crocheted in a colorful abstract sort of pattern. It kind of reminds me of one of her favorite artists. If the artist's medium was yarn and not oil paints.

At one point, Cora even dug out a couple of glass bottles of soda from the outdoor refrigerator. I'd kind of forgotten there was anything in there honestly. Outside of the past few days, I'd spent the last month at Silas's house.

"Is there a reason we're still outside? Hiding from one of your boyfriends?" She sing-songs the word boyfriends and scrunches her face into a silly expression.

"Yeah, you're supposed to be helping me go through everything in here, remember?" I lean my head back, letting my gaze coast to the ceiling with a small laugh. Nana Jo's garage has exposed rafters for storage, not that there's anything up there anymore. But I vaguely remember Grandpa Dalton storing a kayak up there when we were younger.

She tsks. "I thought that was a ruse in case one of your boyfriends was nearby or something."

I roll my head toward her, arching a brow. "Do you think I need permission from my men for my best friend to come to my house?"

Pink dusts the tops of her cheekbones, and the side of her mouth hooks into a smirk. "Well when you put it like that." She toys with the label on her Coke, the paper shredding all too easily now that it's wet. It's hot as hell here in the summers, but the garage is cool enough if we keep the door closed. "How is that working out by the way?"

"How's what working out?"

She waves the glass bottle casually in the air. "You know, the three dicks."

I laugh, this surprised sort of barking noise that has her smirk blossoming into a full-blown grin. "If you ask me about their dick sizes one more time, I'm going to go tell Silas about it."

She rolls her eyes and pitches her voice obnoxiously high. "Oh no, please don't tell the scary biker man that I'm genuinely concerned my girl isn't getting her needs satisfied."

"I genuinely love you so much. So trust me when I tell you

that you're ridiculous sometimes," I tell her, affection wrapping around every word.

She winks and holds up her glass bottle in cheers. "Don't I know it, babe. But you're avoiding the question, and it's not going unnoticed."

"What? What question?" I sputter through another laugh. God I don't even know how long it's been since I laughed like this with anyone, but especially her. No one makes me laugh quite like Cora does. It's different from the kind of fun I have with my men or Hunter. Or even the kind of fun I had with Nana Jo.

Tears fill my eyes as it all becomes so startlingly clear. I've said it before, and I'm sure I'll continue to say it, but Coraline Carter is the sister I should've had. We have the kind of relationship that I wished my *actual sister* and I had. There's something beautiful and heartbreaking about all of it. I blink several times, dispersing the tears and hiding it behind my own bottle.

"You know, the one big happy family thing you have going on here," she says.

"We're not one big happy family. Not without Hunter here," I murmur.

Her amusement settles into something more serious and sincere. "I'm sorry, Evangeline. That you had to go through all of it. I'm really, really sorry." She reaches over and grasps my hand in hers.

"It's not your fault, you don't need to apologize." I shake my head, squeezing her fingers back. "And I hope you know how much I appreciate you coming over today."

"Psh, Jagger told me that Bane told him I need to give you a few days to get settled in. And then Jagger and I exchanged some words."

I don't bother smothering my laugh as I waggle my brows. "Is that a code word for you two or something?"

She slides her hand out of mine and executes a perfect hair toss. "Please, that man wishes."

My brows fly toward my hairline, and I grin at my cousin. "Oh, I'd bet my house he does."

Her brows arch over her dark brown eyes, the color so similar to my own. "You're avoiding the question."

I splay my hand over my chest. "I'm doing no such thing. I'm simply making conversation with my favorite cousin about her on-again-off-again man who happens to be in the same motorcycle club as my men."

"There's no on-again. Jagger and I haven't been *on* for ages. Practically a lifetime in dating terms."

"Mhmm. Whatever you say." Not even she can deny the chemistry they have together. I haven't seen it myself recently, but Lincoln told me he witnessed it a few days ago. Said it was like he could see a string twining the two together, but he also said he hadn't slept in days, so I guess it's possible he was hallucinating.

"Whatever, are we going treasure hunting or just hanging out? By the way, I'm all for hanging out. I feel like I've done nothing but work and worry *for weeks*. In fact, come here." She leans over, bringing her face a few inches away from mine. "See this?" She tilts her head and points to the space between her brows. "That's from you."

A laugh sputters out of me, and I squint, trying to see what she's talking about. "That freckle is from me?"

"No, don't be purposely obtuse. That line is from you. From all the goddamn worrying I did about you."

"I love you, Cora, but there is literally no line there." I sit back with a grin.

She settles into her chair and crosses one leg over the other with a sigh. "I'm going to get Botox and then send the bill to you."

"You know, Nana Jo always said fine lines and wrinkles were a sign of a happy life," I drawl.

"Ah-ha!" She sits up, dropping her feet to the ground and pointing her finger at me. "I knew I had a wrinkle there."

She's so ridiculous that I can't help but tease her. My heart feels light and joyful, and I wish I could bottle this feeling up and uncork it whenever I need a hit. "You're beautiful exactly as you are. I'm just messing with you, but if you want to bill me for your Botox, go for it, babe. In fact, let's go together. I'm going to find Nana Jo's buried gold bars in the backyard, so I'll be good for the money."

She chuckles as she relaxes into her chair. "Damn, do you really think there are gold bars buried in the backyard?"

I lift a shoulder. "I don't know. I kind of got this idea and now I can't stop thinking about it. But I don't know if it's because my mind needs something normal to latch onto or because the idea has merit."

"Yeah, I get that," she says softly before she finishes her soda. She pushes to her feet and tosses the bottle toward the recycling can like it's a basketball. Predictably, it doesn't land anywhere near it. She tilts her head back with a loud groan and trudges over to pick up the bottle off the ground.

"You're lucky it didn't break, you know."

She stands up and tosses it in the bin, pausing as she looks out the window. "I thought you said the guys left?"

"Yeah, Nova and Bane went to work, but Silas should be here still. Why?"

She looks at me over her shoulder slowly. "Because there's a black town car in your driveway."

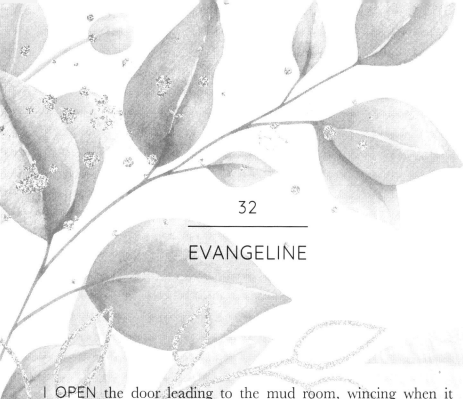

32

EVANGELINE

I OPEN the door leading to the mud room, wincing when it creaks. The sound of chatter floods my ears. I pause with my hand on the door handle, one foot inside the house and the other on the cement stair in the garage. Voices float around the house, male and female. My lips twist to the side as I try to discern whose voices they are.

Cora presses into my back, her hand on my shoulder. "Who's inside your house? Where's Silas?" she whisper-hisses.

I tilt my head toward her and slink inside the house, my heart hammering against my chest. "I don't know."

She keeps pace with me, close enough that I can feel her breathing down my neck. "Well, were you expecting someone?"

"If I was, would I be tiptoeing through the house like this?" I roll my eyes, easing along the wall. I peek around the corner, but the kitchen is empty. I was sort of hoping I'd see Silas sitting at the table.

I can recognize it's a trauma response well-enough, but that doesn't stop the anxiety coursing through my veins at warped speed. It doesn't help me chill out and figure out what to do.

"Well I don't know the kinky shit you get up to with them," she huffs in a whisper.

I shake my head, rolling my lips inward. "Shh. Listen." Both of us pause, our backs to the wall in the kitchen, heads cocked and ears angled toward the sound.

"Is that . . ." she murmurs as the voices get louder. One voice in particular stands out. I'd recognize the disapproving tone anywhere.

I push off the wall, abandoning all pretense of stealth. My intruder anxiety melts away, leaving regular anxiety in its place. Only this time, there's a ring of rage around it like a fire, and I can't tell if it's putting out the anxiety or fueling it like some co-dependent relationship. I stalk toward the front of the house, veering left to stop in the living room toward the four people inside my house.

"Hello, Mother."

"Oh shit," Cora murmurs from behind me. Close enough to give me support but a little breathing room too.

"Evangeline." Virginia Carter stares down her perfect nose at me. Her lips painted in her favorite shade of coral curve into a grin that's too malicious to be anything but a warning.

"What are you doing inside my house?"

Mom wraps one arm around her torso and uses it to prop up her other arm by the elbow. Her nails tap against her chin, the blood-red color stark against her perfectly porcelain skin tone. My mother would never be caught dead with something as common as a freckle. Or god forbid, a sun spot.

She arches a brow, cruelty lining every inch of her presence. "Your house? I don't think so, darling. Tell her, Rupert." She gestures to one of the men next to her with the flick of her wrist, spinning around to look at the bookcase. "Now, this all needs to go. It's dated, and well, even then, I don't think it could ever be considered stylish."

The man, Rupert, scurries toward me, an open leather portfolio in his hands. "If you'll just look here—"

I wave my hand in front of him, walking around him to stop next to my mother. "What do you think you're doing?"

She looks over her shoulder at me, dripping in derision and diamonds. "This is Henri, he's the leading interior designer in California right now."

"I don't give a fuck about him or his accolades."

She tsks, the noise as sharp and grating as I remember. "Ten weeks in Rosewood with those filthy bikers and look at you, talking like some common whore."

There's a gasp, and I honestly don't know if it came from me or Cora or the other woman in the room. I'm doing my best to ignore her presence.

"What did you just say?" His voice is low, that lethal sort of tone I've never heard before.

I don't turn around, I already know Silas is here. There's a tightness between my shoulder blades that eases with his presence. It gives me the courage to face this, face them. And I find myself settling in for a long-overdue conversation with my mother.

Mom doesn't even bother to look at Silas, and I know it's intentional. A power move, if you will. "Oh, let me guess, another one of your charming motorcycling friends, hm?"

"They're not my friends, Mom. They're . . . they're my— they're *mine*." I feel my cheeks warm as I fumbled over my words, but I keep my head straight and eyes locked on my mother, and I fucking brace. Because I know her, and she never misses an opportunity to speak her mind.

"Your what exactly, Evangeline?" She turns to look at me, that cruel smirk a slash across her beautiful face. "Your men? Do you have a menagerie of men here at Magnolia Lane? Such a shame you're going to lose it."

I shake my head and tap my fingers against my thigh, a nervous flutter. "I'm not doing this with you. I'm not going to argue with you. Get out of my house."

She reaches forward and pats my shoulder twice. It's so fucking condescending, that I have to grind my molars not to lash out. "Of course you won't, Evangeline. You never did have what it takes. Not like your sister, Elizabeth." She gestures to the side, where I know my sister is standing.

Still, I refused to look at her. Instead, I point at her general direction. "Get the fuck out of my house, Lizzie, you duplicitous bitch."

"I'm sorry, Eve—"

I look at her now, sending the harshest, most severe look I've ever felt cross my face. "You don't get to call me that. Eve is a nickname reserved for my friends and family. And you are neither."

Lizzie looks as put-together as always. Wearing a sleeveless pale pink jumpsuit that makes her skin look amazing, hair freshly blown out, and her signature stiletto nails painted neon orange. She doesn't look like someone who came begging for help less than a week ago.

"I didn't mean for you to get hurt. I tried to warn you. Coraline will tell you, she was there," Lizzie says, jerking her chin toward our cousin. "And it's not my fault they did what they did. I don't control those bikers."

I watch as Lizzie's gaze slides to Mom, and it clicks into place. She didn't get what she wanted from Bane, so she went crawling back home. I almost feel sorry for her, but then I remember that she literally came to rob me and was going to let that guy hurt me.

I tilt my head to the side, letting the piece of myself out. The version of me that's hellbent on survival. I stalk toward her slowly, feeling like I'm the predator now. "Do you know what I did to the last people who came to my house with intent to harm, Lizzie?" I stop in front of her, giving her a front row seat to my confession. I lean in close and whisper, "I killed them."

She swallows roughly, her gaze darting toward Mom once more.

"Elizabeth, dear, go wait in the car while your sister finishes her temper tantrum. We'll be in the house soon enough," Mom says, shooing Lizzie out of the room with a flick of her wrist. Lizzie obeys her, stalking across the house and slamming the front door as she leaves.

I look at my mother, trying to find a single ounce of maternal blood in her body. But like always, I'm left wanting.

"Get out of my house, mother."

"Evangeline, I grow weary of these outbursts. You really should read the fine print, dear. If you rent out the house, then you forfeit any claim you have on the property."

I shake my head, my hair swishing against my shoulders. "I didn't rent it out."

"Ah, but you did." Her lips curl into a Cheshire-Cat-like grin. "It seems you were gone for three days and you let those biker friends of yours rent the house in your absence." She leans over and pats my shoulder twice again. "It's called a loophole, dear. But you never did catch on easy, did you, hm?"

I smack her hand away from me, momentarily shocked by whatever garbage she's pulling now.

Silas slides in front of me, arms folded across his impressive chest. He towers over my mother, but she only arches a brow at him, unimpressed. "It's going to be hard to do much of anything when you're buried six feet under, Mrs. Carter."

Mom's lips purse and she tries to look over Silas's shoulder at me, but he steps to the side, effectively blocking me from her view.

"No. You had your chance to play nice with her. You failed. Now you deal with me," Silas says.

I'm a little embarrassed to admit it considering the current situation, but a soft flick of arousal warms my belly at his protectiveness.

"Are you threatening me?" Mom scoffs.

"I thought you were the smart parent, Mrs. Carter. Surely you understand a threat, yeah?"

Mom sniffs, jerking up her chin further. "Rupert, Henri. We'll come back another time."

"Don't you ever walk in this house without Evie's permission again. We shoot first in Rosewood, Mrs. Carter, in case you forgot," Silas says.

The clack of her shoes against the floor is the only noise in the house as the three of them leave. Silas follows behind them, and I trail him. He stops at the front door, his body filling the entire door frame, watching them get into their cars.

"What the fuck just happened," Cora whispers.

But I can't take my eyes off of him, not even to answer my cousin. "Did you just threaten to kill my mother?" It should be an accusation, but instead it's more like an awed whisper.

His cheeks turn pink and he crosses his arms over his chest, glancing out the glass-single-paned door. "I didn't mean it."

I step next to him, looking at his profile and daring him to give me his gaze. "Yes you did."

"Nah, I don't think I'd threaten the mother of the woman I just promised I'd try not to be such an asshole. I definitely don't think it would be a good idea to threaten her life not even twenty-four hours after I made the promise to my woman I'd be better." He shakes his head a little, his gaze firmly fixed out the window. As if he's worried the town car is going to come barreling up the driveway again.

But that's not Virginia's style. She's not going to come back with literal guns blazing. She's going to come back with suits and try to bury us with paperwork and lawyer fees and legal terms I've never even heard of before.

"Why does she even want this house so bad? I thought she hated Rosewood," he mutters, his breath fogging up the glass a little bit.

"I don't know. The last time she was here, she said she was going to tear the house down, so it's not really about that. If I had to guess, I'd say . . . spite." My mother is really good at a lot of things. Carefully controlled rage, spite, revenge, etc.

He glances at me finally, a single brow arched in disbelief. "Spite?"

I try to view my mother objectively, as a woman and not *my* mother. It's an exercise I've done plenty of times before, sometimes with more luck than others. But with every time I practice this, it gets a little easier to separate the two. She's flawed like every other human I know, but her flaws seem to have brought out all the worst traits in her.

"If I had to guess, I'd say she has her own childhood trauma she's trying to work through. But that's not really my responsibility to fix it, yeah? It's not my responsibility to fix myself, to change every single thing she perceives as my flaws, just so she fucking loves me. She gave birth to me, but she's never been my mother." I sink my teeth into my bottom lip, releasing it slowly as the next thought feels true, even if it is uncharitable. "Some people aren't meant for motherhood, it seems."

"Some people are," Silas murmurs.

"I'm just gonna go," Cora whispers, but I don't really hear her.

I can't hear much of anything because my heart is thumping loudly in my ears. I turn toward him, but I didn't realize he was so close, and my lips skim across his chest. I suck in a sharp breath when I see his expression. Lips parted, brows even slashes over his eyes bright with reverence.

"Silas." His name is a prayer and a question all in one. And he answers it in the way I'd hoped.

His large hands cup my face as he pulls me closer. His lips meet mine in a passionate, all-consuming kiss that leaves me dizzy with lust.

33

EVANGELINE

"ARE you sure it's okay that we're doing this?" My fingers drum a quick beat against my thigh. The sun casts bright golden light through the tinted windows, highlighting every speck of dust in the air. I always thought it was weird we could suddenly *see* dust floating in a shaft of sunlight, but not any other time.

The two-lane highway stretches into the horizon, tall trees on one side and fields on the other. In the far distance, I can see some houses in a little subdivision.

"I'm sure, sweetheart." Nova answers with the same amount of patience he's had with me since he told me about today's surprise plans.

"And they know we're coming, right? We're not going to sneak up on them and scare him?" I worry my bottom lip, lacing my fingers with Nova's hand resting on my thigh.

He dips his head, his eyes on the road. "They know we're coming. We'll be there soon. About five minutes." He grins, as if he was anticipating my next question.

Which is definitely fair because I was right about to ask him how much longer. I'm normally much better with surprises. But after everything that's happened in the last few weeks, combined with the fact that we're in some strange sort of limbo, and my nerves are shot. I don't know where Hunter and Dixie are, and that's done on purpose. All I know is that we've been driving for nearly three hours at this point. The scenery is beautiful, and the company is great, but I'm just anxious to see him.

"I kinda wish we were on your bike," I murmur, gazing out the window. It's so very green here, almost like we're headed to one of those wooded park areas. I mean, sure, we're on a highway, so it's not like it's totally remote or anything. But I don't know, it doesn't *feel* like we're in a big city.

It kind of reminds me of the place Nana Jo and I would go to for a little getaway every once in a while. They're like timeshare properties in a special community, usually around a lake. I don't even know if Nana Jo owned a timeshare, or if it was something she just rented or borrowed from a friend.

My mind leads me from thoughts of Nana Jo to Magnolia Lane and then to my mother. I still can't believe she just walked in my house like that the other day. It feels more than an invasion of privacy. It feels like a direct hit, even though she hasn't really done anything. Not yet. That's her specialty though, isn't it? It's the not knowing that eats people alive. The constant worry and looking over your shoulder, expecting her to be there figuratively and sometimes literally.

"I'd love to have you on the back of my bike, sweetheart. But we needed a little more protection today."

I nod, running the pads of my fingers over his knuckles. "I know. Maybe when we get home we can go for a ride?"

He grins, and that dimple of his pops out to wink at me. "I'd like that."

"It's a date," I tell him, sending him a bright smile. "Hey, do you think we should change the locks on Magnolia Lane?"

"Bane's on it. But he said no amount of fancy security will

work if we don't lock the front door." He sends me a pointed look.

I roll my lips inward, my cheeks growing warm. "That's true. I guess I've been in Rosewood too long if I forget to lock my front door, hm?" I tilt my head to look at him. The sun shines through his window, highlighting his hair in almost a faint strawberry color. My fingers land on the soft strands, flipping the short length through my fingers.

"Feels good, yeah?" I sink my fingers into his scalp and lightly scratch.

He hums low under his breath as he looks at me for a few seconds, the longest he hasn't had his attention on the road or the mirrors. He's been overly diligent in his focus today.

"Are you fishing for another bath with me, sweetheart?" His lips curl into a playful smile, but there's a dirty curve to it, pulling a chuckle from me.

"Depends. Will you join me this time?"

He drags his teeth over his bottom lip, stealing a glance at me. "You know I will."

I arch a brow. "Will you still massage my head like you did last time?"

"Do you want me to?" he counters, his own brow raised.

I grin. "Hell yeah I do. That felt so good I could feel the tension sliding off of me."

"I'll do anything and everything you want, sweetheart. You know that."

"I know," I murmur.

A minute later, we pull into the driveway of a log cabin style home. It stands tall amongst the surrounding trees, blending seamlessly into its natural surroundings. Its rustic charm is enhanced by the dark wooden beams and panels that make up its walls and roof. It looks cozy and inviting, with a stone chimney rising from its pointed roof.

Before Nova puts the car into park, the front door opens and a blur of color barrels out. It darts across the lawn and practically flies over the stairs. I push open my door and have just enough time to get my feet on the ground and stand up before it collides with my legs.

"Eve!" Hunter yells.

I bend over him, sliding my hands down his back to return his hug. I don't care how awkward it is, or that mosquitos are currently feasting on me right now, nothing could pry me away from him. There's been a vise around my heart for weeks now, and no matter how many times I assure myself I'm safe, it never eased.

I didn't realize why until right now. I wasn't anxious about myself. I was worried about Hunter.

"I've missed you, buddy," I murmur, my eyes getting watery with emotion.

"I've missed you so much," he says.

At least that's what I think he says, his words are a little muffled as he's still squeezing my legs in a tight embrace.

"I brought you a treat. Want to go inside and see what it is?" I smooth my hand around his back in big circles.

He pulls back to look at me, his eyes sparkling a little bit. "Did you bring me cookies?"

I nod, brushing his hair off his forehead. "Chocolate chip ones."

"Yes!" he says, squeezing my legs in excitement. "But wait, I thought we were a cookie team, remember?"

"We are, my little muffin. But since we brought lunch today, I thought we could save some baking for next time. How does that sound?" I ruffle his hair.

He leans back but doesn't let go of the back of my legs. "That depends. What did you bring for lunch? Because I don't like tuna fish sandwiches—yuck." He makes this exaggerated face like he's going to throw up.

I chuckle at his dramatics. Relief sags my shoulders to see him act like the same kid despite everything that happened. Maybe he really was shielded from most of it. I should've asked what they told him about what happened, so I don't stick my foot in my mouth.

"Don't worry, bud, no tuna sandwiches today," I assure him with a grin. "Your Uncle Nova and I brought some pizza! Those really big slices the size of your face, but we have to warm them up. Wanna help me?"

Hunter lets go of my legs to do a jumping fist bump. "Yes! I love pizza!" He turns around and runs back toward the house with nearly as much speed as he left it.

Nova tosses his arms up on either side, calling out, "What am I, chopped liver?"

Hunter's giggles trail behind him.

"You're the best chopped liver I've ever seen, Uncle Nova," I tease him, looking over my shoulder to see his smile soften the edges of worry etched on his face the whole drive.

"Yeah, yeah. Go on in, sweetheart. I'll grab the stuff and meet you inside," he says, tipping his chin toward the house.

"You sure? I don't mind helping."

"I know, baby." He used his soft voice on purpose, because he knows it makes me melt a little bit every time I hear it. "I'll be inside in a minute. I gotta talk to Ma, bring her up to speed on things, yeah?"

I nod, understanding the unspoken request for a moment alone with his mom. As I make my way back to the house, the scent of pine and earth surrounds me, grounding me in this place that feels familiar even though it isn't.

Dixie's waiting for me on the top step, arms open, and eyes misty.

"Evangeline, come on in, honey."

I step into her hug, wrapping my arms around her. "I'm so glad you're okay, Dixie. I've been worried about you two." I try to step back, but she tightens her hold on me.

"Those are my lines, honey." With tears in her eyes, she pulls back, sliding her hands down my arms and holding onto me. "I can never, ever thank you enough for what you did."

"It was nothing." I murmur my standard response, caught off-guard by my own rising emotions. My eyes water, and I have to blink a few times to get them to clear. I didn't think I needed to cry about this anymore, but I guess I was wrong.

"Don't downplay what you did for me, for my grandson. And for your home. You protected it the best you could, and from what my boys told me, you took a handful of those assholes down that day."

I shrug a shoulder. "I tried my best. Turns out, I'm not a great shot. I just got a little lucky."

She rubs my biceps up and down a few times before letting go. "Nothin' a little practice won't fix, honey. Why don't you come on inside before that grandson of mine comes hollering for you. It seems my son has a few things he wants to chat about."

"I'm surprised he's not out here already," I muse, crossing the porch and going inside. It's time to hang out with my favorite five-year-old.

34

NOVA

I SIGH and heft up the four bags Evangeline insisted we bring today. To be fair, one of the bags is just a soft padded cooler. She packed enough food and snacks to last us days, way more than we need for a simple afternoon spent with my nephew. But that seems to be the running theme today: overpacking.

Do I think she's actually going to use whatever is in all three bags? Probably not but knowing her, she'll try to pack as much fun for Hunter in the few hours we've got with him. And if it makes her feel better to be prepared and overpack shit, then that's fine by me. Fuck knows we've all done our fair share of weird shit to cope.

"Here, son, let me grab one of those," Ma says, meandering down the step, coincidentally not made of wood.

"I got it, Ma. You just stay there, yeah. I'm sure you're tired from chasing after Hunter by yourself all week." I adjust the fourth bag on my shoulder again, the straps slipping off.

She chuckles, but it sounds strained. "Well, he does keep me on my toes. But I might need a little vacation when we get back home. Speaking of, any idea when that's going to be?"

I stop next to her at the bottom of the stairs and shake my head. "We're doing all we can, Ma. But—" I cut myself off, sucking my teeth and looking into the surrounding woods—"it's like they just disappeared."

"What do you mean disappeared? The Hell Hounds and Savage Souls just vanished? Isn't that good news?"

I focus on her, searching in vain for some sign that she is biologically my mother. She still looks the same though. Same kind eyes that can turn into a glare on a dime. Same blown-out style and color she's been using for longer than I can remember. Same fierce personality that stops at nothing to protect her family. The anger, it's not going to go away overnight, or even in a month. But it is something I can come to terms with.

"Well, I've found some rats hiding, but it's the big ones we're missing. And that, that makes us twitchy. I'm sorry, Ma, but it's not safe for you to come home until we settle it."

She nods, her smile soft around the corners. "I understand. We're more than fine staying here for as long as we need to. How are you, honey? How's our girl, hm?" She jerks her chin toward the house, where I can hear Hunter and Evangeline's laughter.

I glance at the dark screen door, trying to articulate how I think she's doing. "She's alright. There's some shit coming up with her family. Her ma is a real piece of work. Silas told me he heard the whole thing the other day. You wouldn't believe it, Ma, she just walked in like she owned the place. Brought a couple of decorators and everything. And that shitty sister, too." I wince as soon as the sentence is out of my mouth, my gaze darting toward the open door. "Shit. I don't want to talk shit about my girl's sister, but, Ma, if one of my brothers ever pulled the shit she did, they'd be at the bottom of Whispering Pines by noon."

She chuckles, the laugh lines beside her eyes deepening. "Oh, Asher. I've missed you, son."

The back of my neck grows hot and I shift my weight a little bit. "Yeah, well, it's gonna take some time, yeah? Logically, I know nothing is really different, but I've got this weird organ inside my chest that's been reactivated and shit from a certain brunette. So that stuff takes a little longer to sort out. But I'm handling it, okay?"

She nods slowly, tears gathered on her lower lash line. "You tell them yet?" she asks quietly.

"Nah, haven't found the right time. What am I gonna say: surprise, you thought we were cousins, but turns out we're half-brothers because your mom fucked my dad and then dropped me at Ma's doorstep?"

"Well, that's the truth," she mutters.

"Yeah, well, I'm still pissed that Silas didn't tell me the truth. Or that fucking Bane didn't tell me he was my goddamn brother." It comes out a low growl, anger dancing all over my words.

Ma tsks softly. "Oh, honey, I don't think Lincoln ever knew."

I cut her a sharp look, my gaze roaming all over her face. "You sure?"

Her eyebrows are drawn together in a slight furrow, lips pursed. "He's never given a single indication to me or anyone else that he does. And I think he would have by now. I know the three of you grew up together, raised practically as brothers, but Lincoln"—she pauses and shakes her head a few times—"he really got dealt a hand of shit with his parents. They didn't do right by him."

I never really thought about it much, but she's not wrong. Bane spent a ton of time at our house growing up. I used to think it was just a club thing, except that other club kids didn't have their own rooms at our house. At one point, I remember thinking he was over all the time because he was our cousin, but even that didn't explain why he moved in during elementary school.

"Yeah, I guess." I take a deep breath, the weight of this

revelation is still settling.

"And the compound? Is it running okay? I've been thinking about Helen and her girls. A lot of them don't have a permanent residence, and it doesn't seem right to kick them out to keep them from danger when putting them on the street could very well be their downfall."

I adjust the strap on the bag that keeps trying to slide off my shoulder. "As far as I know, they're still at the compound and doing fine. But Bane has been around the clubhouse more than I have."

"Work keeping you busy, son?" she asks.

"I've got a few customs I'm working on simultaneously to make the deadline. Plus, my extracurriculars keep me pretty busy."

She looks at me, her gaze shrewd as it ping-pongs all over my face. "I hope for your sake that you're being careful. Especially if these assholes are waiting in the wings for us. All it takes is one single moment of opportunity, and then you're fucked." She punctuates her point with a snap of her fingers.

I fight to keep the eye roll in check. "I'm bubble wrap, Ma. I'm safe as fuck."

She clears her throat and looks at the ground for a moment, likely gathering herself together. "And how *are* you? You taking care of yourself?"

I flash her one of my trademark charming grins. "I'm right as rain. Always am."

She rests her hand on my shoulder, squeezing it once. "That's my boy. Let's go in before the bugs really start to come out. I wanna hear more about this whole Ginny and Lizzie situation. We gotta get our girl out from underneath that family's clutches, son."

"I couldn't agree more. They gotta go. But the real question is: how do we get Evangeline on board?"

35

EVANGELINE

I SIGH, flopping onto my couch and staring at the ceiling. "Is it possible to have a hangover from fun? A fun hangover. A fungover. Ugh, that doesn't really work."

Lincoln's chuckle precedes him as he walks into the living room. "Yes, it's possible and no, that definitely doesn't work, but I still like it. I take it you're crashing after having too much fun with Hunter yesterday?"

"Yeah," I breathe. "We made a blanket fort in the loft area and had a pizza picnic. Then we watched a bunch of cartoon shorts on my laptop. It was a great day."

"Sounds like it."

"I can't wait for this to all be over so he can come back home. I didn't really think it was possible to miss a kindergartner this much." I roll my head across the back of the couch and look at him. "On a scale from one to Silas glaring and stalking out of a room, how bad is it going to be when I tell him Hunter and I are officially besties?" I smirk, amusement bubbling inside of me and rejuvenating me a little bit.

He pauses, leaning over the back of the couch with one hand

on each side of my head. The corners of his mouth curl into a sly grin as he looks down at me. "I don't know, sugar, but that's something I'd sure like to see."

I tilt my chin up in a silent question, and he bends over further. Our noses brush together before our lips meet in a soft, lingering kiss. And because he's wonderful and hot as fuck, he obliges. I turn his quick peck into something much more, swiping my tongue along the seam of his lips. He responds eagerly, parting them instantly and deepening the kiss. It feels like we're having our very own Spider-Man style kiss.

The shrill sound of a doorbell fills the room, and he pulls away. "You expecting anyone?"

I purse my lips and shake my head. "The only people who would ever be here for me just walk right in—even the ones I don't want to see."

He sends me a pointed look. "You gotta start locking the door, sugar."

I jump to my feet and wave my hand in the air, dismissing his words. "Yeah, yeah. Nova already gave me the big speech in the car."

He quickens his pace until he's between me and the door. "Behind me, Evangeline."

I tease him with a scoff and pat his back a few times, side-stepping him. "If someone was here to hurt me, they wouldn't ring the doorbell and announce themselves, ya know?"

He sweeps his arm to the side, herding me behind him once more. "Please, sugar," he murmurs.

Some of my amusement fades, recognizing the serious tone. I place my palm in the middle of his back, a gentle reassurance. "Alright, Lincoln. I'll stay behind you."

I hang back a few steps, leaning against the banister at the bottom of the staircase. The soft clink of the lock turning over pulls a smirk from me, but because I'm *the best* girlfriend, I resist the urge to gloat about it.

I try to look around him when he opens the door, but the man's shoulders are so broad, he fills up most of the doorway.

"Who is it?" I stage-whisper.

"No one," he murmurs without turning around.

I take a step toward him, my hand releasing its grip on the smooth wooden banister as I join him at the front door. "Oh, it was a delivery."

"I'll get it," he insists, reaching for the screen door handle and gently moving me to the side.

I shake my head, but it's in fondness not frustration. I've said it before, and I'll probably continue to say it, but I don't think I'll ever get used to the protectiveness. And that's a good thing. The moment I start taking him or any of my men for granted, I hope someone knocks some sense into me.

I hold the screen door open as he crosses the porch to the white box on the edge. Huh, they put it in the blind spot. One of the places you wouldn't be able to see unless you opened the door.

"Who's it for?"

"It's for you, and there's no return address." He looks at me as he brings it inside the house. "Were you expecting something?"

"No, not that I can think of. Unless it's something my mom or sister sent in retaliation for Silas threatening to send my mom six feet under." I raise my brows dramatically.

I still can't believe he went there with her. I mean, I loved it, don't get me wrong. But out of the three of them, that's the kind of thing I'd expect from Nova. Maybe Bane if pushed enough. But brazen threats aren't what I would think of for Silas's style. Or maybe I don't really know his style, and that's exactly the kind of thing he does when it comes to someone he cares about.

That realization sends a warm tingly feeling throughout my limbs as I follow behind Lincoln into the kitchen.

"Should we, I don't know, dust it for prints or something?"

He arches a brow, the corner of his lip twitching as he looks at me. "You been watching those true crime shows again, sugar?"

I give him my most haughty look. "I may or may not have convinced Nova to listen to my favorite podcast on the way home yesterday."

"Mhmm." He grins, pulling out a utility knife. "Well I don't have one of those, sugar. So I'm just going to open it and see what's inside. Let's pray it's not a bomb."

"Jesus, Lincoln," I gasp. My heart pounds as I lunge for him before he can cut the tape on the one side. "Don't touch it."

"Sugar, I was just teasing," he murmurs, holding still.

"Yeah, well that shit isn't funny. Do you remember the last few weeks we've had? I don't want to jinx us."

"C'mere, Evangeline," he coaxes, his voice low and soothing.

My feet carry me toward his side on command, like he's some kind of snake charmer and I'm helpless to resist. Not that I'm trying that hard anyway.

"Silas is going to kill us if we die from a box bomb, you know."

"Nah, it's Nova we have to worry about. That asshole has more untapped aggression to get out than anyone I've ever met before."

I side eye him, thinking our versions of the same man are vastly different. I blow out a breath and look at the box in question. "Okay should we, I don't know, listen or something? Wouldn't we hear ticking?"

His mouth tugs up into a grin. "Sure, sugar. Let's listen for ticking."

"I feel like you're teasing me," I say even as I bend down and press my ear close to the cardboard. "I don't hear anything," I whisper.

His gaze is locked on mine, the dark brown of his eyes looks richer today. It reminds me of freshly melted chocolate, decadent and rich. "I don't either. Are we safe to open it, you think?"

I bite the inside of my cheek, anxiety blaring inside of me that we should be careful. Except that it really does seem like just a box. The kind that someone would ship a couple of hardcover books in. Not too big or too wide.

"It's probably not a bomb, right?"

"No, I don't think it is," he whispers, his lips curving into a small smile.

I stand up with a decisive nod. "Okay, let's open it then."

I hold my breath as he cuts the tape, squeeze my eyes closed halfway as he opens the flaps. But there isn't a bomb inside the box. No, that would've been easier.

Polaroid photos fill the entire box. There must be hundreds of them. They're the big ones, not the smaller, mini-sized photos. On top of all of them sits a white envelope with my name scrawled across the middle. There's something familiar about the handwriting, but I can't place it right away. I pluck the note from the pile, a pop of bright pink catching my eye. Underneath the envelope, the first Polaroid photo on top of the pile is of something pink on a white background.

"What?" I murmur, setting the envelope down and grabbing the photo. It looks like a slightly scrunched up ball of fabric.

No. It's not just any fabric. It looks exactly like a pair of pink panties. And I'd bet my life that this is a pair of seamless high-cut cheeky panties in the color sugar pink.

"What in the fuck is this?" Adrenaline spikes inside my bloodstream, sending my heart racing. I clutch the photo in my hand and run upstairs.

"Sugar?"

I ignore him, but not because I'm trying to ice him out. I don't actually think I can speak right now. Not with the way my mind is racing. My breaths come out in choppy pants, and I'm actually scared I might pass out or something.

"Sugar, what are you doing?" His voice is closer now, and I'm sure he's right behind me. Good. Then he can make sure I'm not losing my fucking mind.

I run into my bedroom, beelining for the dresser. With entirely too much force, I yank open the top drawer and rifle through it one-handed.

"No, no, no. Where are they?"

Lincoln hovers behind me, his warmth a soothing balm against my back. "What's going on, sugar? What are we looking for?"

"These," I growl out, jabbing my index finger against the photo. "These are the same fucking panties that I strangled that asshole with. You know, the person who took me from your house. The same person who knew about your tunnel and then drugged me and took me states away."

I jab the photo again. "And these—these are my favorite fucking pair of panties, Lincoln. I thought it might've been a coincidence, likely just some random kinky thing that asshole was into, ya know? I mean, I'm not going to judge him for it. I definitely judged him for the whole kidnapping though because that shit is fucked-up."

He palms both sides of my face, shuffling closer so he's directly in front of me. "Breathe, sugar. Slow down. Tell me what's going on in this beautiful brain of yours."

I exhale, tears pricking the corners of my eyes. "I can't calm down, Lincoln. Because I'm pretty sure this is a photo of my *actual* panties. Which makes me think I strangled some fucking psychopath with my favorite pair of fucking panties."

"It's alright, don't cry, sugar. We'll get you new ones, yeah?"

"I don't give a fuck about them. I'm mad, and sometimes when I'm angry my eyes leak because they're traitorous organs like that."

He smiles, running his thumbs underneath my eyes and catching any stray tears. "Alright, let's go back downstairs and see what the note said, yeah?"

I nod and sniff, tilting my head to place a kiss along his inner wrist. "Yeah, okay."

He laces his hand with mine and we jog down the stairs and back into the kitchen. I drop the panty polaroid on the island and slide the card from the envelope.

It's a condolences card, and there's nothing written inside, just the pre-printed message.

Wishing you strength and solace in the midst of your grief. With heartfelt condolences.

Lincoln's saying something to me, but it's like I'm having an out of body experience. Pieces are tumbling around on the game board, sliding into place until a bigger picture is starting to take shape. I cross the kitchen and pull out the manilla envelopes of random birthday cards we found a couple of months ago when we were cleaning out the cabinets. They're all addressed to me with nothing written inside, just the pre-printed message.

But the handwriting on the envelopes is the same.

I spin around, crumpling a pink envelope in my fist. "They're the same."

"What is? Walk me through what you're thinking, sugar."

"These." I shake my fist for emphasis, my eyes wide and wild. "The handwriting is the same as that." I point toward the new envelope in the box of photos. "What else is in there? There must be more. Here, help me."

I start taking out the Polaroids, some of them look familiar in the way movie scenes or famous movie quotes are. I recognize them but I can't place from where.

We go through hundreds of photos quickly, and I know I need to take my time and look through them all properly. But I have a hunch, a gut feeling that there's something else in this box. And I'm going to fucking find it. I need a clue—something, anything to help me figure this out.

And there, taped to the bottom of the box, is a single photo. It's me, in the back of that fucking van, unconscious.

And scrawled in the caption area: I warned you.

I stumble back a few steps, my hand covering my mouth in horror.

"Evangeline," Lincoln says, his hands cupping my elbows and his face filling my vision.

But I'm not really looking at him. I'm stuck in my memories, going through everything with a new lens. One that paints an entirely different picture than any of us thought.

The man who abducted me from Lincoln's house has been stalking me for years.

36

SILAS

"REMIND ME WHAT WE KNOW." I lean against the kitchen counter, cradling a neon pink hand-painted mug against my chest. The steam from my fresh coffee wafts up, and the scent of cardamom and cinnamon is kind of making my mouth water. For the last few days, I've been sneaking some of Evie's chai tea latte mix and using it as a creamer.

Bane exhales, running his hands through his hair and falling into the chair at the kitchen table. "This box got delivered today. It's full of Polaroid photos."

"Some of these are mild. Like here's a random tree, and then an iced coffee, and some random brick building. Those could be taken anywhere by anyone. But some of these"—he grabs a different stack and holds them toward me—"these are fucked-up. This is the door to the place she used to work at before she came to Rosewood this summer. This is that box of stationery she found on her bed last month that she swore she got rid of years ago." He tosses each photo down as he lists it. "The Carter family mausoleum in Rosewood Cemetery. The stall at the farmer's market where she bought jam with Hunter. Hamilton tickets. The same bouquet of flowers she bought three weeks ago for our house."

Nova tosses the stack of photos on the island and plants his hands on his hips, his head hanging. "These don't help us figure out who he is. All it tells us is that he's been watching her for a long time."

"There was a graduation announcement in one, which potentially gives us a timeline," Bane adds, his voice subdued.

"Plus the cards, right?" I jerk my chin toward the letter-sized manilla envelope on the table. "How long ago do we think those started?"

Bane shakes his head, covering his mouth with his palm. "Fucking years. A decade maybe?"

I take a sip of my coffee, enjoying the warmth from the chai spices. "So, what do we know about long-time stalkers?

"They're persistent and patient," Evie says from the doorway, startling the fuck out of all of us. She looks like a goddamn wet dream dressed in a matching pale purple lounge set.

"Sugar," Bane says, pushing to his feet. "You should be resting."

She waves off Bane's concern, stepping further into the kitchen with a determined look in her eyes. "I'm not hurt, and I've done more resting in the last two weeks than I have in my entire life. You want to know about long-term stalkers? Well, I just so happen to have watched a few very informative docuseries recently."

Nova stalks across the kitchen, drapes his arm over her shoulders, and guides her to the table, away from the photos. "Alright, sweetheart. Lay it on us. What should we be looking for?"

Evie pulls out a chair, angling it so it faces all three of us. She sinks into it, crossing one of her long legs over the other.

My gaze zeroes in all that smooth, creamy skin on display. It's fucking distracting.

My mouth waters to taste her again, and I must be the biggest kind of asshole to mentally calculate how soon I can get her underneath me again. Or on top of me—any fucking way I can have her, really.

I let my gaze slowly trail over her, drinking in every inch of her. When I get to her eyes, my shoulders jerk in surprise to find her gaze already on me. The side of her perfect mouth ticks up, and I know I've been caught.

I clear my throat and hide my warm cheeks behind my mug.

"So going on the theory that the person who sent the box is the same one who sent those blank birthday cards. And who abducted me. So we know he's persistent. He's obsessive and manipulative, he's not afraid of violence." She pauses as a visible shudder rolls down her body. "He's clearly been around for a long time, which means that he's unremarkable. I didn't see any standout features, which is most likely how he blends in. I probably walked by him hundreds of times without knowing."

"Fuck, for all we know, we've all walked by him without realizing," Nova says, his hand on the back of her chair.

"It's just . . ." She nods a few times, biting her bottom lip and looking at the floor.

"What is it, Evie?"

She clears her throat, giving me her gaze. "I've looked through everything we have, and from what I can tell, the earliest is from eight years ago. The summer I graduated."

I watch as the realization sets in on her face, her eyes widening with a mix of fear and understanding. "I think we need to look into that summer. There might be something I've forgotten or overlooked."

"Who can remember what restaurant they had dinner at eight years ago?" Nova asks, disbelief making his words low.

"Me. I remember every single second of one day eight years ago," Bane murmurs, his gaze locked on Evie.

She turns her head slowly, and I watch something pass between them. Her eyes soften, her lips curving into a small, private grin. There's a spark of jealousy that heats my blood at their visible connection, and I have to fight the urge to lash out just so she gives her attention to me.

I exhale quietly and take another sip of coffee to distract myself.

"Right. I'm going to call Cora. We were damn near inseparable that summer, so maybe she remembers something I forgot," she says, pushing to her feet.

Bane's eyes never stray from Evie as she leaves the room, worry and longing etched into the flat line of his mouth.

"While that information is good, I don't know how it's going to help us figure out who this motherfucker is before he decides to pay our girl another little visit," Nova says, sitting in Evie's chair.

I swallow the last bit of my coffee and rinse out the mug, infusing calm into every movement. As I dry my hands on the hand towel covered in labradoodles, I turn to Bane.

"Call Diesel and cash in on another favor."

Bane's brows rise. "What're you thinking?"

"We need to borrow his expertise and find that fucking car. We find the car, we find the man."

"Then we kill him," Nova says with a feral sort of smile.

Bane's boots thud against the kitchen tiles as he nods and strides to the other side of the island, leaning against it. He presses a button and drops his phone in the middle of the island without a word. Shrill ringing fills the air, tension rising.

"Bane," Diesel says with a laugh. "I gotta say, man, I'm surprised to hear from you so soon. I thought you'd be holed up with the nanny for at least a few more weeks."

"Diesel," Bane grunts. "You're on speaker with Silas and Nova."

Diesel laughs. "Ah, I get the whole family? Damn, now I really do feel special."

My patience frays with every second that we're wasting with idle chit chat. I brace my hands on the island and lean toward the phone. "We need a favor."

"That'll cost ya."

"Fine," I snap.

"What can I do for the Reapers?" Diesel asks casually.

Bane catches my eye and nods toward the phone. "Remember that situation we found at our doorstep a few weeks ago? I need you to find a car for us."

Diesel laughs, but there's nothing unkind about it. "Don't you have some people on your payroll for that shit? I mean, I'll take the favor, but I can do that shit in my sleep, man."

"Not this kind of shit. This is . . . tricky." I'm careful not to reveal too much. I don't think we're being tapped, but I feel like I don't fucking know anything anymore.

Diesel's laugh tapers off. "Alright, I'm listening."

Bane clears his throat, and my adrenaline spikes like I'm about to run a half-marathon or something instead of standing here in the middle of Evie's kitchen.

"We're looking for a car. It crashed in a ditch next to a cornfield," Bane says, dragging his palm down his face and exhaling a long breath. "We don't know if it was a reported crash, but it would've happened roughly two weeks ago."

Diesel tsks. "Curious timing. So this does have something to do with your nanny then, hm?"

Nova stretches his neck from one side to the other, and his eyes narrow on the phone. "Check nearby chop shops, junk yards, impounds—the works. And be discreet."

"Alright. Location?" Diesel asks.

Bane shakes his head. "We don't have one. I'd guess a day's drive from Rosewood in every direction."

Diesel whistles under his breath. "Damn, man. Don't make it easy on me, yeah? I don't suppose you have plates for me."

"Nah, man. No plates. But the driver was six-foot or so, dark blond, caucasian, total psychopath," Bane continues.

Diesel laughs. "Is that a physical trait now—psychopath?"

"You know it is. They have that look about them, ya know? Their files are usually fucked-up, too."

"Too true. Alright. I'll hit you back when I find something."

The call ends and the three of us look at one another, a fragile sort of understanding passing between us. Gratitude softens the hard edges of my soul as I look between the two men I trust my life with.

More importantly, the two men I trust her *life* with.

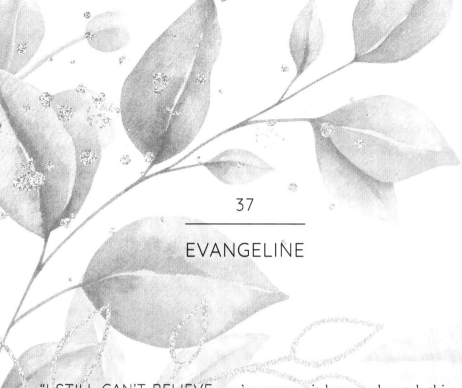

37

EVANGELINE

"I STILL CAN'T BELIEVE you're gonna sit here and watch this with me. And with popcorn too," I muse, tossing a few kernels of popcorn in my mouth.

Lincoln grins, tossing his arm over the back of the couch. His fingers twirl around the ends of my hair. "It's no trip to Disney, but I thought you could use something fun to take your mind off things."

My smile slips a little bit at the reminder. It's been two days since we found the box of Polaroids. We're no closer to figuring out who's behind everything, and no matter how many times I try to think about anything out of the ordinary from that summer, I come up empty-handed. I've even picked Cora's brain a few times, but we're both drawing blanks.

It's exhausting to try and fish through memories, but it's nearly impossible to try and find something conceivably inconsequential to me at the time. It's a conundrum and a paradox.

"Well, I'm happy for the distraction anyway. I don't want to think about all that stuff until tomorrow. And maybe not even then."

"Ignoring it won't make it go away, sugar."

I roll my head across the cushion to look at him. "I know. But for tonight, in here with you, I'm going to pretend it doesn't exist —that *he* doesn't exist."

His fingers twine in my hair, tugging gently. "In here, it's just you and me, yeah?"

"Yeah, I like that," I breathe out, a little distracted. I can't help it when he looks at me like that. It gives me all kinds of things the two of us could do instead of watch a movie about sparkling vampires. I clear my throat and focus on the screen as the opening credits start. "Who's your favorite character?"

"Despite the fact that you couldn't walk ten feet without running into this franchise, I've never actually seen it before. For years, it was all everyone talked about, so I think I got the gist anyway."

I grin around another mouthful of popcorn. "Nah, you can't understand the fandom if you were never in it. I wanted an Edward poster on my wall so bad, but my mom never let me put anything up on the walls. So I taped it to the inside of my closet instead."

He chuckles. "Spend a lot of time in the closet, did you?"

"Nah, not really. It only lasted a few days before someone tattled on me. I came home from school and it was gone."

Lincoln tugs on the ends of my hair, and I look at him. "I'm sorry, sugar."

I lift a shoulder and let it fall. "It's just a poster. Besides, I could plaster the entire first floor with memorabilia from that franchise now if I wanted to."

He smiles, but it's a little pained. "You could."

The first scene starts, and I scoot closer to him. He made me my own bowl of popcorn, but I just like being next to him. Plus,

I'm acutely aware that we have the house to ourselves for the first time in . . . I don't even know how long.

Nova is in his studio, working late tonight to catch up on some orders. And Silas is out doing whatever Silas does. I honestly don't know. He mentioned something about errands and the sheriff, though he was quick to reassure me everything was fine.

"Oh, look, this is one of my favorite parts. It's so cheesy, but I still love it so much. It's nostalgic, ya know? And I can still remember how hard I swooned when I first saw these movies."

Sweet nostalgia wraps around me like a warm blanket on a cold winter's night. It's such a complicated emotion, intertwining threads of happiness and sadness.

"You ever read the books?"

I side-eye him, my brows crowded low over my face. "Of course I did. Everyone knows the books are always better than the movies, Lincoln." I playfully scoff and return my gaze to the TV.

"Have I ever mentioned how much I love the sound of my name on your lips?" he murmurs, closer to me than a second before.

A small smile plays around my lips as I give him my attention once more. "Oh yeah?"

He grins, gently pressing his lips against mine. It's not a kiss, not yet. "Yeah, sugar."

I lean in closer to him, a mischievous grin spreading across my face. "Okay, *Lincoln*."

And then I make the first move, tracing my tongue along his bottom lip. He responds immediately, parting his lips and sliding his tongue against mine. It's a playful kiss, but the connection between us is undeniable.

All too quickly, it deepens. His hands start to wander, sliding over the curve of my hip when I clutch the fabric of his tee. The movie fades into the background as everything else disappears except for him.

Time seems to freeze as we explore each other's mouths, savoring the taste of our mutual lust.

"I thought you wanted to watch the movie?" he murmurs, his lips sliding over my jaw.

"I changed my mind. I want to do this instead." I slide off the couch and stand between his legs with my hands on his knees. I drag my palms up his thighs, marveling at how big his thigh muscles are.

Jesus, since when did I find a man's *thigh muscles* attractive?

I look at him from underneath my lashes, biting my lip when I see his hungry gaze already locked onto me. He looks so attractive, eyes dark and lips pink from my kiss. There's a possessiveness inside of me, this small little creature that's only ever come out to play when it comes to the St. James men. And Lincoln's feeding it now with his legs spread wide in that stupid-hot man-spread thing, hair mussed, and kiss-swollen lips.

"Goddamn," I whisper, dragging my thumbs along the seam of his jeans on his inner thighs. My right thumb dances over his hardening dick, and a rush of desire floods through me. My mouth waters at the thought of getting to explore.

My fingers tremble as I unbutton his jeans and grip the metal of his zipper, slowly pulling it down and revealing his black boxer briefs. I ghost my fingertip down his cock, my touch featherlight through the fabric of his jeans.

I drink in the sight of his eyes darkening as his gaze stays glued to my hand. His chest rises and falls quickly, like he's holding himself in check and letting me take my time.

It only makes me want to reward him for his patience.

I scoot closer, leaning up toward his mouth as I palm him through his pants. "I need your help, Lincoln."

"Anything, sugar."

I whisper my lips along his, nipping at the corner of his mouth. "Your jeans are too tight, Lincoln."

"You tryin' to tell me something, hm?" A smirk tugs at the corner of his mouth before he lifts himself up slightly from the couch.

My fingers eagerly trail inside his pants. The moment my hand wraps around his dick, I hear a low, guttural groan escape his lips.

I pull him out, eager to see the expression on his face as I stroke him slowly. His eyes are dark with desire as his gaze slides from my hand wrapped around his cock to my eyes and back down again. He watches my hand move up and down, and he bites his lip.

"You're so hard already, Lincoln," I whisper.

His cock is thick and long, and I have a moment of panic at the idea of fitting that whole thing inside my mouth. But I'm going to give it the old college try and use my hand to make up for the rest.

The head is flushed and glistening with pre-cum, a bead of it sliding down the underside of his shaft. I lean down and drag my tongue along his length, tasting the salty sweetness of his arousal.

"Fuck me, sugar," he groans, this low rumbling sound in his chest. "Your mouth feels so fucking good."

I flatten my tongue and swirl it around the head. His body shudders beneath me, and I see his hands clenched at his sides, like he's holding himself back.

Using my free hand, I grasp one of his fists, and place his hand on the back of my head. He threads his fingers into my hair, but doesn't apply too much pressure. I take him deep into my throat, gagging slightly as I go further than I've ever gone before.

"Alright, sugar, you've had your fun," Bane says with labored breaths. "But if you don't stop, I'm going to fucking come down that pretty throat of yours."

I let his cock slip from my mouth with a pop. I grin even as I continue to stroke him. "Good, that's kind of the point."

He chuckles darkly, a wicked grin darkening his face. "I've got a better idea, sugar. Hop on up, we're going to come together."

I stand up, and sink into his lap, grateful to past-me for choosing a dress to wear today.

"Let me take care of you first," he murmurs, dragging his lips down my neck and sliding his fingers underneath my panties. "Jesus, sugar, is this all for me?" he murmurs, playing with my arousal.

He sinks two fingers inside of me, and I reflexively tighten my grip on his cock. He makes this sound that's halfway between a grunt and a groan, his hips flexing. So I do it again, and again.

"Fuck me, sugar. That's too good." He palms my waist, scooting me forward until I'm poised over him.

I hold his gaze as I slowly lower myself, torturing both of us with pleasure. Our moans mix together in the air, creating a symphony of desire. Every movement sends sparks of electricity dancing through my body, tingling with anticipation for what's to come.

In this moment, nothing else exists except for us, lost in the pure bliss of each other.

38

EVANGELINE

THE BACKDOOR SLAMS, the loud crack of aluminum on wood sharp enough to yank me from utter bliss. I freeze at the sound, my thighs flexing as I hold my position poised over Bane.

Panic sings inside my veins at the idea of someone walking in on us like *this*. Me, frozen with my knees on either side of Bane's thick thighs, straddling him with the first couple of inches of his hard cock inside of me.

And the alarm waging war with my arousal has nothing to do with shame and everything to do with the current minefield that is my love life. And my complete lack of navigational skills.

Multiple men aside, there are a lot of people who have access to this house that absolutely do not need to see me in such a compromising position. At the top of the list are his aunt and his nephew, both of which frequently walk in, as improbable as it is —it's the most detrimental. Then there's my cousin and apparently my mother. And let's not forget my backstabbing sister.

In fact, I should probably preemptively crawl into a dark hole and possibly never emerge again, sparing all of us the awkward situation.

"You here, sweetheart?" Nova calls.

Relief hits me hard, and I sink onto Bane's lap with an exhale. He grunts his appreciation, his hands smoothing up along my ribs. The relief is short-lived as panic of an entirely different kind blossoms inside of me. It bursts into full bloom like one of those yellow wildflowers in the backyard.

"Shit," I whisper-hiss. "Shit, shit, shit." My thoughts scramble in slow-motion, my brain begging my body to catch up. But she's still riding high on those delicious endorphins.

It's one thing to say that I have feelings for all three of them, but it's another thing entirely for them to have a front-row seat, to witness it. Not when they all run through random bursts of jealousy.

I won't lie and say that there isn't a little part of me that preens under their possessiveness. But I never want it to get out of control, and I would hate myself if I ever came between the three of them.

So, yeah, the idea of Nova walking in here and seeing me ride Bane like this makes me feel a little bit like a trapped butterfly. I flex my thighs and push to my knees once more, intent on *dismounting* off of Bane and sitting next to him instead.

I'm still wearing my dress for fuck's sake, so I've already convinced myself that I can sell this. I don't even know why I'm freaking out so hard, just that I *am*. And I don't know how to stop.

Bane's warm hands glide along my ribcage, soothing the rapid thumping of my heart. His gentle touch eases my panic, as if he can read my thoughts and knows exactly what to do.

"It's alright, sugar," he murmurs in that low tenor that does stupid things to my brain. "Trust me, yeah?"

My eyes widen as they meet his. The dim light of the living

room turns his deep brown eyes nearly black, and I can't look away. They draw me in, hypnotizing and endless like the night sky in the heart of winter.

As the movie continues to play on the TV behind me, the blue-green glow from the screen washes over his face. It highlights his sharp jawline and the small bump in the bridge of his nose. Despite the fact that it would make anyone else look like some extra in a zombie movie, the blue-green cast only makes him more attractive.

I nod, a couple quick dips of my chin in acknowledgement. "I do."

"I know, sugar," he says to me, his eyes soft as he holds my gaze. He flexes his hips, burying his cock deep inside of me once more. The sensation is intense, almost too much too fast as he fills me completely. Shivers of pleasure roll over me, lighting me up like little sparklers on the Fourth of July.

God damn, the man is fucking me from the bottom with such ease. A flood of arousal sinks into my skin, smothering the flickers of anxiety.

"Oh god," I gasp, pitching forward and bracing my hands on the back of the couch.

"That's right, Evangeline. Let me take care of you." He tilts his head back against the cushion, spreading his legs wider. The angle changes, and he hits some neglected part inside of me that has bright white spots of euphoria flashing in front of my eyes.

"We're in here," Bane says calmly, like his cock isn't buried balls-deep inside of me right now. Like I'm not nearly panting from desire on top of him.

My nails dig into the fabric of the couch cushion, keeping me grounded as arousal floods every inch of me like someone opened up the dam, and my body pulls taut.

Insatiable lust replaces the panic entirely, and suddenly, the very idea of Nova walking in on me like this has me reaching for my orgasm with both hands.

Nova's footsteps are even as he rounds the kitchen table and stops behind the couch.

Bane slows to shallow thrusts, his hips just barely rocking against mine. He doesn't move from his slouched down position, and I can't tell if it's another one of their power plays or if he's just willing to see how this plays out.

Or fuck, maybe he just likes his current view. Nearly eye-level with the tops of my tits spilling over the top of the sweetheart neckline of my dress. Regardless, it gives me an unobstructed view of my other boyfriend. And fuck me, does he look downright edible.

Dark blond hair tousled like he just got off his bike, tattoos crawling over his exposed skin, and those fucking veins standing out in his forearms. I'll never understand why it's so goddamn attractive but my god it is. It really, *really* is.

He saunters the last few feet until the toes of his boots thud the back of the couch. His teeth sink into his bottom lip as he gives me a blatant perusal. And just because I can, I tilt my chin up, giving Nova an unobstructed view of the lust painting my mouth like my favorite shade of gloss.

He sucks his teeth, the sharp noise loud in the otherwise quiet house. "There she is," Nova murmurs, his eyes darkening as his gaze leisurely wanders over my face.

"Why are you here?" Bane grunts.

"Now, is that any way to greet your brother?" Nova's voice takes a dark edge.

"You wanna talk about that shit when I'm fucking my girl?" Bane drawls, snapping his hips to punctuate his point.

"*Our* girl," Nova drawls like he isn't bothered in the least. I don't buy it for a second, not when his face broadcasts his very unwelcoming thoughts flying across his face.

I blink and all that rage is replaced by casual unaffectedness. A soft chuckle leaves Nova's mouth as he leans down, bracing his arms wide on the back of the couch, palms on either side of me.

"Ain't that right, sweetheart?" Nova's low murmur washes over my lips like a physical caress, his lips twisting to the side in a secret sort of smirk.

My tongue darts out, swiping across my bottom lip as my throat runs dry at the promise curving his lips. I'm not sure if this is some kind of pissing match between these two, but if it is, they're going to be disappointed when I intentionally choose both of them.

At the same time, even.

Logically, it should feel wrong to want so many men. But my desire rages on. It builds and builds, casting a net wide enough to entrap all three of the men I want.

The men I need.

And I can't think of a better time to try to stop making apologies for it, including to myself.

"Yes," I hiss, my eyelids closing with the weight of that acknowledgement.

"Good girl," Nova murmurs at the same time Bane runs his big palm down the center of my back.

I roll my hips, a primal sort of instinct taking over as I grind against Bane's cock. My clit brushes against his pelvis with each movement, sending electrifying sparks of pleasure through me.

"Oh," I breathe out. I let my head fall to the side as I lose myself a little rocking against Bane. Someone grunts, pulling me out of reverie and my eyes fly open.

"Now, don't stop on my account, sweetheart." The slow drawl of Nova's deep voice sends a shiver down my spine. It leaves a thick trail of lust in its wake.

Despite his low tenor, the tension in the room unfurls further, expanding wide enough to blanket the entire first floor. Bane's fingers flex around my hips, and I feel his cock inside of me twitch. I don't bother concealing the pleasure skirting across my face.

Bane's fingertips skim the sensitive skin above my hips as he rocks into me. "You feel so perfect, sugar. Like you were fucking made for *me*."

I angle my face toward Bane, my mouth parting in surprise when he bumps against that place deep inside of me again. A strangled moan coasts from my lips as my vision goes white-hot with pleasure.

Strong fingers lift my chin, and Nova's too-handsome face comes into view. He brushes his lips across mine, and I tip toward him, chasing his mouth.

He tilts his head to the left, teasing me again. "Ah, brother, you're just in time. Our girl is about to get her first of the night. Take a seat, yeah?"

The unmistakable sound of footsteps echoes through the empty kitchen, their pace never quickening.

A surprised noise flies from the back of my throat, and I clench my internal muscles on instinct. Anticipation fills the air like a heavy fog, and I'm so amped up I'm a little afraid that I might spontaneously come or something.

"Jesus, fuck, sugar," Bane groans against my chest, his fingers digging into the curve of my waist.

Before I can look or even reply to Bane, Nova gives me his attention once more. He's too close for me to see his features clearly, but I don't need to. I can tell by the slight curl of his lips that he's smiling.

"Remember what you said, sweetheart?"

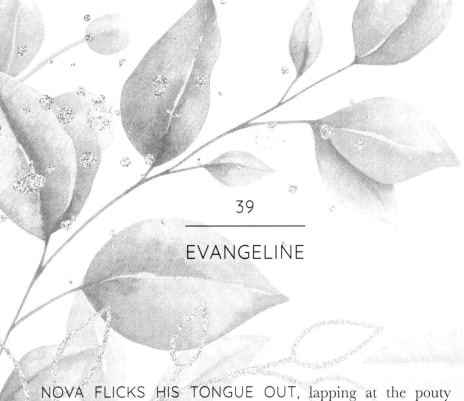

39

EVANGELINE

NOVA FLICKS HIS TONGUE OUT, lapping at the pouty center of my bottom lip. It's gone too soon.

My brows sink together as my lips part in protest. I'm too distracted, the first pricks of frustration starting to sink into my haze of lust. I need Nova's lips on me more than I've needed anything in a long time.

He cocks his head to the other side and nips at my jaw. "Hm?"

"Stop teasing me, Nova." I meant for it to come out strong and demanding, but it falls flat. It sounds like I'm pleading with him, which isn't that far off, to be honest. I do feel a little desperate, my orgasm *just* out of my reach.

Warm heat envelops my nipple through the thin fabric of my dress, sending tingles dancing across my skin. The layer of cotton does little to shield me from the alluring sensation of Bane's mouth on me.

I feel both heavy and light at the same time, like I'm suspended mid-air with gravity threatening to sink me at any moment. My body is soft and pliable under their combined touch, but deep inside of me, a powerful yearning begins to build, threatening to consume me. As if on cue, my back arches, pushing my tits closer to Bane's face, desperate for more of his intoxicating mouth.

My right hand leaves the back of the couch, flying to Bane's soft dark hair. My fingers tangle in his locks. It's the perfect length, just long enough to grasp between my fingers. The image of him on his knees between my legs, with my hand twisted in his hair flashes into my mind, and something inside of me clenches tight.

Bane's muffled grunt momentarily distracts me from the tease of Nova's tongue and teeth against the sensitive skin on my neck. But it's not enough. I want more.

"Kiss me, Nova," I plead.

Shame threatens to implode this little bubble of ecstasy. Fear of what kind of person it makes me to beg a different man to kiss me while another one is inside of me. My breath hitches, and my nipples tighten into hard peaks. I rock against Bane, urging him with my body.

Nova's grin hitches up on one side, his goddamn lethal dimple winking at me. "Nah, that's not what you said, but it's alright, sweetheart. I'm happy to remind you. But first—"

He cuts himself off by sealing his lips to mine in a fierce, dominating kiss that steals my breath. There's nothing gentle or slow. This isn't an exploration, it's a possession.

His tongue sweeps through my mouth, tangling with mine in a dance that threatens to unravel me. As Nova pulls away, his eyes smolder as he murmurs, "Do you trust me?"

I don't care how eager it looks, I start nodding before he even finishes talking. I'm rewarded with one of his more feral smiles. The kind of expression that says *I'm going to eat you now*.

But god damn, I would let him. I'd let him consume me whole if I could.

As Nova walks around the couch, Bane slides his palm around the back of my neck. He pulls me into a soul-searing kiss that leaves my lips tingling and my heart pounding. Jealousy wisps from his tongue, but it's quickly overshadowed by carnal hunger.

"I believe it was along the lines of Bane fucking your mouth while I ate my favorite meal: your pretty pussy," Nova says, his voice right behind me. "But since you two started without us, we'll have to improvise a little on your fantasy, sweetheart."

Nova slides his fingertips underneath the thin straps of my dress, his touch featherlight and cool against my overheated skin. He runs his touch down my back, letting the straps slip off my shoulders. The fabric drapes around my décolletage, pooling low enough that the very tops of my nipples are visible.

Nova's fingers tiptoe up my spine, tracing a few patterns along my shoulder blades.

I pull back from Bane, tipping my head back to gulp in much-needed oxygen. I feel the heat of Nova's breath along the tender skin behind my ear as he whispers, "You're in control, sweetheart. We go at your pace, yeah?"

Excitement ignites inside my body, adding to the calamity of lust and arousal.

"Yeah," I breathe, tipping my head towards him.

Nova drags the blunt edge of his teeth along the tendon in my neck. It's a distraction really, something to occupy me as he deftly unzips the hidden zipper on my dress along my rib cage. My dress drops into a puddle of fabric in my lap, exposing my tits completely. A soft breeze from the ceiling fan wafts over us, and it feels exquisite.

Nova hums as his hands round the curve of my hips, settling

on the globes of my ass. "Do you have any idea how perfect you are?"

I shake my head a few times, my hair swishing over my shoulders. I'm trying to split my attention between Bane's cock almost lazily rocking inside of me, his tongue toying with my nipple, and Nova's fascination with the curve of my asscheek. And I'm not doing that well.

I guess that means I just need more practice.

Nova taps my hip twice with the pad of his index finger. "Hop up for a sec, yeah?"

"What're you doing?" Bane growls but not at me. No, his gaze is fixated on Nova behind me, his eyes promising retribution for whatever Nova has planned.

Nova uses his grip on my hips to lift me off of Bane's cock, so I can balance on my knees. My pussy nearly cries in protest, the urge to keep him inside me until I come a couple more times is nearly uncontrollable. But I know they won't edge me forever. And at this point, I'm so close, my skin so sensitive that the breeze from the ceiling fan might make me come.

"Lean over Bane, sweetheart," Nova murmurs, applying a little pressure to get me to bend forward.

On trembling hands, I bend forward and place my hands wide on the back of the couch once more. My tits hover just above his face as I brace myself, feeling the wet heat of his tongue lave at my nipples.

I let out a shuddering moan as Nova drags his fingertips up along the backs of my thighs, teasing me with his touch. I rock toward him, eager to feel the full weight of his palms on me.

The air around us thickens with desire, a collective hunger the four of us are creating together. Later, I might feel conscious about it, but right now all I feel is free.

Alive and hungry.

I'm fucking starving for these men.

"More, Nova." I rock back into Nova once more, a noise of impatience clicking from the back of my throat. It draws a slow chuckle from his mouth, and he rewards me immediately.

His touch turns possessive as his palms glide up the inside of my thighs. He drags his fingers through the oddly ticklish crease between my hip and my pussy, down and around, over and over again. He touches me everywhere except where I really need him.

"*Please*," I beg, rocking into his touch.

"Begging already, sweetheart? But I've only just begun," Nova murmurs.

There's some rustling, and I imagine Silas adjusting his cock, palming it a little too long as he stares at me. I imagine his hungry gaze, like he's a hair trigger away from pouncing on me and dragging me somewhere to keep me all to himself.

Nova's fingers trace along the sensitive line between my ass cheeks, sending a warm shiver down my spine. Anticipation tastes like cotton candy on my tongue, overly sweet and dissolves too soon. I can't help myself, I buck my hips against his touch, silently asking for more.

Nova's mouth on my ass cheek is his answer to my silent question—a silent kiss that sends lightning bolts straight to my core. He nips at the curve of my ass, leaving a trail of fire in his wake.

"Nova," I let out a soft whimper, closing my eyes and rocking my ass toward him, yearning for more.

Bane drags the end of his teeth along my hard nipple, the pressure hard enough to drag my attention to him. My eyes widen as I take in the sight below me.

Bane's hand wrapped around his hard cock, my nipple between his teeth, his gaze locked onto my face with a predatory hunger that burns deeper than I've ever seen.

I moan softly, unable to resist the sight of him.

Nova palms both of my ass cheeks, spreading me open for him. I can feel his breath wash over my most sensitive area, and I'm suddenly aware of how vulnerable I am. But it's not fear that courses through me—it's desire. White hot and ravenous.

Nova edges his tongue around my asshole, teasing the entrance with little flicks. I exhale sharply, my hips bucking involuntarily. He tightens his hold on my ass cheeks, keeping me open for him.

His tongue dips inside me then, a slow, deliberate plunge that makes me gasp. The sensation is unlike anything I've ever felt before.

Nova groans, this long, drawn-out masculine sort of noise that feels like it reverberates around the room. "You taste so good, baby."

Bane watches me, his eyes never leaving mine as Nova continues to eat my ass like it's his favorite dessert.

And then another pair of hands creeps along my inner thighs, but his touch doesn't tease. It doesn't linger and taunt, holding me on a razor's edge. No, Bane doesn't make me wait. He slips two fingers inside of me, thrusting deep. I gasp, lifting my head and arching my back further.

Nova's touch remains soft, tantalizing, and playful in his exploration of my ass.

But Bane delves deep, curling his fingers and seeking out my g-spot. And with each caress, wave after wave of ecstasy rolls over me.

I knew this was going to be intense, but I didn't expect it to be all-consuming. With Nova at my back and Bane at my front—and just knowing Silas is here somewhere, *watching*.

It's enough to send me soaring high. My breaths come out in thready pants, my heart a thundering drum against my ribcage. I feel powerful in this moment, like I've finally woken up. And I have this newfound hunger that's consuming. A hunger for their touch and attention and adoration.

I've never felt this desired before, this *alive*.

This feeling is dangerous—it's the kind of thing that could easily become an addiction.

And these men? I fear I'm already addicted.

40

BANE

"PUT YOUR HAND ON HER THROAT." It sounds like someone reached down Silas's throat and ripped the words out against his will.

I spare him a single glance, noting he hasn't moved from his perch on the edge of the armchair. It's about all I can offer him when so much of my energy is tangled up in concentrating on how good she feels.

Her pussy flutters around my fingers as she rides out her orgasm on my hand and Nova's face. Sweat beads along my brow as my dick aches, weeping to slide inside of her again. I'm fucking dying to feel her pussy strangle the life from my cock, and we're in agreement that it's the only acceptable way to go. Death by Evangeline's perfect cunt.

Sign me the fuck up.

In fact, if I knew I was gonna be six feet under, I'd choose to spend every last minute buried inside of her. A bonafide heaven.

Every moment with her feels like claiming ownership of eternity, as if the universe itself recognizes that she belongs to me. The familiar flush of possession flashes through me, and I have to curb the instinct to haul her up and hoard her somewhere they can't find us. Just for a little while, at least.

"To punish me," Silas grunts the words, shifting to brace his elbows on his knees. His focus is entirely on the woman straddling me. On the woman who's owning me with every innocent gasp and low moan.

I don't even blame him.

Even now, she's all I see.

I don't really even know what the fuck they're going on about, but I'm sure I'll figure it out soon enough.

Nova stands up behind her, dragging his mouth along the slope of her shoulder. He palms the exposed expanse of her throat and tilts her chin up toward him. "You hear that, sweetheart? My brother seems to think this is sufficient punishment. But you know what I think, hm?"

I watch through half-lidded eyes as my girl exhales a shuddering breath. Yeah, I know that look. I fucking love that look. She's still hungry, my girl. She's momentarily sated, but she's not full yet.

I was worried about how she was going to react when Nova tossed her words back at her. Asshole must've hacked the security cameras I set up and watched our conversation.

"It's not enough," she says, her voice a sultry purr as she tilts her head to the side. She looks from my cock to my eyes, swiping her tongue almost absentmindedly across her bottom lip.

Her right hand leaves the back of the couch, and I expect to feel her fingers gripping my cock. But I should've known better than that. My girl is full of surprises.

She slips two fingers inside herself, right alongside mine, and we groan in unison. It's impossible to disguise the wicked smirk that spreads across my face as I watch our fingers slide in and out, in and out. The sound of her arousal fills the room, and I decide it might be one of the best noises I've ever heard.

Nova's lips brush the corner of her mouth. "I don't think it's enough either. Bane?"

"No." I grunt, as she pulls her fingers from her pussy and grips my cock. My breath hisses out between clenched teeth when she coats my dick with her arousal.

Her strokes are firm and deliberate, her gaze locked on mine, a sort of challenge in their dark depths. One I'm more than happy to meet.

"I think he's too far away to really appreciate you. You're the most exquisite masterpiece I've ever seen," Nova says, dragging his mouth down her neck. "It'd be an absolute tragedy to deny him the pleasure of observing."

Her fist chokes my cock and sweat beads along my brow. The leash on my self-control is shortening by the minute. But I'll be damned if I'm going to ruin her fucking fantasy for her.

So I tell my dick to calm the fuck down and wait his goddamn turn. She needs at least two more.

"So come on over, Silas. Take a fucking front row seat, yeah? Watch our girl fall apart on my fingers and then on my cock."

EVANGELINE

I DON'T REALLY UNDERSTAND the dynamic of what's happening, but I'm too far gone to really care right now. Tomorrow, I'll corner one of them and ask what the hell is going on. But for tonight, I'm going to live out my fantasy that somehow everyone seems to know about.

I imagine the three of them getting together over tea and cookies and comparing notes. But then it morphs into the three of them shirtless, each staring at me while fisting their cocks.

I hold out my free hand. "C'mere, Silas. Please," I beg softly. I know I'm asking a lot of them, especially him, to openly share me like this.

His hand slides into mine a moment later, and he sits on the couch next to me. I slow my stroking, still holding Bane's cock, and lean toward Silas. He meets me halfway, taking my lips in a brutal kiss. It's the kind of passion that has an edge to it, and I'm fucking here for it.

Nova eases inside of me, feeding me one inch at a time until he is flush with my ass. His hands smooth over the soft curves of my body as he murmurs to himself, "So fucking perfect."

Silas swallows my groan, returning my kiss tenfold. One of his hands tangles in my hair, holding my face to his as if I'd try to leave.

Nova's fingers dance over the space our bodies connect, gathering my arousal and dragging it up to swirl around my asshole. It feels so fucking good, like overstimulated in the absolute best way possible.

And then I feel someone's curious fingers pinch my clit, and I'm fucking gone. I astroplane somewhere far above my body as I orgasm harder than I ever have in my life. And it keeps going and going and going, my muscles cramping and my breath freezing in my lungs.

I finally understand why the French call it *let petite mort*.

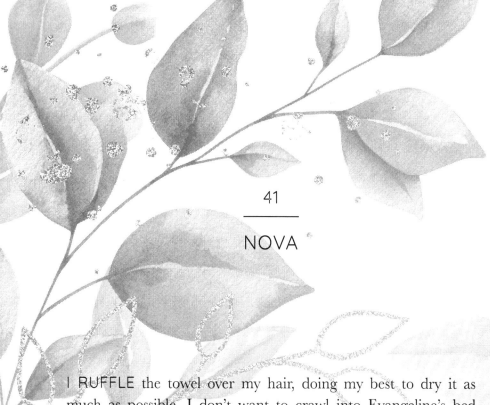

41
NOVA

I RUFFLE the towel over my hair, doing my best to dry it as much as possible. I don't want to crawl into Evangeline's bed soaking wet tonight. The air conditioning is working overtime in this house lately, and it's blessedly cool at night.

The bathroom door bursts open with a dull thud, and I instinctively reach for the gun I left on the counter. I started carrying it around with me ever since the fateful trap we walked into. The only time it's out of my reach is when I shower.

My shoulders sag with relief when it's not a Hound or Savage in the doorway. It's just my brother.

Well, one of them.

I leave my gun on the counter and pick up the towel again. "You need something?"

Silas steps inside the bathroom and kicks the door closed with the heel of his boot. "Yeah, yeah, I fucking need something."

I drape the towel around my neck, gripping the edges and turning to stare at him. "Well? What's so important that you had to barge in the bathroom while I was showering?"

Silas's face contorts into a scowl. "Fuck off, Nova. You're not in the shower anymore, and no, this shit can't wait. What the fuck is your problem, hm? I went along with that shit because I know Evie wanted to try it, but what the fuck is going on?"

I glance in the mirror and run my fingers through my hair, trying to tame it a little bit. "Don't know what you're talking about, *brother*."

"*There*," Silas seethes, pointing his finger at me. "That shit right there. What in the fuck, Nova?"

I take my time making sure my hair isn't going to dry in some weird-ass position. When I'm done, I find my brother practically vibrating next to me. His energy is frenetic and growing by the second. "Damn, Silas, you seem a little wound up."

Okay, so even I can admit that was an asshole thing to say. At this point, I'm just goading him into a fight. I don't even know what I'm expecting him to say, but every time I think about the fact that he's never said *anything* about it, it fucks me up a little bit. Like not a single thing in all these . . . however many fucking years he's known. It makes me wonder what other secrets he's kept from me.

The door opens before he can respond, and Bane stands in the doorway, his face like thunder. "You wanna tell me what the fuck is going on in here? If one of you assholes wakes my girl up, I'm going to put fucking centipedes in your beds tonight."

My mouth drops open at his very creative, very alarming threat.

"What the fuck, Bane?" I hiss, wrapping the towel around me tighter as if that will protect me from those fucking evil bugs.

"Our girl," Silas says slowly.

Bane slices him a dark look, but Silas looks unfazed. "What? She is."

"You wanna tell me what the fuck you two are yelling about in the middle of the night in the bathroom?"

I shrug and paste a grin on my face. I can feel the sharp edges and brittle shape of my smile, but I don't fucking care. "Nah, not me. I'm not yelling, that's my half-brother Silas over here."

There's a moment of silence then, like the universe itself is holding its breath. I fold my arms across my chest, acutely aware that I'm only wearing a pair of athletic shorts for this conversation.

And to make shit just a little bit weirder, Bane slides inside the bathroom and shuts the door quietly behind him. The bathrooms at Evangeline's house aren't small, but they sure as fuck aren't that big. And right now, the three of us are bumping into each other's personal space too quickly.

"Fucking explain. Now," Bane snaps, looking at me.

"Nah, *brother*. I think you have it mixed up. *He* should be the one to do the talking." I shift my gaze to Silas, noticing the stricken look painted on his face. "Oh, shit. He didn't tell you yet? Turns out, the three of us"—I circle my fingers in the air between us—"we're all half-brothers. Fucking wild, yeah?"

I rock back on my heels, an angry smirk curling up the corners of my mouth as I study Bane's expression. His eyes widen with shock, eyebrows drawn together. I watch, a little fascinated, as his eyebrows smooth out and his face falls into that neutral expression of his. My gaze slides to Silas, and I'm surprised to find an equally surprised look on his face.

"What?" Silas grunts.

"Details," Bane barks at the same time.

"You want the details of how Margaret Thorne, Ma's best fucking friend and better known as Aunt Maggie, fucked Raymond St. James, dad of the year? 'Fraid I don't have those specifics, brother."

Bane steps toward me, aggression shattering that perfect blank expression of his. "Is this a fucking joke to you?"

I tilt my head to the side, giving him a flat look. "Do I look like I'm fucking joking, Lincoln? I've had to sit with this knowledge for weeks, but that motherfucker has known for years and years," I seethe, pointing toward Silas.

"Bullshit. I didn't know about this," Silas blurts out.

Bane and I turn to glare at him as one. Silas exhales and looks at the ceiling for a moment. "What I meant was I didn't know it was Aunt Maggie, okay? I only knew that you weren't, you know, Ma's biologically."

I flinch at the reminder, even though it's been on a loop inside my head for too long. "How? How long have you known?"

He looks at me, regret softening his face. "I was home sick one day in middle school, and some woman came to the house. There was yelling and screaming, and I crept down the stairs at one point, sure I'd find the house a mess or something. Shit was so loud, I was convinced Ma was wrestling a whole pack of bobcats." He pauses and drags his hand over his head. "But when I got downstairs, Ma was crying in the kitchen. She was on the phone with Pops, and she was saying something about some woman coming over and trying to take Asher back, that she was ready to be his mom again. But Ma was inconsolable, so I knew Pops would be home soon. And I went back into my room and pretended it never happened."

I bark out a caustic laugh, shaking my head at his easy explanation for the fucking complicated situation. "But it did fucking happen, Silas. And you should've told me."

"I was a fucking child, and I was scared, okay?" Silas's gaze darts around the room, never settling on one thing. "I thought if I told someone what I heard, they'd take you away."

"What?" I mutter. His confession pierces the balloon of rage I've been harboring. It doesn't pop, but it loses some of its steam.

"I don't fucking know. Some kid at school had to leave his parents and he was separated from his little brothers, so maybe that shit was in my head. Honestly, I haven't thought about this for years, Asher."

The use of my real name isn't lost on me. He only ever uses it when he wants me to listen.

"That's fucked-up, Silas," I mutter.

"Nah, you don't get it. You were my brother, Asher, and it was my job to protect you. It's still my fucking job. So if telling you meant that you'd get taken away from me, then—" He cuts himself off, shaking his head. He slides his hands into his pockets. "I'm sorry, man. You can hate me for what I did, and I'll accept it. But to me, you've always been my little brother. Regardless of who your biological mom is."

Fizzy emotion seeps through the cracks of my anger, and I fucking hate that there's a tide of relief too. It was fucking exhausting being angry at him all this time.

But it feels too easy to just accept his apology and move on like it didn't happen.

I take a deep breath, trying to gather my thoughts and identify those pesky little emotions slithering around inside of me. "Well, I didn't expect you to have such a compelling reason. Asshole," I mutter, side-eying Silas.

The corner of his mouth ticks up, and he might as well have shouted *hooray*.

"Well, *I'm* fucking pissed at you for the way you handled this, you know." Bane looks at me, gaze narrow and lips pursed. "There are about a hundred different ways you could've gone about this, starting with, oh, I don't know, fucking talking to us like adults."

"Instead of stomping around the house for the last month, throwing out tiny barbs because you're lashing out like a child," Silas drawls. He has the audacity to look at me with wide eyes, like he's fucking innocent in all this.

I shrug, uncomfortable with the weight of the accusation because it has fucking merit. "Yeah, well, I guess I'm not all that mature sometimes. But I didn't really know how to process this shit, and it felt like my family wasn't my fucking family anymore."

"You're a fucking idiot," Bane mutters.

"Fuck, man, don't hold back now." I roll my eyes and crane my neck from one side to the other. But I can't shake the feeling of relief that gnaws at my gut. There is something liberating about finally having it all out there.

Bane shrugs. "I'm not. Look, I get why you're angry, and I'm not getting in the middle of that shit between you two. But me? I'm gonna take this as a boon."

"Your ma steps out on your dad, and you're going to just smile and nod?" I ask, incredulous.

"First of all, fuck you. She's *our* mother, and she's not even qualified to have that title. And secondly, I meant because I've always wanted siblings, asshole. And the three of us, we've been tight our whole lives, but it pales in comparison to the two of you," Bane says, jerking his chin toward me and Silas.

My cheeks grow warm under his reprimand.

"Fuck you too, man. You've always been our brother, and you know that," Silas chides with a slow grin.

"I came to pee, but I'd really like to know why you three are having midnight meetings in the bathroom," Evangeline mumbles, shuffling between the three of us. "And phew, do you guys smell that? It reeks of feelings in here." She waves her hand in front of her face, like she's wafting away a bad smell. But I don't miss the broad grin curving across her face. "Now, I love you all, but get out. Some boundaries shouldn't be crossed, yeah?"

42

SILAS

THERE'S a knock on the doorframe into the small office inside RGRC, Rosewood Garage and Repair Company. I glance over my shoulder, dragging a wet paper towel across my face and the back of my neck. It's hot as fuck today, and that fucking air conditioner still doesn't work.

Sheriff Redford stands in my doorway, looking ten different shades of awkward, and I have to resist the urge to grin at his discomfort. I haven't seen or heard from him in a couple weeks, not since he came to my house and tried to throw around his weight.

"Something you need, Sheriff?"

"Yeah, uh, Silas. I was wondering if I could have a word?"

I grin at him, but it's nothing like the charming smiles Nova tosses to everyone. Nah this one is too rough around the edges to ever be considered friendly. But I don't have the patience in me to put on pleasantries. Not when my boy has to be separated from me for his safety, the garage is behind and the compound is recovering and there's a fucking stalker after my girl.

I check the clock on the wall, noting that the demo crew will be at the house in fifteen minutes. I hired a small team of guys to do what they have to in the house to take the ruined shit out and save as much as they can. I offered to pay for them to do Bane's house too, but he's dead-set on bulldozing it to the ground. If he ever peels himself away from our girl, I mean.

Not that I fucking blame him. Being with her will always outweigh most things. And it's definitely better than slowly cooking to death inside this fucking oven of a garage.

"Sure, I got a couple minutes for my old pal, the sheriff." I toss the dirty paper towel in the garbage can and lean my ass against the edge of my desk. Arms folded over my chest and one ankle crossed over the other. "Have a seat, Redford." I jerk my chin to the chair next to me. "You look like you need to sit down."

Redford smoothes his palm down the front of his shirt, a nervous habit of his. I can't tell if he has bad new for me or if he's just fucking squirrely because the last time we saw each other I implied that I was going to kill him.

He drops into the chair with a grunt, straightening his shirt once more, as if he suddenly has misaligned buttons on the front.

"Well? The clock's ticking. I have somewhere to be."

Redford clears his throat. "Yeah, see, that's why I'm here."

My brows fly toward my forehead and I tilt my head to the side. "You got a problem with me renovating my house?"

He shakes his head. "What? No. Of course not. That's your property, your business."

I nod slowly. "Okay, then break it down for me, Redford."

He clears his throat, his gaze darting around the room before settling on mine. "See the thing is, there's been some chatter lately."

"Chatter," I deadpan.

"Yep, mm-hmm, some citizens are real concerned about the

fallout of what's happening here with the Reapers and the Hell Hounds and the Savage Souls."

"Citizens are concerned about the Hounds and the Savages. What about exactly?"

"Well, it seems your, uh, attempt to clean up the streets isn't flying under the radar like last time."

"Speak plainly, Redford. I just put ten hours in the garage without any fucking air conditioning."

He winces and clears his throat. "Seems the other sheriffs are concerned that you picking off the enemies is going to create a problem for us. Blowback, ya know."

I sigh and pinch the bridge of my nose. "So let me get this straight. We're cleaning up a mess we didn't start, and you're in here asking me to, what? Stop cleaning up the mess? Stop making this town a safer place?"

"Well when you put it like that," he says, shifting in his seat.

"It *is* like that."

"Well, I understand what you're doing. I really do. But it isn't up to me anymore. I'm retired in two weeks, Silas. The transition has already started, and Ethan, I mean Sheriff Bellfleur, has already made arrangements."

"What kind of fucking arrangements? What about our existing arrangement?"

Redford holds up his hands, palms toward me. "I can't make him do anything, Silas. I already told you that. Our arrangement stays between us. It doesn't roll over like a vacation fund, going to whoever becomes sheriff after me."

"He's your goddamn protégé, Anthony. What the fuck were you thinking?"

He straightens in his seat. "I was thinking that I came here as a professional courtesy to let you know that Bellfleur is making moves, so you're not caught unaware."

I can feel my blood pressure rising with every second of this conversation. We need another complication like we need a fucking hole in the head. "What kind of moves? So far all you've done is say a lot of words without saying much of anything."

He clears his throat. "The kind that involves the sheriffs from the Diamond."

"Fuck," I curse under my breath, dragging my palm across my jaw. "What does that mean exactly?"

He shakes his head. "I don't have all the details yet. But I pulled a few strings, and it seems like they're forming some kind of co-op, a treaty of sorts so no one gets hurt."

"And what does that mean for us?"

"It means you better tighten ranks, Silas. And keep your men in Rosewood for a while."

"And what happens if someone wanders into Rosewood? Are we supposed to just let them roll up on us twenty-five deep like that again? Do I need to remind you who was in my fucking house at the time?"

"No, no. I remember. Look, all I'm saying is that expect Bellfleur to be knocking on your door soon. He's gonna have some demands, and if I were you, I'd think long and hard about complying. You wanted out five years ago, and you did it. Don't undo all the hard work, all the sacrifices you made to get here now."

"You don't need to tell me what we sacrificed for peace. Don't forget that we didn't start any of this. We didn't want a war."

"I know." He nods his head slowly. "I'm just saying, remember to weigh the cost of everything Bellfleur says before you act."

I nod, my mind already spinning to figure out how the fuck we're going to navigate this upcoming development. "Thanks for the head's up, Sheriff."

"Yep. Be seeing ya, Silas." Redford pushes to his feet and leaves my office with a backward wave.

43

SILAS

TWO HOURS LATER, I'm standing in the middle of my wrecked front room. Thinking. I want to go home—to go to Evangeline's home, but I can't yet. I made her a promise to reel in my shit, and I'm going to do my damndest to keep it. So that means hanging out here for a little while longer until I can take a full breath without wanting to punch something.

The crew is gone already. Turns out, it doesn't take all that long to tear shit out of a house. It's going to take so much longer to redo everything. To patch the walls and put in new furniture and make it feel like my home again.

There's a knock at my front door, and I yell "come in" without looking. I'm sure it's one of the guys looking for me. It seems I'm needed endlessly, especially lately, and normally I can easily weather it or shove it off to Nova or Bane. But it's only me here right now, and as much as I never wanted to be the president of the Reapers, I'll be damned if I shirk all my responsibilities.

A low whistle slices through the air, and I pivot instantly, grabbing my gun from the back of my pants in the same breath.

Ethan Bellfleur is standing at the threshold of my living room with his hands in his pockets and a slimy little grin on his face. I lower the gun slowly, hoping he reads the disrespect in the move.

"What do you want?"

"Now is that any way to greet your new sheriff?"

"You're not the sheriff yet, Ethan. So what the fuck are you doing in my house?"

He whistles again. "I heard about this, but I haven't had a chance to see it until now. They sure did a number on your house, hm?"

"I'll ask one more time: What do you want, Ethan?" I widen my stance, my fingers still taut around the grip of my gun.

"Just came by to give you a friendly heads-up, that's all. There's a new sheriff in town, St. James, and he doesn't play by the same rules as the old one."

My head rears back and I narrow my eyes at him. "Why the fuck are you talking about yourself in the third person like that? Get to the fucking point."

His face reddens, and he smooths his dark-blond hair back with both hands before exhaling and shoving them into his pockets. It's a fucking strange little series of movements I just witnessed. And for the first time, I start to think that Nova might've been onto something about this guy.

"The point I'm trying to make is that we're gonna do things differently around here. Starting now."

"Redford's still sheriff for two weeks."

Bellfleur shrugs, rocking back on his heels. "He decided to take an early retirement package."

"When? I just talked to him this afternoon."

"Retirement moves fast apparently. I don't fucking know. That's not the point. The point is we're doing shit my way now. And you won't be able to buy me off with bribes and shit like you did with Redford. He was weak. A fucking coward who didn't have what it takes to keep this town safe. But not me, St. James."

The implication is there, but I don't fucking buy it. Still, Redford's advice rings in my ears. I school my face into my most neutral expression, locking all my shit down tight. "Why are you here?"

"We're starting something new. A new-age co-op. The Diamond's coming together to agree to a peace treaty. Good for the many and all that."

"And this warranted a house visit? Fucking call the clubhouse next time, Bellfluer."

"I'm here because your presence is required. You, your cousin, and your asshole brother. That's it. Don't roll up with your whole fucking club, or you're all going to go to jail."

I let the Nova comment slide for now. "For what?" I scoff. "Driving?"

"Nah, St. James. For trespassing and violating the curfew laws I'll set just for you."

My blood roars in my ears. "You threatening me Bellefleur?"

"Threatening?" He shakes his head dramatically. "Gosh, no. As an officer of the law, I wouldn't dream of such things. But"—he sucks his teeth, dipping his head in an exaggerated shrug—"as an officer of the law, it *is* my duty to uphold it. So if I find you in violation of it, I'm gonna have to take you in. And then I'm going to have to take in your cousin and your shithead brother. And then I'll probably have to shut down your little boys club. And who knows what'll happen then. I hear you got quite the pretty nanny too. Maybe she'll need a new job. I'm sure I can rustle up a few kids for her to look after."

My body vibrates with anger so potent I half-expect to look down and see my skin blistering from the inside out.

"You have two seconds to get the fuck out of my house and off my property. Because in case you forgot, Bellfleur, we live in

Rosewood. Which affords me the right to defend my house against intruders by any means necessary. And Bellefleur? Right now, you're looking exactly like the kind of guy I saw trespass with intent to harm. Be a real shame to never see your swearing-in ceremony, yeah?"

His jaw clenches and his jovial fake fucking grin slips into something decidedly sinister. Good. Now we're fucking getting somewhere.

"Be at the summit, St. James. Or I'm going to have to assume you're unwilling to comply, and then I'll really fuck you, your family, your bullshit club, and that pretty piece of ass. *Yeah?*" he mocks me. "Two days. Three Crowns Tavern. Three p.m. Don't be late."

He strolls out of my house, whistling some fucking jaunty little tune like he's out for a stroll in the park, and it takes everything I've got not to follow through on my threat and take care of this little problem right here, right now.

I pull out my phone as I watch the sheriff-elect stroll toward his car. It's not a police car, but one of those undercover SUVs. He grins, a feral flash of his overly white teeth, and gets into his car.

"Yeah?" Bane answers on the first ring.

"We got a fucking problem. Get Nova and Evie and meet me at Magnolia in a half hour. There's a fucking coup happening."

44

EVANGELINE

"I DON'T FUCKING LIKE THIS," Silas mutters for the fifth time in the last ten minutes. He drums his fingers against the steering wheel, his body vibrating with nervous energy.

I lean over the center console and rest my hand on his forearm, giving it a gentle squeeze and hoping to ease his nerves. "I know, but it's the only option."

His gaze flies to the velvet scrunchie around my wrist, eyes narrowing as he glares at it. "What's that, Evie?"

I rotate my wrist, like I'm showing it off while keeping my fingers on his forearm. "Oh, this? Strangest thing, Silas. I found all seven of my missing scrunchies in your nightstand earlier today."

Quiet laughter rumbles from the backseat, and Silas's cheeks tint pink.

He focuses back on the road, and he grunts, "I don't know how that happened."

"Bro, what are you even doing with all her velvet hair thingies?" Nova asks around a laugh.

"Scrunchies," I offer.

"Twenty says he's hoarding them like some kind of dragon mating ritual," Bane muses.

Nova chuckles. "Nah, no way, man, a hundred says he's jerking off with them."

Silas's neck flushes pink and he grunts. "Fuck off, both of you."

I waggle my eyebrows and stage-whisper. "Can I watch next time?"

"Oh for fuck's sake, baby. We're about to wade into some serious shit. Don't encourage them," Silas says, but there's no real heat in it.

"It's called comic relief, bro. Check it out sometime, yeah?" Nova leans forward and taps the middle console twice.

I run the pads of my fingers along his arm in soft, sweeping lines. "I know it could get dangerous, but we agreed this was the best option."

"But it's not the *only* option," he counters as we stop at a red light. He looks at me, his gaze a physical touch as it roams over my face.

He doesn't have to say it, I know he's worried. Just like I know the men in the backseat are humming with the same anxious energy.

I push onto my knees and lean into him, brushing my lips against the corner of his mouth. "I'm not going to be left behind again, yeah?"

"Yeah, but we could be walking into another ambush, sugar," Bane says from the backseat. There's resignation in his voice, and something darker.

I brush my lips along the other corner of Silas's mouth, and answer him, "True, but being alone at Magnolia Lane to be ambushed there isn't a better option."

Nova grunts from behind me, shuffling closer until I can feel his body heat. "We're just worried about you, sweetheart."

As soon as the light turns green, Silas accelerates and takes a left, his grip tightening on the steering wheel once more. I ease back into my seat, keeping my face toward Nova's.

The tension in the car is off the charts today, nearly suffocating me as I try to breathe through the heaviness of it. I can feel the weight of every glance, every exhale, every fear of theirs seeping through their pores.

"I know, but I'll be fine. I'll stay in the car, remember?" I keep my voice calm and even. I'm doing my best to alleviate their anxiety, not add to it. It has the added benefit of not allowing any space for my own anxiety to take root. It's still there, but it's like I've cut off access to it.

Nova bites the inside of his cheek and shakes his head. "Nah, I don't think so. I think you should be sandwiched between us. I don't trust those fuckers not to blow the car up or something as a distraction."

"You got your gun, sugar?" Bane asks.

I lean forward and lift up the back of my tee, showing him where he gave me a hands-on instruction on how to tuck my gun in the back of my jean shorts. I let the fabric flutter back down, and settle into my seat, wiggling my feet a little bit. I wore Nana Jo's favorite cowboy boots today. I don't know if I did it for luck or comfort, maybe I just wanted something pretty and fun. But I do feel better wearing them, so there's that.

Nova stays hovering behind me, his hand lightly brushing against my shoulder before settling on my chest. His fingertips brush over the skin above my heart, like he needs reassurance.

"Alright, you're with us at all times yeah? Superglue, baby," Silas murmurs, his gaze dark as he focuses on the road. "At the first sign of trouble, I want you to run. Take the car or steal a car, I don't fucking care. You get your ass outta there, and you go to Ma and Hunter."

My heart flies up into my throat as my breath hitches. A chill runs down my spine at the idea of leaving without them.

"I'm not leaving you," I vow. "So if you want me to walk away from this little meeting today, you better make sure you do the same."

Silas's gaze flies to the rearview mirror, and I glance over my shoulder to see him exchange a loaded look with Bane and Nova. It's one in a long line of many heavy looks the three of them have been trading over the last few days. I still don't know what the fuck happened in the bathroom that night I found all of them having what seemed like a heart to heart. But after Silas told us about what the new sheriff said, it's been tense as fuck around the house.

Admittedly, I don't really understand what everything means. Like the politics of the Reapers or how it works with the sheriff or even the people of Rosewood, let alone how it works with other clubs. I told Lincoln I wanted to be brought in on everything, and since then, they mostly have. But there is still so much that I don't comprehend. I think it would take me months, maybe even years, to fully understand their dynamic within Rosewood and beyond.

"That goes for all of you, yeah? I'm not leaving any of you there, so get any heroics out of your heads right now. We're going home today, and then we're going to find that motherfucker who stole my panties *and then* stole me. *And then*, we're going to bring Hunter home." I'm on a roll by the end of my little pep talk. I didn't intend for it to start out that way, but I can't deny that it makes me feel better knowing we have a plan. Regardless of how arbitrary it is. Even the best plans go to shit sometimes.

"Perfect timing, sweetheart. We're here," Bane says.

I sit up and try to take in the scene. Men standing in small groups, some smoking cigarettes and some chatting with the other guys around their motorcycles. There are clear divides here, and you can spot each little group easily enough by the three-foot buffer of space.

"I thought there was only supposed to be like twenty people here or something?" I ask, glancing at Silas.

"That's what he told me. He said the three of us, so I assumed he meant just the board for the other clubs too, which would put us at roughly twenty. Plus the sheriffs, so maybe twenty-five," Silas says, pulling into the gravel parking lot of what looks like a bar that recently had a fire.

I wonder what happened here?" I murmur, eyeing the blackened exterior walls with peeling paint and broken windows. Two giant red dumpsters are next to one side, and one of them looks full. I imagine how much damage is inside for it to look this bad on the outside.

Silas swings the car into a makeshift parking spot at the edge of the lot. A strategic move so it's close to the exit for a quick getaway, I'm sure.

"Savages and Hounds torched it earlier this summer," Nova says with a sigh. "Even though this is neutral territory."

Fear snakes up my back, sinking its poisonous legs into each vertebrae. "Then why the fuck are we meeting here with them?"

"Why, indeed," Silas mutters as he turns the car off and pulls the keys. He taps the visor with two fingers. "Spare's in here, yeah?"

"Knock it off, Silas. I'm not fucking leaving you here," I growl out. Fear has burned away my faux calm.

Bane glances at his watch and makes a low noise in the back of his throat. "It's three o'clock. Let's do this."

"With me, Evie," Silas says as he pushes open his door.

I get out of the car, letting Nova throw his arm over my shoulder and huddle me close to his side. He leans down and murmurs, "This is supposed to be a peaceful meeting, sweetheart.

But you don't fucking hesitate if they open fire, yeah? We're not asking for permission today."

I nod my understanding and look at the men we're walking toward.

"Good girl," he says, dropping a kiss to the top of my head.

"So good of you to join us."

My heart stops inside my chest and I freeze, like my feet are suddenly glued to the ground.

"Sweetheart? You okay?" Nova asks.

I think he says something else, but I can't be sure because my head is ringing. I shield the sun from my eyes as I look around for the speaker, the man whose face belongs to that voice. My gaze flies over everyone, quickly dismissing each one until it lands on him.

There.

Only he doesn't look exactly like the last time I saw him. I shake my head a few times, trying to make sense of what my body has already figured out. My gun is out in the next breath, aimed at him with my finger resting next to the trigger.

"Ah, it seems you brought an uninvited guest. I thought we all understood the rules for this little meeting, St. James. Do I need to remind you, hm?"

"Shut your fucking mouth before I shoot it off," I seethe, taking two big steps toward him. There's still twenty feet between us. Plenty of room for something to happen.

His smile turns into a leer and he tilts his head to the side. "Ah, there she is. What did I tell you, Evangeline, hm? I told you that I was going to help you. And look at you now," he crows, throwing his arms to the side as if he's showcasing me. "You look magnificent, princess." There's genuine pride in his voice, and that freaks me the fuck out more than anything.

It's then that other noises start filtering in. The low murmur of conversation mixed with a couple engines revving. It's a symphony of masculine sound and energy, and it's too fucking much.

"Shut up," I snap.

And then their voices pierce the cacophony.

"What the fuck is going on?" Silas yells, stepping closer to me.

"You better get your fucking gun off my girl, or I'm going to rip it off your fucking body, Moore," Nova growls at the Hell Hounds president, malice dripping from his voice.

I see the Hell Hounds in my peripheral vision, that twitchy sort of tension filling the parking lot. It's probably not my best idea to pull a gun on the man who drugged me and drove me two states away, but I'm not exactly thinking rationally right now.

I'm acting on instinct, and everything inside of me is screaming to mete my revenge.

"Talk to me, sugar," Bane urges from right behind me.

It's then that I realize he's quite literally behind me, hovering close enough that I can feel his chest brush against my back with every exhale.

"Ah, you didn't tell them about me? I'm not surprised. You always did like your secrets, hm? But don't worry, princess, I've got it all taken care of."

"Shut up," I snap, my hands trembling as I hold the gun.

His smile turns cruel as he strolls across the divide, eliminating the space between us by half. "You know, I didn't plan for you to come today, but I should have. You liked to surprise me, keep me on my toes. I always knew you did it to keep my skills sharp, to make me prove to you how worthy I am." He sighs, this happy little sound that fucks with my head. And then he whistles as he pivots on his heels, stalking across the parking lot to stand by Sheriff Redford.

"I was hoping I wouldn't have to do this, but c'est la vie and all that shit."

"What's going on, Ethan?" Redford turns toward him, a scowl painted across his face.

My abductor pulls out a pair of gloves and puts them on with fast precision. A moment later, he's holding a gun I didn't even see him grab. I hear the gunshot before I even see it, and Redford falls to his knees on the gravel, clutching his chest. Blood blooms across his chest, and his hands try to staunch the bleeding, but it's in vain.

"Wh-why?" Redford croaks.

Everyone around seems to lean in, as if collectively waiting to hear his reasoning for what the fuck just happened. But not me. I don't need to hear his reasoning. In fact, I can't think of a single reason why I shouldn't shoot him.

So I pull the trigger.

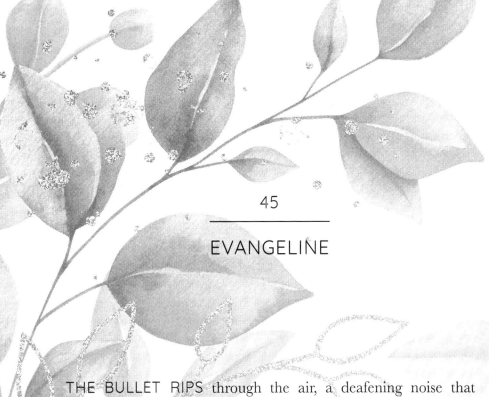

45

EVANGELINE

THE BULLET RIPS through the air, a deafening noise that echoes in my ears. Or maybe it's all in my head. It hits my abductor, who's name I still don't know, in the shoulder, and he jerks back a step.

"Fuck, Evie," Silas curses, stepping into me and sending me careening into Nova. "You just shot the fucking sheriff."

My men close ranks around me, and I feel them draw their weapons. I can't pull my eyes away from the man in front of me as he clutches his arm with genuine hurt in his eyes.

"Princess?" The sheriff cocks his head to the side. "Did you . . . fucking shoot me?"

"Don't do it, Bellefleur. I don't understand what the fuck is going on, but if you take a single fucking step, I'm going to send you to meet your maker faster than you can blink," Silas snarls.

My abductor, Bellfleur, keeps his eyes on mine as he points the same gun he shot Sheriff Redford with at me. "But can you shoot me before I shoot her? That's the real question."

"Somebody better start fucking talking," some guy wearing a Hell Hounds kutte snaps. "I don't give a fuck about your petty

Rosewood politics or who's fucking who. I thought we were here to discuss peace."

"Ah yes, of course," Bellfleur says, nodding and tapping his chin with the end of his gun. "I forgot about you for a second." Without another word, he pivots and shoots Moore in the head.

Time seems to slow down as the gunshot rings out through the air. Moore, crumples to the ground and blood pools around his head, staining the gravel. Bellefleur stands above him, bleeding from the arm and gun still in hand, a hint of a smirk on his face.

Before Moore even hits the gravel, a barrage of bullets erupts from everywhere at once.

My men converge on me, herding all of us toward the car, but none of the bullets fly toward us. No, they're all aimed at the Hell Hounds. Or what's left of them.

I shuffle back a step and glance at the bodies on the ground, horror crawling up my throat and stealing my voice.

"What the fuck, brother? I thought we agreed to let Moore live. He was fucking useful," Deran Masters, the president of the Savage Souls, snarls.

Bellfleur puts his hand up, halting Masters. He strolls in front of us, like he's putting on a one-man performance. "Now you've gone and done it." He scratches his head with the barrel of his gun, his face pinched in annoyance. "I had this whole speech prepared, a better way of introducing her to you and telling her my origin story, asshole. A beautifully crafted story about my mother's affair with your father. See my mother, the incomparable Olivia Bellfleur, fell for lowlife scumbag, Elliot Masters."

"Fucking watch it," Masters growls. "That's my father you're disrespecting."

"To the fucking car, now," Bane hisses out of the side of his mouth. Like we're one entity, the four of us walk backward, never taking our eyes off of the devastation unfolding in front of us.

Bellfleur concedes with a dip of his chin. "Quite right. Our father was a piece of shit to my mother, much like he was to my half-brother Deran." He grins now, this maniacal flash of too many teeth. "But then it went the way these kinds of things always go. Big brother over here grew up, and one day, he fought back. Luckily for him, his half-brother was a respected member of the police force."

"Jesus fucking Christ, he's gonna monologue us to death," Nova grumbles under his breath as we shuffle back another step.

"So when we reunited, I did him a solid and took care of his little problem. Nothing bonds you quite like murder, am I right?" Bellefleur flashes me a Cheshire-Cat-like grin and winks like we're bonding or something. "One thing leads to another, yada, yada, yada—I'm skipping around a bit, princess, because it seems like I'm losing your attention, and I don't want to have to start shooting people until I'm ready, yeah? It'll ruin the grand finale."

I freeze when he looks at me, my hand flying out to stop Silas from taking another step. The threat feels as tangible as Silas's stupid-hot forearms underneath my palm.

Bellfleur pivots and starts pacing again, resting one arm behind his back and letting the injured one hand. "Now, where was I? Oh, yes. So big brother over here told me all about his childhood in Rosewood, and I was curious. And that's where you come in, princess."

I swallow around the lump of fear in my throat and force my lips to tip up on the sides. "How so?"

"Good," he says with a decisive nod. "You're listening. I would hate to have to force compliance, but I will if I have to." He stops pacing and closes his eyes, tipping his chin toward the sun. "I can still picture your face, you know. The little flared skirt you wore and the way your hair shined in when you wrote your name in the air with sparklers. The way you laughed when you burned your marshmallow over the bonfire."

Fear churns inside my gut, around and around until I'm sure I'm going to vomit. I can picture those moments with the same amount of startling clarity. It was the night I met Lincoln.

Bellfleur opens his eyes and looks directly behind me, at Lincoln. "I saw every signal you sent me that night, but no matter how hard I tried, I never had an opening." His gaze slides to mine again. "So I waited and waited and waited some more. Watching over you until you were ready. But how long is a man expected to wait, hm? Don't you think eight years is long enough?"

I shake my head, my mouth parting but no words coming out. It sounds fantastical, like some shit I'd hear on a podcast or see in a movie.

Bellfleur exhales loudly, tossing his hand up and letting it smack against his thigh. "Well now look at what you did, Deran, she thinks I'm fucking crazy."

Deran Masters grunts, eyeballing me like he's not sure I'm worth the trouble. "She looks fine to me, brother. Let's get on with it, yeah. I'm fucking starving."

Bellfleur taps his forehead with the end of his gun, glaring at his brother and then us. "Princess," he says, his face softening when he looks at me. "I can't believe you shot me."

"I was aiming for your head," I mutter.

Nova elbows me in the side. "Fucking hell, don't provoke him, sweetheart."

But Bellfleur only chuckles. "I'm so proud, princess. Don't worry, I'll help you practice your aim. C'mere, we can start right now. There are a few more things that we need to take care of."

"Hard pass, you Polaroid panty-stealing fuck."

"Oh for fuck's sake, sugar," Bane mutters under his breath.

Bellfleur clears his throat. "What I meant to say was, get your ass over here before I shoot your boyfriend in the fucking head." He flashes me a manic grin. "Is that better?"

I take a step forward, and three hands latch onto me at the same time.

"Ah ah ah. You're outnumbered here, boys. If you don't hand over my woman, you're going to die and I'll still go home with her. This way, you at least get to go home. But my princess stays with me." He beams like he just pitched the deal of a lifetime.

"Don't you fucking dare, Evie," Silas seethes quietly. "You know the plan. Stick to it."

But I'm already shaking my head. "I told you I'm not leaving here without you."

Bellefleur snaps his fingers. "Right, how rude of me. Yes, of course, take a moment to say goodbye to the St. James family, princess. I'm afraid you won't be seeing them again."

Well, I don't like how fucking ominous that sounds. But I take the gift anyway, spinning around and throwing my arms out wide and planting my forehead against Bane's chest. "I can take him," I whisper.

"Baby, your aim is shit," Silas whispers, despair thick on his tongue.

I place a kiss on Bane's chest, turning to do the same for Nova and Silas. "Trust me."

"I do, sugar. It's those fuckers I don't trust," Bane says, discreetly tilting his head toward the gaggle of Savage Souls.

We're outnumbered, eight of them and three of us. Technically there are four of us, but Silas is right, my aim leaves a lot to be desired. The truth is, I got lucky as fuck the day they stormed Silas's house.

"Make it count then, yeah?" I grin at him. "I'm ninety-five percent confident that Bellfleur won't shoot me, so all I have to do is incapacitate him so he doesn't shoot you three. Easy-peasy."

"Make him bleed, sweetheart," Nova adds solemnly.

I squeeze Nova's bicep as I turn around. I take my time strolling across the space until I stop right in front of him.

Bellfleur licks his lips, eyes dark and pupils blown. "So glad to see you're learning. You're not going to give me a hard time like you did in Bane's basement, are you?"

"No." I shake my head and force my face to fall into something submissive, relaxing my shoulders and looking at my feet. My pulse thunders in my ears, echoing the frenetic beat of my heart like a battle cry.

"C'mere, princess. Give your man a hug." I let him pull me into his chest, and I have to breathe through my nose so I don't vomit all over him.

I wait a beat, then two. Then I bring my knee up hard enough to crush his fucking balls into raisins. He lets go of me, drops his gun to clutch his crotch, and doubles over with a wail.

And then I hear the sweet sound of gunfire. Never thought I'd think that, let alone feel grateful for it. I don't turn around, trusting them to take care of the Savage Souls. And I don't want to take my eyes from the asshole on the ground.

Bellefleur groans as he rolls from side to side in the gravel, but it's not enough. I kick his gun away, and when he reaches for it, I panic and stomp on his outstretched hand.

"I'm not your fucking princess, and you're not my man," I seethe. And then I bring my heel down on his dick for good measure.

He wails, this high-pitched sound of pain that grates on my ears, and I look around and take in the carnage.

Three people are left whole and standing, and relief hits me so fiercely, my knees wobble.

They jog over to me, the three of them converging on me and making sure I'm unharmed. Once they're satisfied that I'm okay, they give me a little breathing room.

I look around, feeling overwhelmed by everything. "What are we going to do about all this?"

"I'll call in a few favors, get it taken care of," Bane says, pulling out his phone.

"And him?" I nod to the wailing man at our feet.

"Up to you, Evie. We'll back whatever you say," Silas says.

I nod a few times, dragging my teeth over my bottom lip. "I don't know if I can ever relax knowing he's out here somewhere."

"You know, I've heard the lake is beautiful this time of year," Nova says with a conspiratorial grin.

"Now what?" I murmur, feeling exhausted down to my very bones.

"Now we go get our boy, and we bring him home," Silas says, wrapping his arms around me and curving me into his chest.

"I CAN'T TELL you how happy I am to see you here, honey. My boys, they told me you're okay, but I worry, you know? You can always talk to me about anything."

I take a drink of the iced tea, letting the sounds of the cicadas and the breeze rustling the leaves in the trees ground me. I've been anxious and jumpy ever since the little showdown at Three Crowns Tavern yesterday. I wanted to come get Hunter right away, but Silas convinced me that showering, eating, and sleeping needed to happen first.

He wasn't wrong, even if I grumbled about it the whole time.

I exhale and try to articulate why I'm still feeling like there's a hoard of wasps cruising around inside of me, occasionally stopping to sting me.

"It's just, we got the bad guys, right? And the guy who was stalking me. And my mother seems to have relented, at least for this week. So why am I still feeling all . . ." I flap my hand around, trying and failing to find the right words to describe what I'm feeling. "It's just, now it's real, you know. This thing between me . . . *and them*. And now there's nothing to distract us from the fact that we're in an extremely unconventional relationship."

"Do you love my boys?"

"Yes," I reply easily.

"Then the rest is easy," she says, patting my leg with affection.

"What if it's not though? What if I mess up? Or mess Hunter up? I'm not a mother." Emotion swells inside my throat, making it hard to breathe.

Dixie arches a brow. "Who says you're not?"

A wry laugh falls from my lips. "Uh, everyone?"

Dixie places her cup down on the table to the right and reaches over to clasp my hand. "Motherhood isn't defined by biological records or length of time or any other arbitrary definition we place on things. It's a feeling. A conviction. A desperate need to do anything and everything you can to protect your child."

Tears prick my eyes as I let Dixie's words roll over me in a cool wave. They're a soothing balm to the cracked and bleeding parts of my soul. I listen to her voice talk about motherhood as I watch Hunter and Nova race around the front yard, jumping over imaginary obstacles as they play super heroes.

At some point, Silas joins in on the fun, chasing both of them around and growling like he's some kind of animal. I'm not entirely sure he understands the game they're playing, but he's having fun.

And eventually, Bane brings out a kickball and some plastic bases. Dixie and I watch as the three grown men squabble like children over foul balls and bad plays while Hunter tries to coach them diplomatically.

I love every single second of it.

And for the first time in my life, I'm grateful for every hardship I faced. Every disparaging comment from my mother. Every holiday spent alone. I'm thankful for each and every low point in my life, because it led me there, to them. And it was worth every second.

Epilogue - Silas

Later

"HELLO?" I call out the moment my feet cross the threshold of our house. Anxiety tightens my gut when no one responds right away.

The abduction left a mark on me that no amount of time has been able to erase. And since our house is big as hell to fit our entire family comfortably, as unconventional as it is, it's nearly impossible to be heard everywhere. Though Evie usually tries to be close by so she can holler when I come home. But she's been distracted lately, and with good reason.

Instead of that rationale soothing me, it only amps up my anxiety.

"Evie? Hunter? I'm home," I yell, pitching my voice louder. Not that it would fucking matter if she was on the other side of the house.

I toe off my work boots, shuffling them to the side of the entryway where Evie and Hunter's one-of-a-kind bench. It's sage green with hand-painted daisies on the sides.

The low hum of air conditioning pumping through the vents answers me, but it does nothing to cool the sweat stuck to my skin.

I stalk through the house on a mission, looking for my wife

and son. The kitchen and living room both turn up empty, which usually means one place: the home theatre.

It was one of the only things Bane insisted on when we built this house. He watches more movies than anyone I know. I might've protested at the pretentiousness of it all, but even I can admit it's a great space. We find ourselves in there more than the living room or any other place outside of our respective bedrooms.

The sounds of some lyrical singing comes from the open door to the theatre room. It fills the hallway and I can just make out the words to the song Hunter's been singing nonstop for the last two weeks.

I stop inside the threshold of the door, giving myself time to take in the sight before me. To calm my racing heart with the sight of them sprawled out on the modular couch in the middle of the room. Soft snores punctuate the mellow melody of the song, and I let out a sigh of relief.

It's this unspoken agreement the three of us made a few months ago after the waffle debacle. Nova had mentioned Evie's recent snoring habits as she was plating chocolate chip Belgian waffles her and Hunter had made. But by the way she reacted, you would've sworn he told her she shits the bed every night. She glared at him and fixed her and Hunter's plates like nothing happened. Then she left the three of us in the kitchen, hungry and waffle-less. To add insult to injury, Hunter raved about those waffles for two fucking weeks.

Annoyance simmers under my skin when I think about how it took me nearly eight weeks to convince her to make them for me again. And you better believe I threw my asshole brother under the bus faster than he could backpedal. He should've known better than to bring that shit up when she was already so conscious of all the changes her body was going through.

I stop next to her, slipping my phone from my pocket without taking my eyes off of her.

She's the most beautiful thing I've ever seen.

It's a revelation I find myself experiencing daily.

I swipe up to open the camera app and snap photos from a few different angles. One that showcases her growing belly. Another one that frames her beautiful face, her freckles deeper from all her time in the sun. I take a step back to get the full photo: Evie slightly propped up, head angled to the right, and our boy tucked in tight next to her. His hand rests on the top of her belly, and I switch my phone into video mode quickly.

I crouch down to get the perfect angle and hit record. A smile blooms so fucking wide my cheeks ache. *There*, there it is. Baby kicks again, pushing right at the spot where Hunter's hand rests, his index finger moving like he's tapping in Morse code.

I reign in my snicker at how fucking cute it is. How fucking cute my boy is.

He's getting big now, growing like the weeds they pull from the back flowerbeds. I used to worry that I was robbing him of a real childhood. That despite my best efforts, having a Reaper father would age him, smother his sweetness too soon.

But Evie nurtures his youth, giving him space to be a kid. To be kind even when faced with cruelty. To be sweet and caring. She shields him from everything, and I can never thank her enough for it.

Though I do try, usually on my knees, and as often as she lets me.

I'll never forget when Hunter's school called to tell us he was suspended for fighting. Evie marched down there in her bright pink sundress with her sweet-as-pie smile and told the principal he was a fucking idiot, so it's mildly threatening but southern sweet.

I'd asked her why she came in swinging, and she replied simply, "I'm his mother."

I take a few more photos and add them to my Evie folder on my phone. She doesn't know I've been sneaking photos of her like a fucking stalker, but I can't stop myself. I got the idea from one of those parenting magazines I found tucked under her pillow one day.

I ease myself onto the couch next to her, and she stirs a little, her lashes fluttering before her eyes focus on me.

"Silas?"

"Shh, baby, close your eyes." I tuck in close to her and lay my palm over her stomach, my fingers resting over Hunter's.

"What time is it? We need to get dinner started," she murmurs, her eyes already closing.

"We will, Evie. First, let me say hi to my baby. I haven't seen her all day." Joy wraps around my words, weaves between each letter. An elbow or maybe a foot bumps against my hand, and I swipe my thumb across the fabric of Evie's dress. "Hi, baby. I'm here. Daddy's here," I croon softly.

Evie tsks, this soft noise in the back of her throat, and I already know what she's going to say.

"You're going to confuse her, you know." Her voice is raspy with sleep.

"Nah, she won't know that there are three of us."

She cracks an eye open and arches a brow. "Babies one hundred percent recognize voices, Silas. Surely you, of all people, know this."

I grin at her with a wink. "Exactly, Evie. Why do you think I've been reading to her every night? I got a bet with them, and I'll be damned if my baby girl comes out recognizing their voices over mine."

She laughs, and it's the sweetest sound I've ever heard. "You guys are ridiculous. So possessive already."

I brush my lips across her stomach with reverence. "Only with you, Evie. Only with you."

EPILOGUE

SILAS

one year later

"Hello?" I call out the moment my feet cross the threshold of our house. Anxiety tightens my gut when no one responds right away.

The abduction left a mark on me that no amount of time has been able to erase. And since our house is big as hell to fit our entire family comfortably, as unconventional as it is, it's nearly impossible to be heard everywhere. Though Evie usually tries to be close by so she can holler when I come home. But she's been distracted lately, and with good reason.

Instead of that rationale soothing me, it only amps up my anxiety.

"Evie? Hunter? I'm home," I yell, pitching my voice louder.

Not that it would fucking matter if she was on the other side of the house.

I toe off my work boots, shuffling them to the side of the entryway where Evie and Hunter's one-of-a-kind bench. It's sage green with hand-painted daisies on the sides.

The low hum of air conditioning pumping through the vents answers me, but it does nothing to cool the sweat stuck to my skin.

I stalk through the house on a mission, looking for my wife and son. The kitchen and living room both turn up empty, which usually means one place: the home theatre.

It was one of the only things Bane insisted on when we built this house. He watches more movies than anyone I know. I might've protested at the pretentiousness of it all, but even I can admit it's a great space. We find ourselves in there more than the living room or any other place outside of our respective bedrooms.

The sounds of some lyrical singing comes from the open door to the theatre room. It fills the hallway and I can just make out the words to the song Hunter's been singing nonstop for the last two weeks.

I stop inside the threshold of the door, giving myself time to take in the sight before me. To calm my racing heart with the sight of them sprawled out on the modular couch in the middle of the room. Soft snores punctuate the mellow melody of the song, and I let out a sigh of relief.

It's this unspoken agreement the three of us made a few months ago after the waffle debacle. Nova had mentioned Evie's recent snoring habits as she was plating chocolate chip Belgian waffles her and Hunter had made. But by the way she reacted, you would've sworn he told her she shits the bed every night. She glared at him and fixed her and Hunter's plates like nothing happened. Then she left the three of us in the kitchen, hungry and waffle-less. To add insult to injury, Hunter raved about those waffles for two fucking weeks.

Annoyance simmers under my skin when I think about how it took me nearly eight weeks to convince her to make them for me again. And you better believe I threw my asshole brother under the bus faster than he could backpedal. He should've known better than to bring that shit up when she was already so conscious of all the changes her body was going through.

I stop next to her, slipping my phone from my pocket without taking my eyes off of her.

She's the most beautiful thing I've ever seen.

It's a revelation I find myself experiencing daily.

I swipe up to open the camera app and snap photos from a few different angles. One that showcases her growing belly. Another one that frames her beautiful face, her freckles deeper from all her time in the sun. I take a step back to get the full photo: Evie slightly propped up, head angled to the right, and our boy tucked in tight next to her. His hand rests on the top of her belly, and I switch my phone into video mode quickly.

I crouch down to get the perfect angle and hit record. A smile blooms so fucking wide my cheeks ache. *There*, there it is. Baby kicks again, pushing right at the spot where Hunter's hand rests, his index finger moving like he's tapping in Morse code.

I reign in my snicker at how fucking cute it is. How fucking cute my boy is.

He's getting big now, growing like the weeds they pull from the back flowerbeds. I used to worry that I was robbing him of a real childhood. That despite my best efforts, having a Reaper father would age him, smother his sweetness too soon.

But Evie nurtures his youth, giving him space to be a kid. To be kind even when faced with cruelty. To be sweet and caring. She shields him from everything, and I can never thank her enough for it.

Though I do try, usually on my knees, and as often as she lets me.

I'll never forget when Hunter's school called to tell us he was suspended for fighting. Evie marched down there in her bright pink sundress with her sweet-as-pie smile and told the principal he was a fucking idiot, so it's mildly threatening but southern sweet.

I'd asked her why she came in swinging, and she replied simply, "I'm his mother."

I take a few more photos and add them to my Evie folder on my phone. She doesn't know I've been sneaking photos of her like a fucking stalker, but I can't stop myself. I got the idea from one of those parenting magazines I found tucked under her pillow one day.

I ease myself onto the couch next to her, and she stirs a little, her lashes fluttering before her eyes focus on me.

"Silas?"

"Shh, baby, close your eyes." I tuck in close to her and lay my palm over her stomach, my fingers resting over Hunter's.

"What time is it? We need to get dinner started," she murmurs, her eyes already closing.

"We will, Evie. First, let me say hi to my baby. I haven't seen her all day." Joy wraps around my words, weaves between each letter. An elbow or maybe a foot bumps against my hand, and I swipe my thumb across the fabric of Evie's dress. "Hi, baby. I'm here. Daddy's here," I croon softly.

Evie tsks, this soft noise in the back of her throat, and I already know what she's going to say.

"You're going to confuse her, you know." Her voice is raspy with sleep.

"Nah, she won't know that there are three of us."

She cracks an eye open and arches a brow. "Babies one

hundred percent recognize voices, Silas. Surely you, of all people, know this."

I grin at her with a wink. "Exactly, Evie. Why do you think I've been reading to her every night? I got a bet with them, and I'll be damned if my baby girl comes out recognizing their voices over mine."

She laughs, and it's the sweetest sound I've ever heard. "You guys are ridiculous. So possessive already."

I brush my lips across her stomach with reverence. "Only with you, Evie. Only with you."

WANT MORE OF SILAS, Bane, Nova, and Evie?
Get all the BONUS SCENES here!

AUTHOR'S NOTE

Dear reader, thank you so much for picking up my Midnight Salvation!

I sincerely hope you enjoy Evie's story with her St. James men!

And I hope you're loving Rosewood as much as I am, because I'm not quite ready to leave yet! It seems we have a few characters that are begging to have their stories told!

Keep your eyes peeled for Cora and Jagger's story this summer! Eep! I'm absolutely obsessed with them, and I hope you join me on their whirlwind romance! Preorder it here!

As always, my DMs are open if you need to chat!

Happy reading!
xoxo—pen

A NOTE FROM PEN

As many of you know, when I sat down to start plotting Rosewood, I knew Nana Jo was going to be a big part of Evangeline's story. And I knew that she was already gone when we meet our heroine.

See, Nana Jo is largely inspired by my own grandma. We had a close bond, and even though she's been gone for several years now, I still miss her like crazy. Some days more than others, sparked by the most random events.

And then while I was writing Moonlit Temptation, we lost Grandpa Black.

Suddenly and tragically.

Many of you might remember the funny stories I'd tell about Grandpa Black and the moments he chose to tell me what chapter he was on. Usually at a family dinner. It usually went something like: "Can you pass me the potatoes? Say, Penelope, I'm on chapter twenty-five, by the way."

And then I would blush, murmur a thanks, and be distracted for the rest of dinner until I could sneak away and check what chapter he was on. I'm not kidding when I tell you, it was almost always a spicy scene.

Grandpa Black was funny like that. I like to think he skipped over the especially spicy scenes, though. Or maybe he got a kick out of them.

And then right when Shadowed Obsession released (right before Christmas), we got sudden and devastating news about Grandma Black. Her prognosis wasn't good, but you wouldn't know it by her energy.

She was committed to live, laugh, loving the rest of her life with her family. Usually with a big slice of chocolate cake and a scoop of chocolate ice cream. One of the last things she said was: "I'm sorry, honey, but I don't think I'm going to be here to read book three. Will you tell me what happens now? I don't want to leave not knowing how your story ends."

I cried that day. And for a lot of days after that.

We lost Grandma Black in early February.

See, Grandma Black has read every single one of my books. (Except for In A Little While. I refused to download that all-spice-no-plot novella to her kindle and then have to sit across from her at family diner and act like she didn't read the *twin sandwich scene*) We'd talk about the plot and her favorite characters and if she saw a plot twist coming or not. Mostly, she celebrated every single book I released like it was the first one, never wavering in her pride.

It feels like I've done a lot of crying in this series, tapping into my own grief to shape and fuel Evie's. (And in case you were wondering, I'm definitely crying typing this.)

I hope I did Evie's grief justice, and I hope you enjoyed her story.

Thank you so much for reading.

ACKNOWLEDGMENTS

There are so, so many wonderful people in my life who continue to support me and lift me up every single day. And for that, I'm forever grateful.

Special shoutout to my absolutely amazing assistant, Jen! She's the literal best, and I honestly don't know what I'd do without her. Forever sending you the biggest air hugs for your endless patience when I routinely send five-minute voice memo answers to very simple questions.

To my beta besties: Tracey, Elaine, Dorothy, and Allie. Thank you for your continued and unwavering support. I'm so grateful for you all!

To all my author besties, y'all are the real MVPs. I can't wait to squeeze all of you at our next joint signing! Our little corner of the world is one of my favorite places, and I'm eternally grateful for you all.

Special shoutout to my sprinting bestie Cali, who quite literally battled me to complete this book. You're def stuck with me now, sorry (not sorry!)!

Big, big thanks to Mr Black for being the stuff book boyfriends are made of. And for continuing to nurture my passenger princess life every time I claimed my muse needed a dirty chai latte and vegan doughnuts.

And thank you to my tiny humans for always being constant forces of light in my life. My son, who routinely asks me about my characters. And my daughter, who likes to keep track of my word counts. You'll never read this, but I love you both so, so much.

And to my readers: thank you for standing by me while I clawed my way out of burnout for Rosewood. I hope the St. James men help make up for that. I'm forever awed by your continued love and support for me and these stories.

Printed in France by Amazon
Brétigny-sur-Orge, FR